❧ LONESTAR SANCTUARY ❧

ALSO BY COLLEEN COBLE

Smitten

The Under Texas Skies series
Blue Moon Promise (Available February 2012)

The Lonestar Novels
Lonstar Sanctuary
Lonestar Secrets
Lonestar Homecoming
Lonestar Angel

The Mercy Falls series
The Lightkeeper's Daughter
The Lightkeeper's Bride
The Lightkeeper's Ball

The Rock Harbor series
Without a Trace
Beyond a Doubt
Into the Deep
Cry in the Night

The Aloha Reef series
Distant Echoes
Black Sands
Dangerous Depths

❋

Alaska Twilight
Fire Dancer
Midnight Sea
Abomination
Anathema

❊ LONESTAR SANCTUARY ❊

COLLEEN COBLE

Thomas Nelson
Since 1798

NASHVILLE   DALLAS   MEXICO CITY   RIO DE JANEIRO

© 2007 by Colleen Coble.

All rights reserved. No portion of this book may be reproduced, stored in a
retrieval system, or transmitted in any form or by any means—electronic,
mechanical, photocopy, recording, scanning, or other—except for brief
quotations in critical reviews or articles, without the prior written permission
of the publisher.

Published in Nashville, Tennessee, by Thomas Nelson. Thomas Nelson is a
registered trademark of Thomas Nelson, Inc.

Thomas Nelson, Inc. books may be purchased in bulk for educational,
business, fund-raising, or sales promotional use. For information, please
e-mail SpecialMarkets@ThomasNelson.com.

Publisher's Note: This novel is a work of fiction. Names, characters, places,
and incidents are either products of the author's imagination or used
fictitiously. All characters are fictional, and any similarity to people living
or dead is purely coincidental.

ISBN 978-1-40168-577-5 (value edition)
ISBN 978-1-59554-761-3 (HDA)

Library of Congress Cataloging-in-Publication Data
Coble, Colleen.
  Lonestar sanctuary / by Colleen Coble.
    p. cm.
  ISBN 978-1-59554-549-7 (pbk.)
  I. Title.
PS3553.O2285L66 2007
813'.54—dc22

2007021347

Printed in the United States of America
11 12 13 14 15 QG 6 5 4 3 2 1

For my brother, Rick Rhoads,
*who should have been a cowboy
and whose strength and loving heart inspire me.*

PROLOGUE

THE RODEO CROWD, REEKING OF BEER AND PEANUTS, FINALLY REELED OFF into the night. Allie Siders heard their good-bye calls faintly through the faded cotton curtains. The twin bed sagged under her weight as she sat down and slipped off her worn cowboy boots. She smelled like horse—not a bad smell, but pungent nevertheless. A hot shower would ease her muscles, taxed with riding around barrels all day.

Her five-year-old daughter, Betsy, slept with one fist curled under her cheek in the youth cot next to Allie's bed, and Allie watched her sleep for a moment. So innocent, so beautiful.

So damaged by the blows life had dealt.

But things would get better soon. They could hardly get worse. Once Allie won the barrel-racing championship, the money would come rolling in, and they'd have a better place to live than this old, broken-down trailer.

Allie dreamed of the day she and Betsy would have a real home again. They had one once upon a time, until the rough seas washed the sand castle away. But she'd find a way somehow. Betsy deserved more.

Allie slipped out of her dusty jeans and padded to the hall in her bare feet. The floors of the tiny travel trailer creaked and groaned under her weight as she tiptoed toward the bathroom. She left the door open a crack in case Betsy called out for her, though the chance was unlikely. The little girl hadn't spoken a word in nearly a year.

The tiny bathroom was spotless except for the rust stains Allie couldn't get off the worn fixtures. The Lysol she'd sprayed still lingered in the air, and she resisted the urge to sneeze.

She stared at her reflection in the mirror. The rodeo queen's smile was one that vanished with the crowds.

She went to the tub and turned on the shower. The hot spray sputtered from the rusty showerhead and struck her sore arm, soothing it, enticing her to step fully into the welcoming warmth.

Straightening, she tugged her shirt over her head. A creak like someone stepping on the weak floor came from beyond the door. She whirled in time to see it slam shut. Allie jerked her shirt back down. Gooseflesh pebbled on her arm when the creak came again.

"Yolanda, is that you?" she called.

Her friend's cheery voice didn't answer. Allie wet her lips. She was being a nervous Nellie tonight. The noise was probably the old trailer settling. Her hand gripped the bottom of her shirt again to remove it.

Something scratched at the door, and she caught her breath.

"*Aaaallieee*," the taunting voice whispered through the door. The scrape sounded once more. "*Aaaallieee*."

A man's voice, low and guttural, maybe even deliberately pitched so she wouldn't recognize it. A sharp edge under the low, cruel voice vibrated. That voice could cut to the bone without a weapon.

Allie took a step away from the menace, her back pushing away the wet shower curtain until water sprayed her neck. It was like a wet slap, bringing her back to what mattered most.

Betsy!

She grappled with the embrace of the wet shower curtain and managed to disentangle herself from it. She leaped to the door and grabbed the doorknob, yanking hard, but the door didn't move. With her hand on the cold metal knob, she could feel his movements on the other side.

"Let me out!" she screamed, pounding and kicking at the door.

"You want out?" He chuckled, the razor edge of his voice contrasting with the smooth laugh. "Your sister wanted out."

The room felt close, airless. Her lungs strained to pull in enough oxygen. She wanted to scream for Betsy but didn't dare call the man's attention to the fact that her daughter was in the bedroom.

"You sure you want out, Allie?" he whispered.

Terror whirled inside like a mounting tornado. She forced it deep, down to the dark place where she kept all the things she feared. For Betsy's sake she had to keep herself together.

Maybe she could get out, circle around to Betsy's window, and get to her. She spun around and ran to the bathroom window, but it was too small to allow even her tiny frame to exit. She turned back to the door and tried to open it again. It opened a crack against the force of his hand holding it to on the other side, then slammed shut before she could get it open wide enough to get her leg through.

"Let go of the door!" She tugged harder, kicked at it. Her fear morphed into a cold anger. If she could face him, she'd tear at his face with her nails. She would allow no one to hurt her baby girl.

The man's laugh—if such an evil sound could be called laughter—whispered through the door again. "Your sister was so pretty. Not nearly as pretty as you, though. Especially not now." A knife poked through the crack. "She screamed when she saw the knife. Are you going to scream, Allie?"

Allie stared at the blade slicing through the door. It wasn't true, couldn't be true. He was just trying to scare her.

Tammy had walked in on a burglar.

The knife blade danced in the crack, moving forward, then pulling back long enough to make her think he was leaving. Then it reappeared, the edge sharp and dangerous.

She pulled on the knob again. "You coward," she yelled. "Face me like a man! Quit hiding behind whispers and phone calls."

"You might faint if you saw my face," he whispered. "Just like Tammy did."

The fear tried to surge out of the box she'd stuffed it into, but Allie tightened her control. Her sister's face flashed through her mind, and sorrow welled in her eyes. Had this man really been the one? She couldn't let herself believe it.

Allie laid her head against the door. "What do you want?"

"I want you to pay," he said, his whisper harsher. "I'm going to take everything you love, just like you destroyed the things that mattered to me. What matters most to you, Allie?"

Betsy, he would take Betsy!

Allie's frantic gaze ran around the room. What could she do? Though she knew it was so late no one would be out there to hear, she ran to the window and screamed, "Help, somebody help me!" Her cries fell into the silent yard. No one answered her scream.

"Don't do that," he growled.

Allie ignored his commanding tone and raised her voice so loud it hurt her throat. "Help! Please, someone help me!"

Then she heard the sweet sound of another voice. A shout answered her, feet shuffled through the dust toward her trailer. Help was on its way. She whirled and leaped back to the door. The knife was gone. This time the knob turned easily under her fingers, and the door flew open.

The hallway was empty.

Allie bounded from the bathroom and raced across the hall. "Please, oh please, God, let Betsy be all right." She rushed into the room and saw Betsy's tousled dark curls on the pillow. "Bets?" she whispered.

Betsy stirred and rubbed her eyes, then rolled over and went back to sleep.

Allie sagged against the doorframe. Her legs trembled, and she wanted to crawl into the bed herself, pull the covers over her head like she used to when she was afraid of the boogeyman.

But this was a real-life monster.

Someone pounded on the front door hard enough to make the whole trailer shake. She tottered down the hall and threw open the door.

Her best friend, Yolanda Fleming, stepped through the door. "Allie, what's wrong?"

Allie clutched her. "He was here, in my house!" Aware she wore only her shirt and underwear, she backed down the hall. "My sister. He said he killed Tammy!"

Horror began to dawn on Yolanda's face. But even as Yolanda hugged her, Allie knew none of her friends would be able to protect her and Betsy. There was only one thing she could do.

1

HIS BOSS DROVE WITH BOTH HANDS ON THE WHEEL, SLOW AND STEADY AS A
tortoise. Some days Elijah DeAngelos's attention to detail drove Rick
Bailey crazy, but today wasn't one of them. He had other things to
worry about.

Interstate 10 stretched out east, straight and nearly empty of traffic. Sage and creosote had greened up with the winter rains. The old
man turned the steering wheel in his gnarled hands, and the truck
rolled down a narrow dirt path toward a broken-down barn a quarter
of a mile back.

"Look there," Rick said. His hand gripped the door handle, wish-
ing he could wring someone's neck. The call had come in two hours

ago about these horses, but he'd hoped the caller was wrong about how bad their condition was. Everyone in the area knew to call Bluebird Ranch when a horse was in danger.

The two horses, one a pinto and the other a dun, stood on the other side of a gate that hung cockeyed on its post, their heads down. They could easily have gotten out, but they didn't have the strength. The ribs of both animals showed through their rough, dull coats. They barely mustered the will to turn to look at the vehicle.

They were so far gone, it would be a battle to save them.

Rick flung open his door and strode to the trailer they'd hauled here. Opening the back, he reached in for the bucket of high-protein dog food and sweet feed, a combination of oats, steamed cracked corn, and cottonseed pellets, all covered with molasses. The quick energy would be crucial to saving the mares. He carried the mixture to the animals. Elijah followed with a bucket of water.

Rick watched the feeble horses try to feed, and he fisted his hands. If he could find the man who had starved these horses, Rick would bloody his nose. He told himself to take a few deep breaths. Getting mad wouldn't help these animals.

He stepped to the dun and ran his hand over her patchy coat, wincing at the protruding bones. "I'm not sure we can save them," he admitted.

"I fear you might be right." Elijah held the bucket of water under the pinto's lips, but the mare refused to drink.

Rick heard the sound of an engine and turned to look. "The vet's here." He stepped to meet Grady O'Sullivan. "Thanks for coming all this way." The ranch was two hours from town, and Grady was the only vet he trusted to come this far.

The large man had red hair that stuck up like Woody Woodpecker's crest. About Rick's age, his big hands and feet matched his bulk. Dressed in jeans and a T-shirt, with feet thrust into sandals, he could have been at home on the Gulf beach.

He was also the pastor of the church Rick attended. He knew more about Rick than any man except Elijah.

Grady's gaze was on the horses, and he just nodded as he got out his bag. "They look bad, Rick."

"They are." Rick followed the vet to the two mares.

The dun's front legs buckled, and she went down. Rick knelt on one side, and the vet on the other. Grady ran his hands over her, checked her eyes and mouth, then prodded her stomach.

Rick knew the verdict before the man said anything. His gut clenched in a painful spasm, and he exhaled until it released. He'd hoped to reach her sooner.

Grady shook his head. "They're too far gone. I doubt they have the strength to make the trip. This one will die in the next couple of hours. She's just been starved too long."

"What about the pinto?" Elijah asked. The other mare had managed to get down some water and a handful of sweet feed and dog food. She stood swaying, her head down.

"Maybe, but it will take a miracle," the vet said.

"Those we have had before," Elijah said.

"Do what you can, Grady," Rick pleaded. "For both of them."

The vet heaved a sigh and opened his bag. "I'll start an IV of electrolytes and add in some B12. Then all we can do is pray."

Rick had already started that, and he knew the other men had as well. He watched the vet insert the IV and get the fluid going. The minutes ticked by, and he swatted at the horseflies congregating around the desperately ill mares. Squatting by the dun, he rubbed her head and neck, but half an hour later, she blew a final puff of breath into his palm, then . . . nothing.

No, no! He couldn't lose her. He blew in her nostrils and massaged her stomach, but the great chest stayed motionless. His head dropped. Pain pulsed behind his eyes. "She's gone," he said.

Feeling older than his thirty-four years, he stood and went to check on the pinto. Elijah was at her side, coaxing her into eating another handful of the high-calorie feed. "She looks a little stronger," he said.

Elijah nodded. "This one, she will make it."

"Another hour and the prognosis would have been different," Grady said. "She's a nice mare. Small, but good lines. The kids at the ranch will love her."

Rick looked back at the dun. He'd failed that one. "Can we take her home now?"

"Give her another hour and some more feed, then see how strong she is. Wait until she's not wobbly. And leave the IV in until the second bag is empty." He closed his supply case. "Call me if you need me."

"Thanks, Grady. Tell Dolly I appreciate her sparing you on your day off."

"No problem." Grady carried his bag to the car, and Rick walked with him.

Over an hour later, Rick and Elijah decided the mare was strong enough to attempt the trip. The men got her loaded into the trailer, then climbed into the truck.

"We'll have to stop and feed her a few times," Rick said.

For now Rick could be glad Elijah was a slow and careful driver. The mare couldn't handle much jarring. "How can men be so cruel?" he asked softly once they were out on I-10 again. "We see so much of this neglect. People think they want a horse but don't stop to realize how much care one requires. When they're tired of it all, they just abandon their responsibilities."

Elijah gave him a quick glance. "Somehow I do not think you are speaking of the man who did this to the horses. It brings back memories of your mother, *sí?*"

The scars on Rick's back throbbed at the word *mother*. The woman didn't deserve the title. His thoughts raced to the woman who'd scarred him. It was her fault the county had taken his brother, Chad—Rick had never found him again. If he'd had a real dad, like Elijah, and a loving mom, what might he have done with his life?

Those kinds of doubts could drive him crazy. Rick was doing what he wanted, saving the horses he loved and helping kids turn out right.

THE SUN HAD ALREADY CONVERTED THE TRAILER INTO A SAUNA, THOUGH A slight breeze relieved the heat a tad. Allie swiped away the sheen of perspiration on her forehead with the back of her hand before tossing a handful of socks into the suitcase.

"But where are you going?" Yolanda blocked the doorway.

About Allie's age, Yolanda was a pretty African-American who could ride like Dale Evans and rope like Roy Rogers. Yo would go far in the rodeo. Ice curled around Allie's veins at the realization she wouldn't be around to see it.

She glanced up from packing and forced a smile. "It's better if you don't know," she told Yolanda. "You're safer that way."

Familiar sounds and smells wafted in through the window: shouts from the stock crew, steers bellowing, the jingle of horse tack, the good scent of horse and cattle. Allie would miss the rodeo. And El Paso. Even this little trailer had come to feel like home after so many years.

Yolanda flopped onto the bed, her black cornrows bouncing on her shoulders. "I'm scared for you, girl. You'll be alone, without anyone to help you with Betsy. Let me tag along for luck."

"You're going to win the barrel race this year, Yo. I can't take that away from you. We'll be fine." Allie's purse sat on the nightstand with only a hundred dollars in it, and she prayed it would be enough to get them to the Big Bend. Yolanda would give her anything she had, but Allie couldn't ask.

It was bad enough that she had to give up her dream of winning the barrel race this year herself. She wouldn't dream of torpedoing Yo's chances as well.

"Did you talk to the cops?" Yolanda asked.

"What good would it do? The police have done nothing to stop whoever this guy is." A lump crept up her throat, but she swallowed it down and focused on her packing.

"They're trying. The guy is slick."

Allie zipped her old green suitcase closed. "I have to disappear."

The worry in Yolanda's dark eyes intensified. "I know we've gone over this before, but, girl, you have to have *some* idea who could hate you so much."

"Hernandez is the only one with something against me, and he's dead."

"What if it's someone he met in the clink?"

Allie set her suitcase on the cracked linoleum floor. "Why would someone take on his vendetta? Whoever this guy is, he's *killed* three people, Yo. That takes a lot of hatred. And I'm not waiting around for him to get to Betsy."

After her parents died when her father's plane went down, the calls started. An eerie voice taunted her on the phone, telling her he had killed her parents and would take everything she loved. She'd been sunken in despair and grief, bowed down with more than she could bear until the guy started calling.

Strangely, his calls infused her with the determination to protect the rest of her family. The threats gave her purpose.

Only one person could help her now. She hadn't wanted to go to him—not with him working for the one man she wanted to avoid—but now he was her best chance.

"How do you think Betsy will handle the change?"

Allie glanced out the open curtains to the melee going on outside. Her daughter stood on the first rung of the fence, watching the cowboys practice throwing their ropes at the stationary stands. Dust billowed from the horse's hooves. "I hope the place where I'm taking her will make her well."

Yolanda's forehead wrinkled. "Some place that will make her talk? What kind of place would that be?"

Allie wagged her finger at her friend. "Don't try to find out any more."

"What if Betsy's grandparents show up? What should I tell them?"

"The truth. That you don't know where I am. If they can't find me, they can't serve me with custody papers." She picked up her suitcase and dragged it toward the door. "I packed too much," she panted.

"Let me help." Yolanda sprang toward her.

"Just get the door."

Yolanda opened the door, and Allie dragged the bulky luggage out onto the dirt. She opened the tailgate of her old pickup and heaved it into the back with the ragtag assortment of rope, bridles, empty Pepsi cans, and old blankets.

"What if the police have questions?" Yolanda followed Allie toward the paddock. "And all your friends from church will want to know you're okay. Girl, it scares me to think about you being off on your own with no support."

"I'll call and check in occasionally. I can't let that guy find me and Betsy." Allie stepped to where Betsy stood at the fence. She scooped up her daughter and inhaled the scents of red licorice and little girl.

Betsy was all she had left of Jon. Allie would give her every possible reason to talk again. "Ready to go, Bets?"

Betsy shook her head so hard her ponytails flipped against her cheeks. She set her chin, and her lips quivered. Even the threat of leaving everything she knew and loved didn't break the wall of silence that had encased her for a year.

Allie set her on the ground and took her hand. "We'll come back for a visit. Come along, honey." Betsy's feet scuffed along the dirt, but she followed her mother to the truck.

"Call me, girl." Yolanda grabbed Allie in a tight hug.

Allie clasped Yo back, closing her eyes and imprinting the musky scent her friend wore in her memory. It would be all she'd have to hold her until they met again.

She was going into hostile territory.

"I'll call when I get there." Allie's eyes burned, and she knew she had to get out of there. Tears would upset Betsy. She got in the truck and buckled her seat belt, just a lap belt, the thing was so old. "Fasten up, Bets."

As the truck pulled away from the stockyard, Allie forced herself not to look in the rearview mirror and watch her ten-year dream dissolve in the distance.

2

BLUEBONNETS. THOUSANDS OF THEM. THE CARPET OF BLUE UNDULATED over the hills, melding into the distant haze of the mountains. Those peaks had been growing ever since she left the Del Norte Mountains behind and pressed closer to the Rio Grande.

Allie rubbed her tired eyes. Even Eddy Arnold belting out "Gonna Find Me a Bluebird" failed to energize her. Six hours on the road with the dust blowing in through the open windows had left her eyes dry and gritty.

She glanced in the rearview mirror. No other vehicles meant no pursuit. They had time to enjoy this, make a memory. She lifted her foot from the accelerator. "Look, Betsy, let's get your picture taken in the bluebonnets!"

Dark curls tied up in red holders hid Betsy's face from view. She plucked at the frayed edges of a hole in her jeans and didn't answer.

Allie would *not* allow despair to take hold. She would root it out, trample it underfoot, burn it to ash. Her daughter would talk again, laugh again, find joy again.

She forced a bit of cheerfulness into her voice. "I'll stop here and get your picture."

Something clanked in the old Ford's underbelly when she parked it at the side of the road. "Come on, sweetie," she coaxed. She hung the camera around her neck and turned to her daughter. "I'll show you the picture of me in the bluebonnets. I think I was about five at the time too."

She remembered the day so clearly. Her mother's smile, her scent. Allie's hands gripped the wheel in a spasm of agony. Nearly a year after her parents' deaths, the pain still threatened to swamp her. She shook off the memory and got out of the truck.

The sweet aroma of the thousands of flowers wafted around her. The wildflowers tossed their blue heads in the breeze and lifted their faces to the fading sunlight. How could Betsy not be moved by this place?

These hills felt like a sanctuary, a place of healing for them both.

Allie went around to the passenger door. The latch was always a bit tricky on this side, but she managed to wrench it open. Betsy's wide eyes were as blue as the wildflowers carpeting the landscape. Allie could see Jon in those eyes.

She lived for the day when those blue depths didn't hold fear. "It's okay," she said. "There's no one here."

Betsy hiked one leg out the door and looked around before she stood and put her small hand in Allie's. Allie led her into the bluebonnets and sat her down. The flowers almost looked like hyacinths, and the fragrance was divine, the sweetness intoxicating. The flowers stood tall on bright green stalks and came up to Betsy's chest, where they contrasted with her yellow shirt. Dusk was only a few minutes away, and the lighting was perfect.

"Just a minute." Allie turned on her digital camera, a gift from her parents, and snapped several shots of Betsy sitting stone-faced in the flowers. "Smile, Betsy," she called. But of course her daughter's lips stayed straight and sober.

Allie would give anything to hear the little girl giggle again.

"Let's go, sweetie."

Betsy jumped to her feet and ran to the truck. She slammed the door shut, then got out her coloring book and crayons.

Allie inhaled the fragrance one last time and slid under the steering wheel. She twisted the key. The engine did nothing but grind. "Come on, come on," she muttered. Releasing the key, she let the engine rest a minute, then tried again. The sound of the engine softened as the battery weakened.

If she had the money, she would have gotten a new battery before she left El Paso.

"Please, please." She leaned her head against the steering wheel. They couldn't be stuck out here. It would be dark in another hour, and the ranch had to be miles away.

Her gaze went to Betsy, who was lost in coloring the bluebirds in the Cinderella picture. Betsy would freak if they were stranded in the dark. Her night terrors were bad enough without actually being in danger.

Allie tried the engine again, but the grinding slowed until all she heard was the clicking of a dead battery. The empty highway stretched out to the horizon ahead and behind. Marfa was at least twenty miles behind her. There was no one she could call for help, even if she had a cell phone.

Leaning across the seat, she unlocked her daughter's door. "Let's go for a walk, Bets. I want to get a few more shots of you in those blue-bonnets, and there's a great patch just a little ways down the road."

Betsy shook her head and locked the door. Hating to be firm, Allie bit her lip and got out of the car. She went around to the passenger door and unlocked it with her key. "Come on, it will be fun."

Betsy's lip trembled, and tears filled her eyes, but she got out and took Allie's hand in a death grip.

Allie hit the lock on the door with her other hand, and they started toward the darkening mountains. "Just a little ways farther." She'd get Betsy to go about half a mile, then they'd take some pictures, then walk some more. Once the truck was out of sight, Betsy would quit looking behind.

"Your daddy was the strongest man who ever lived," Allie said. "One time the car fell off the jack when his friend was under it, and your daddy lifted it up with his bare hands so his friend could get out."

Betsy smiled, obviously drinking in the story. For a second she looked up at her mom instead of at the ground.

Their feet made a lonely sound on the pavement. "Look at the bluebirds, Bets." Allie pointed out a flock sitting along the electrical wires along the road.

Betsy rewarded Allie with an expression of interest as she craned her neck to watch the birds. She adored all things with feathers, and Allie took her bird-watching as often as possible. Maybe if she pointed out birds along the way, she'd be able to get Betsy to walk until dark without too much coaxing.

Allie watched the bright mountain bluebirds herself a moment.

She'd once thought she found her own bluebird of happiness, but it flew away, never to be found again. Now all she could do was put one foot in front of the other and keep going. Keep Jon's memory alive for Betsy and honor the amazing man he was.

The light was beginning to fade, and the birds would be finding spots to sleep soon. Then what?

Allie quickened their pace. They had to find help. The road rose to meet them, and the steep incline ahead didn't look pleasant. She tried not to worry about how many deserted highway miles lay ahead.

"Race you to the top!" She started to let go of Betsy's hand, but the little girl clutched it more tightly and slowed her steps. "Don't want to race?"

Betsy shook her head and made a drinking motion with her hand. Allie slapped her forehead with her palm. How could she have forgotten to bring water? She had a case of bottled water in the truck, and they'd walked off and left it. Casting her gaze back, she couldn't see the truck in the gloom that was whisking away the last of the light. They'd lose even more light if they went back.

She stood in the middle of the road and tried to figure out what was the best thing to do. A road sign was just ahead. She studied the words, figuring them out in her head. Big Bend 10. Bluebird Youth Ranch was supposed to be nine miles from the national park, so maybe the road to the place would be right up ahead. They were closer than she thought. That would be faster than going back.

"There will be water at the ranch," Allie said, tugging Betsy onward. "Let's hurry."

A rumble sounded behind them, and she turned to see lights shining out of the gloom. Her initial relief dimmed as she realized how isolated they were. Maybe they should hide in the bluebonnets.

The way Betsy clutched her hand told her the little girl was frightened too. "Let's hide in the wildflowers, Bets," she whispered. "The ranch isn't far." Praying the driver was too far away to see them, she dashed toward the flowers with Betsy in tow. They hit the dirt, and without warning, a line of bumblebees flew up from their ground nest.

Right toward them.

Allie shrieked and leaped to her feet, jerking Betsy with her. The little girl's mouth opened in horror as the bees descended, but she didn't scream. Allie felt a sharp pain on her cheek and another on her arm. The loud buzzing disoriented her, but she reached for Betsy. Four or five bees clung to her top. Allie swatted them off, too intent to even flinch at the stings in her fingers.

Maybe there were some under the fabric. Allie pulled the T-shirt over Betsy's head and found two more bees clinging to the underside. She shook them off, then grabbed her daughter's hand and ran. Another bee stung her in the back of the arm, and she swiped at it, knocking it to the ground. They reached the road and left the bees behind. Silent tears rolled down Betsy's face, and she held her arm.

Allie slipped the top back onto her daughter. "Oh Bets, I'm sorry. It was my fault. Do the stings hurt?" She pulled Betsy close. The little girl wrapped her skinny arms around Allie's neck and buried her face in her chest. Allie rubbed the soft skin of the little girl's arm. The stings were already swelling.

Allie thumbed Betsy's tears away. "Let me check for stingers. There might be some left in your skin."

"I saw what happened." A man's voice came from the truck idling five feet away. "The little girl okay?"

Allie had forgotten all about the approaching vehicle. She glanced around for a stick or some kind of weapon. There was nothing. Edging her daughter behind her, she backed up.

"That was a pretty stupid thing to do." His voice went flat. The truck door opened, and a man stepped out and moved into the headlights.

Allie's nails bit into her palms, and she struggled to hold back the words she wanted to say. With the lights blinding her, she got only a brief impression of his bulk and height. Betsy sounded like she was about to hyperventilate.

"Stop, don't come any closer!" Allie edged further away. "I've got a gun." She put her hand in the pocket of her jeans like there was really something there.

He squatted near Betsy. "Are you hurt, honey? Let's go get something on those stings." His voice was surprisingly gentle.

Betsy edged her wet face around Allie's waist, and her death grip loosened. Allie stared at her daughter. She didn't trust easily, but she pulled away from Allie and stepped toward the man. Anyone who coaxed a bit of trust from Betsy deserved a second look.

"She has several stings," Allie told him. Her own fingers throbbed with stingers, but she'd get them out on her own. Putting her fingers to her mouth, she pulled one out with her teeth.

"Let me see. Come in front of the headlights." He leaned into the truck and rummaged in the glove box. Carrying a first-aid kit, he moved to the front of the vehicle. "It won't hurt," he said to Betsy, who lowered her head and moved slowly. "Show me the stings."

Betsy held out her arm without looking at him. "Looks like the stingers are still there." He pulled out his wallet and extracted a credit card, which he swept over the marks. "Got them!" He opened the kit and pulled out a can.

"Is that deodorant?" Allie asked.

"Yep. Meat tenderizer is better, but aluminum chlorohydrate reduces the effect of bee venom too." He sprayed Betsy's arms and neck. "Better?"

Betsy nodded, still not looking at him.

He stood and nodded to the north. "Was that your old rattletrap down the road? You need some help?"

"I could use a jump," she said. She kept her voice cool. Rattletrap indeed. Maybe it was, but the comment held too much contempt for her liking.

"Hop in."

Her trust would only go so far. "We'll meet you down there. Who are you, anyway?"

His sigh was loud and exasperated. "Look, lady, I'm not an ax murderer. Just get in the truck, and I'll give you my résumé later."

Betsy shrank back at his harsh voice and buried her face in Allie's waist.

Instantly, the man squatted. "I'm sorry, honey. I'm not mad." Betsy peeked at him from between her fingers, and he smiled. He stood and put his hands in his pockets. "It's not safe to walk out here by yourself. I'll let you drive my truck back and I'll walk."

"How about you ride in the back and let me drive?" Allie didn't think he'd agree, but she didn't feel right about making him walk.

If only Jon were here.

"Okay." He tossed her the keys and strode to the pickup's rear, where he put one boot onto the wheel well and vaulted into the back.

The guy was a mountain. Allie didn't like big men. They made her feel even smaller than she already was—and more inept.

She stared at the keys in her hand and forced a smile. "Let's go get our truck, Bets." She opened the driver's-side door, and Betsy climbed in, then scooted across the seat. Allie slid inside after her daughter. Nice wheels. The vehicle wasn't new, but he'd taken good care of it. Its gray interior didn't hold a speck of dirt.

She started the truck, turned around, and drove back toward her pickup. The headlights picked out the silhouette. When she reached it, she angled the man's vehicle so the headlights shone on her hood.

The man jumped out and opened the hood of his truck, then fiddled with something inside. She watched him walk around to her truck and open the driver's door. She thought she'd locked it. No, only Betsy's door, she remembered.

She got out to help. Only one boot showed under her open driver's door. The battery clicked, then he exited the vehicle.

"Lady, you're out of gas," he said with a disgusted thrust to his lip. "Don't you have any sense at all? Dragging a kid out into the middle of nowhere without gas, putting her in a nest of bumblebees, and not even taking any water with you."

He had no idea what she'd been through. Stiffening her back, she stared at the man until he looked down.

"Sorry, it's none of my business," he said.

"No, it's not. We're on our way to Bluebird Youth Ranch. Is it close?"

His head came up at the mention of the ranch. "I work at the ranch. It's just a mile down the road. We weren't expecting any visitors."

"I know. I've come a long way to talk to someone there." Two men actually, but he didn't need to know the details. If she had the nerve, she'd ask him if he knew Rick Bailey, the foreman.

The surly man stalked to his pickup and flipped down the tailgate. Tight-lipped, he stalked back with a gas can in his hand. He drained it into the gas tank, then went back to his truck. Revving his engine, he called out the window, "Try it now."

Allie ran to the truck and slid under the wheel. "Please, please start," she muttered under her breath. She cranked the engine. It ground slowly, then picked up speed and turned over. It was running so rough that the truck shook, but at least it would go.

"Come on, Bets," she called. Betsy ran to get into the passenger seat.

The man's pickup pulled away, the tires spitting sand and dust. Allie dropped the transmission into drive and followed him. The blackness of night cloaked the land as she followed him into a wide dirt lane, hard and packed from the weight of vehicles. At a distance, the lights of the house and four outbuildings shone a welcome, and Allie felt the weight of fatigue press heavier.

So this was the Bluebird Ranch. Even the name had intrigued her when her mother talked about it. A longing for home and family rose, and she squelched it. She had to stay focused.

Surely they wouldn't turn her away tonight.

The man switched off his engine and walked back to her truck. "I'll take you to Elijah. He's probably in the barn. Cupcake is about to foal. Come with me."

Grabbing Betsy's hand, Allie leaped from the truck and followed the man's long steps toward a big white barn. It had a hipped roof, and white paddocks stretched as far as she could see in the moonlight. The last building was a hangar that held a small plane.

"Who's the pilot?" she asked, pointing to the plane.

"I am. The distances are so great out here, it makes sense to fly when we can."

A border collie, tail wagging, came to meet them. The animal rose on its hind legs without touching either of them. The joyous expression of the dog's excitement brought a smile to Betsy's face.

"Nice dog." Allie said, pausing to pet the collie. "Male or female?"

"Jem's a male. Don't spoil him. He's a herd dog."

"He's gorgeous." With a last pat, she and Betsy followed the man.

The good scent of horses and hay lifted her fatigue when they stepped into the barn. The man led them to the back, where they found a short, sinewy old guy tending to a laboring horse. The bay mare was down in the straw, and the man had her head on his lap. His brown skin was leathered with age and sun, but when the dark eyes under the cowboy hat met her own, she saw a depth of love and compassion that made her feet move toward him.

This was Elijah? She tried to hide her curiosity but was unable to look away. She hadn't known he existed until her mother died.

His stare seemed a bit intense for just having met, then his gaze settled on Betsy, and his face softened even more. "Hello, *niña*. Do you like horses? We're going to have a colt soon."

Betsy nodded, her gaze locked with the old man's. Allie's hope surged. Betsy's face held more interest than she'd seen in a year. The little girl stepped forward with her hand out, then pulled it back.

"You can pet her." Elijah's voice was gentle.

Betsy knelt and touched the mare's nose. The horse blew her breath into Betsy's hand, and she scrambled back. A huge yawn erupted from her mouth.

Mr. DeAngelos nodded to the corner. "It will be a long night. There are blankets for the *niña*. You both look tired."

"Want to lay in the hay, Bets?" Allie wouldn't have minded curling up in that soft mound herself.

Betsy nodded. Allie led Betsy to the hay in the corner and sat her down with a blanket over her lap. Dust motes danced into the air when the little girl rustled in the mound. Betsy kept her gaze fastened on the horse, but her lids drooped, and Allie knew it wouldn't be long before she would be asleep. Then she could make their case to the old man.

And then she would find Rick Bailey.

Elijah glanced up at the other man. "Rick, would you get us some hot coffee? The stuff in the kitchen has been sitting there since morning, so brew some fresh."

Rick. Allie sank into the straw next to Betsy. How could Jon have told her to come to this tight-lipped man for help? The only assistance he'd give would be to escort her right out of here.

3

RICK MUTTERED UNDER HIS BREATH AS HE STRODE ACROSS THE YARD TO the ranch house. Jem did his little air dance at Rick's side, then stopped at the front door when he went inside. Women like that one gave the word *mother* a bad rap. Some just weren't born with a maternal instinct.

She had only been thinking of herself.

And what was wrong with the kid? Betsy hadn't said a word. Something weird going on there, and it was likely the mom's fault. Everyone that pretty had entitlement problems anyway. She wasn't much bigger than a kid herself, and she'd probably used her tiny stature and big blue eyes to her advantage.

He was going to advise Elijah to get rid of her as soon as he could.

He stepped into the kitchen and threw together some sandwiches while the coffee brewed. He put them in a knapsack along with some apples and bottles of water. The most he would do is feed them. After pouring coffee into a thermos, he started back to the barn.

To give Elijah and the woman more time to talk, he stopped at the smaller barn to check on the horse they'd hauled back this morning. Scooping up the sweet feed mixture, he offered the mare another handful. The dull eyes looked at him, then her teeth nibbled at his palm. She was far from out of the woods.

The wind changed and brought the odor of manure to his nose. He winced as memories of another stench washed over him.

He was back in Fallujah, moving past puddles of raw sewage running in the streets. Joking with his buddy Jon and tossing pennies at the children who ran shouting and laughing beside them.

At one time, he'd thought to save the world. Right now, saving this horse would make him happy.

ELIJAH RUBBED THE MARE'S BELLY. "MY FOREMAN IS NOT AS GRUFF AS he seems."

Allie didn't believe the old man, though she wished she could. Allie glanced at Betsy. She was asleep. Now was the time.

She wet her lips. "I've come a long way to talk to you, Mr. DeAngelos."

He held up his hand. "Please, call me Elijah." He nodded to Betsy. "The *niña* has been hurt."

Allie nodded. "My name is Allie Siders, and this is my daughter, Betsy." The old man made a sudden movement, and she stopped. "Is anything wrong?"

"No, no, continue."

Was it her imagination or had he paled? She hoped he didn't have some kind of heart condition. When he didn't move, she went on. "She hasn't talked for a year. I've taken her to therapist after therapist, and there's been no change. I've tried everything I know to help her. You're my last hope." Especially now that she knew she'd rather die than ask Rick Bailey for anything.

"How did you hear about us?"

She hesitated. How could she explain without telling all? "One of your hired hands came to a rodeo I worked in El Paso. He told me about this place. I had to try it." She decided to see if she could get a reaction out of him. "I found a scrapbook about this place in my mama's things."

"Your mother? She stayed here?"

Allie nodded. "Her stage name was Anna Morgan." Something seemed to shift in the room when she said the name, but everyone reacted that way.

"The barrel racer?"

"Yes."

"She is dead now, killed in a plane crash."

Allie took a deep breath. It had been the worst day of her life. "A year ago."

Her mother had been as beautiful and flamboyant as a flamenco dancer. Her half-Hispanic blood was further diluted in Allie, who had her father's blue eyes and calm temperament. Her mother brought passion and excitement to everything she did, and Allie's life seemed to be lived in dull black and white since her mama's death.

She studied his impassive face. Did he know his Selena had changed her name and become famous? Until Allie found the scrapbook and began the research, she thought her grandparents were dead. She found no evidence the old man knew he was her grandfather.

"You are hurting too, *mujercita*. What happened to you and the *niña?*"

He'd called her "little woman," and she drew herself up to her full five foot two. "It's Betsy I'm worried about. She's been like this for a year, and I've tried everything. I don't have any money to pay you, but I'll work. I know horses. I've grown up in the rodeo. I can cook, clean, anything you need." She rushed on, certain he would refuse when he found out she had nothing.

He didn't have to know she'd sold everything—her horse, her new car. She had some pride left.

"I was once a bronco buster," Elijah said. Then his gaze shifted as the horse groaned, and the hay darkened with fluid. "Ah, our foal is coming. Sleep. There will be time to talk tomorrow."

Allie squatted beside him. "I can help you."

"Cupcake is an experienced mother. She'll do it all herself."

"I'll wait with you then." If she could show how much she knew about horses, maybe he'd find her a job. It was no secret Rick Bailey wouldn't be in favor of that. But Betsy needed Allie to do this. Though Elijah couldn't help the other things that threatened them, if he could heal Betsy, it would be enough.

Elijah lifted the mare's head enough to ease away. He stood back and watched the horse labor.

Rick came back in carrying a coffee thermos and Styrofoam cups. A knapsack was slung around his shoulder. He set the cups on a bale of hay and poured out a cup of coffee. Digging in his jeans, his hand came up with small containers of creamer. He still hadn't said a word.

"Thanks." Allie accepted two creamers and dumped them into her coffee. The aroma made her mouth water. Then the hot liquid filled her empty stomach. She'd been hoarding the last of her money to make sure Betsy had enough food and hadn't eaten herself since breakfast, part of an omelet in a greasy spoon at nine this morning. Even then, she hadn't eaten until Betsy was full.

Rick slipped the knapsack off his shoulder and unzipped it. "Turkey sandwiches," he said, handing her the sandwich wrapped in plastic. "There's fruit in here too." He handed her an apple.

Maybe he had some compassion to spare for adults after all. Allie smiled at him, but he still hadn't looked her in the eye.

"Let me see if Betsy wants some first."

"There's plenty for you both," Rick said. "And more where that came from. Let her sleep."

He was right, but Allie felt wrong to eat when her daughter might be hungry. A peek in the knapsack reassured her. There were two more sandwiches in it, and four apples. She took a cautious bite. Relishing the hot sting of horseradish on her tongue, she devoured the sandwich.

Food had never tasted so good.

She swallowed the last sweet bite of apple and looked up to find both men watching her. "Thanks," she said, clamping her lips against the explanation that pressed against her teeth.

Without a word, Rick held out another apple. She took it and squirreled it away in her backpack. Betsy might need it later. She did the same with the rest of the food. If Rick and Elijah turned down her plea for help, she and Betsy would be in desperate straits.

She settled on the hay to wait for the foal's arrival. With a full tummy, her lids drooped and her breathing eased. Maybe she'd close her eyes for just a minute.

4

"GOOD LINES," RICK SAID, EXAMINING THE WET ARRIVAL. CUPCAKE nudged the colt. The small, black foal stood on wobbly legs. He moved a few feet along her flank and nosed her belly before beginning to nurse.

Elijah grabbed a pitchfork and began to clean the wet, soiled straw out of the stall. Where did the old man get his energy? "I'll do that," Rick said. "Why don't you go on into bed? It's after two."

"Many hands make light work," Elijah said.

Rick shoveled with him. When they were done, he hung the pitchforks on a nail. "What about those two?" he asked, nodding toward the sleeping woman and girl.

The girl looked like a miniature of her mother. Fine, dark hair, blue eyes, dimples that flashed. At least the mother's dimples had flashed. Betsy hadn't smiled yet.

"You don't like Allie," Elijah observed.

"It's hard to like stupidity," Rick said. "She doesn't have an ounce of sense." He told Elijah how he'd found them fighting off bees in the bluebonnets. "And she didn't even have any water for the kid. I'll bet she did something to make the girl quit talking. Now she wants you to fix it."

"A snap judgment, Rick? You should get to know them before you point fingers."

A slow anger burned his belly. "You're going to let them stay? It's because she resembles Maria, isn't it?"

"I realize she is not my daughter, Rick. I would not be taken in so easily. And wasn't it you who just told me you weren't going to do the cooking anymore?" Elijah was smiling. "You have lost weight since Rosa left us. A woman's cooking might fatten us both up."

"For the slaughter," Rick said. "She'll steal you blind in the night."

The woman raised his hackles for some reason. For one thing, she was too pretty. He'd never seen eyes such an electric blue. In his experience, beautiful women expected pretty things handed to them. She just showed up here and expected Elijah to take her in. That whole wolfing down of the sandwich was probably an act to get Elijah's sympathy.

And it worked. Rick could see the softness in the old man's eyes. Elijah was a sucker for a sob story.

"Someone once told me the same thing about you," Elijah observed. "Trust my judgment, *hijo*."

Rick gave a grudging nod. "You made up your mind to help her when she ate her food like a starving street person."

"No, it was when she put the food away for the *niña*. You can't tell me that you were untouched by that, Rick."

He didn't want to be moved by her love for the child, but the gesture had affected him. "Yeah, I saw it too. It's the only reason I haven't thrown her out on her ear. The kid needs help."

"And so do we." Elijah went toward the door. "Let them sleep. If we wake them to move to a bed, the *niña* may have trouble getting back to sleep."

Rick followed his boss out of the barn to the ranch house. Stepping into the living room, he looked around, seeing it with fresh eyes. He couldn't remember the last time one of them had mopped the scarred wooden floors or dusted the battered furniture. Last autumn maybe?

A stale odor hung in the air as though the windows hadn't been opened in months. And maybe they hadn't. He should clean it up a little before Allie took over. But not tonight. Fatigue weighed down his legs. He'd do it in the morning.

ALLIE STOOD WATCHING THE SUN COME UP OVER THE MOUNTAINS. THE morning air made her shiver, but she couldn't go inside yet. Not while the sunrise gilded the peaks and valleys, and the air smelled like sage and creosote. Her hair still uncombed, Betsy stood beside her with their hands locked.

"You like it here, Bets?" Allie asked.

Betsy nodded and pointed. A flock of bluebirds blanketed the grass and pecked for insects.

Allie drank in the sight. If only finding the real bluebird of happiness was as easy as following a flock of birds. "I've never seen so many in one place. I wonder if this is a migration spot for them. We should ask Mr. DeAngelos."

Betsy nodded, her gaze still on the birds.

The old man had to let them stay. The bluebirds told Allie she and Betsy were in the right place. Betsy would talk again, and no one would find them here. She'd been careful to cover her tracks, and the faceless man wouldn't know where she'd gone. They would be safe here.

"I don't think they're up yet. If the door isn't locked, we'll go in and fix breakfast." Allie glanced at her watch. It was nearly seven, so the lack of lights in the house surprised her, but the men might have been up most of the night with the mare.

The thin, sandy soil felt cool under her bare feet, and she avoided the cactus in the path as she stepped toward the house.

A male voice spoke. "You made it."

Allie turned to see a fresh-faced young man. He looked like a fourteen-year-old trying to act twenty-four. A big rodeo belt buckle on his waist glinted. With his thumbs hooked in the pockets of his jeans and his cowboy hat pushed back, he stood with one worn boot on the fence rail as if posing for a documentary about cowboys.

Poor kid. If he only knew trying to make an impression on her would get him nowhere. He'd tried it at the rodeo last month, and though she hadn't caught his name, he was the one who told her about this place.

"We never introduced ourselves when we met at the rodeo." She extended a hand. "I'm Allie Siders, and this is Betsy. We came in last night."

"Like I'd forget a honey like you. I'm Charlie." He put his propped foot back on the ground, shook Allie's hand in a strong grip, then knelt in front of Betsy. "Hey kid, want to see some horses?"

Betsy buried her face in Allie's waist and didn't look at him.

"She's tired," Allie said. "Maybe later."

The young man straightened. "I made a run to Marathon after oats yesterday," he said. "When I saw that old truck parked beside the barn this morning, I wondered who had blown in while I wasn't looking."

"I don't think anyone in the house is up yet."

He nodded. "Cupcake foaled. I think the boss was up most of the night. Otherwise, there'd be breakfast on the table. I could rustle us up some grub."

"Let me do it." Allie took Betsy's hand and moved toward the house again. "I was about to try the door when you called to me."

The house looked like it had grown out of the red soil, but as she neared, she saw red dirt coated the stone face of the home. The big pillars that supported the massive porch of the two-story dwelling sported a fresh white coat of paint. The place was bigger than she'd thought at first, easily three thousand square feet.

She followed Charlie up the stone steps and across the porch to the entry.

"It's always unlocked." Charlie twisted the doorknob and pushed open the door. "Go on in."

She stepped onto an oak floor, its patina of old age as fitting as the well-worn boots on her feet. Stucco walls painted a soft green invited her in, but they were bare of any ornamentation that would have enhanced the effect of the color. Heaped under the window was a jumble of discarded socks, boots, and shoes. They gave off a pungent odor, and Betsy wrinkled her nose.

Allie took Betsy's hand and moved down the hall to the door at the end. "Is this the way to the kitchen?"

"Yep. Don't mind the mess. The housekeeper left last fall."

Mess was an understatement. As Allie moved past the living room, she caught a glimpse of a large den littered with newspapers and piles of books. Some kind of video game controller lay on a recliner, its wires stretching to the TV.

She averted her eyes and stepped through the swinging door into the kitchen. And stopped short. Had no one cleaned the kitchen since the housekeeper left?

The sink overflowed with pots and dishes. Several cupboards hung open to reveal empty shelves. Every dish in the place must be dirty.

Charlie seemed oblivious to the chaos. He went to the refrigerator and opened it. "I know we've got eggs and bacon. There's bread for toast. I think there might be hash browns in the freezer."

"I'll figure it out. First I'd better do some dishes." Allie rolled up the sleeves of her blouse and went to the sink. "I can't cook in this . . . dirt." She eyed the stove, thick with grime.

Charlie's smile was weak. "Yeah, it's bad."

"Want to dry the dishes?"

"Uh, I'll go feed the stock." He backed out of the kitchen.

THE SETTING OF THE SUN ONLY SLIGHTLY COOLED THE BRUTALITY OF THE Fallujah heat. Rick tossed his cards onto the battered wooden table. "You win," he told his best friend.

"I always win." His buddy grinned at him and began to gather up the cards. "I'm done. I need to write to my wife."

"You write to her every night." Rick's tone was sharp, but in his heart he wished he had someone to write to every night. Someone who cared if he lived or died.

His friend's smile faded. "I worry about her. What if I don't come back?"

Rick shuffled on his chair. "Don't talk like that. We're both going to get on that plane next month and fly home."

"Tomorrow's mission is dangerous, buddy. Promise you'll look out for my family—if the worst happens."

"You'll take care of them yourself." Rick stood and pushed his chair under the table. "I don't want to hear this."

"I know what will happen if I don't come home. My parents will try to get my daughter. And that can't happen. Not ever. Promise me you'll make sure."

"If I promise, will you drop it?"

"Promise me," Jon said again. "I know you're a man of your word."

"Okay, okay, I promise. Now shut up about it!"

His friend's shape began to morph. Red spots bloomed on his chest, his face grew pale and stricken. Rick saw breastbone protruding through the skin before he awakened with a start to hear an echo still lingering in his room.

I promise.

He sat up and wiped the sweat from his forehead. His heart was thumping in his chest like he'd just had a fright. He drew a few deep breaths until he got control of his racing pulse. It was over, he reminded himself.

Maybe these nightmares were going to continue until he checked on his buddy's family. This was the second dream in a week, and he always woke drenched with dread. Shaking off the effects of the dream, he climbed out of bed and pulled his clothes on.

Rick's nose twitched when he opened his bedroom door. Was that bacon? The tantalizing scent pulled him from the room and down the steps. His stomach growled, and he spared a glance at his watch. Holy cow, was it really that late? Though he'd only had about four hours sleep.

He heard banging in the kitchen. Charlie was sure loud this morning, but bless him for making breakfast. Rick stopped in the doorway and saw the tiny woman at the sink. The kitchen sparkled, even the tile underfoot. Every dish and pot was in place. Bacon sizzled in a skillet, and the eggs and hash browns looked crisp and tasty.

Allie whirled to face him. Her welcoming smile faded. Rick felt his own smile falter.

"Where's Charlie? I thought he was fixing breakfast."

"He's feeding the livestock. You're up late," she said.

He squinted at the clock on the wall. "I think it was four when we got to bed."

"Is Elijah up?"

"No, he's still out." He frowned. "You think you can win him over by cleaning the kitchen?"

Allie opened her mouth, then closed it again. That would put her in her place. Did she think she was Martha Stewart, coming in here and taking over?

She turned back to the stove. "Breakfast is ready." She ladled up a plate of food and handed it to him.

His stomach, traitor that it was, rumbled loudly in the kitchen. He took the plate without a word and sat down beside Betsy, who was finishing up her own serving of eggs and toast.

The little girl gave him a shy glance, and he tried to coax a smile from her. "Hey Betsy, have you seen the new baby?"

Betsy nodded, but the smile he wanted didn't break out. He glanced at her mom. What had she done to this kid?

"We saw him," Allie said.

Rick frowned. "You always answer for her?"

"She doesn't talk."

"She won't ever talk if you don't let her."

"I'm her mother. I think I know how to behave around her better than you do." Allie turned her back to him and turned off the burners.

Touchy. She made him tense just by being in the same room. That was the trouble with women—they came in and upset everything. He'd woken up in a good mood, and now he could tear the head off of a bear with his hands.

Betsy tugged on his hand and pointed to the door. "You want to go watch cartoons?" Rick asked. The little girl nodded. "Okay, but don't turn the TV up very loud. Let's let Elijah sleep."

The wooden chair legs scraped across the tile, and Allie settled into the chair. She wet her lips, and her eyes looked uncertain. "I thought I'd better formally introduce myself," she said. "I'm Allie Siders."

She paused as though she expected the name to mean something to him. That's when it hit, and when it did, his pulse leaped like spurred horse.

Siders. Jon's wife was named Allie. It couldn't be. The egg in his mouth formed an immovable lump.

"I'm Jon's widow," she said quietly.

Rick choked, then managed to swallow the bite of eggs. "Jon's widow?" His gaze locked with hers. Jon Siders. Even hearing the name made the grief and guilt well up like a spring. The promise he'd never kept had come here searching him out.

His promise to Jon rose up to mock him. He'd tried halfheartedly to find Jon's widow but couldn't. The Bluebird Ranch became his refuge, the safe haven where he could lick his wounds. His selfishness shamed him. Jon had sacrificed everything for him, and Rick was all too quick to abandon his promises.

Her eyes never left his face. "I know I should have called or written first, but there wasn't time." She finally looked away and cast her gaze to her plate.

The words he wanted to say locked behind the muscles of his throat. He wanted to ask her to forgive him, he wanted to ask her what she wanted, he wanted to tell her everything would be all right.

He choked back the confession of guilt and forced himself to cast a cool gaze on her face. "Why are you here?"

"Jon told me to come to you if I was ever in trouble." She said the words with an edge of reluctance.

"Are you in trouble now?" So he wasn't ready to honor that promise, even now. The responsibility loomed like a mountain.

"I'm in big trouble." She shut her mouth, then finally lifted her gaze. "I didn't even want to say anything. You've made it clear what you think of me. But I don't know where else to turn. Even if Elijah gives me a job, there's another . . . issue."

The silence echoed in the room. The words he needed to say stayed lodged behind his teeth. He had to wonder what kind of trouble would bring her clear out here to what the Mexicans called *El Despoblado,* the land of no people.

Guilt seized him in its sharp teeth. Whatever it was, he had to help. He'd promised Jon.

"Aren't you going to say something?" she whispered, finally raising her gaze to meet his.

The color had leached from her face, and her blue eyes looked murky with an emotion he couldn't name for sure. Maybe fear and grief. His own grieving had thinned until all that was left was a wisp of fog that dissipated every day.

Her revelation brought it storming back.

He wet his lips. "Jon was my best friend."

Allie smiled then. "I know. His letters from Iraq were filled with stuff about you. He loved you like a brother. I—I always wanted to thank you for trying to save him. I heard you were wounded trying to get him out."

Her blue eyes warmed then, and the gratitude in them was hard to take. He knew the truth.

"I failed him," Rick said, his voice harsh. Confession would be hard. She would hate him when she found out what really happened.

"You tried. That's all anyone could do."

"No." He pushed back from the table. "I wanted to contact you when I got back, but I couldn't find you." The silence seemed to grow louder before he finally broke it by clearing his throat and saying, "What's the trouble?"

"It would be a shorter list to tell you what's going right." She blinked rapidly. "It's been hard since Jon died, but we were doing okay. I was making the rodeo circuit in barrel racing—and doing great. I worked at the rodeo as well. Then my parents died in a plane crash, and a month ago my sister was killed. There's no one left to turn to."

Rick wasn't good at platitudes. First Jon's death, then the rest of her family. Pity stirred in his heart. "You need money?"

"No! I'm able-bodied, and I'll support us. I don't want a handout." She looked down at her hands, clasped in her lap. "Jon's parents are trying to get custody of Betsy. My world would end if I lost her." Her gaze came up to stare at him with a pleading expression. "One of your hands told me about this place, that it could help Betsy. I'd been coming here to see you anyway."

Just as Jon thought. He'd been adamant they shouldn't have a hand in raising his daughter.

"They've got grounds?" Though he framed it as a question, his tone suggested he'd have no trouble siding with someone who thought her unfit. It was hard to let go of his initial judgment of her. Elijah was right—Rick shouldn't have assumed so much.

Lifting her chin, she stared him down. "None. But they say the rodeo isn't a fit place to raise a child, especially for a single mom. They want her to have a stable home with two parents." The fire in her eyes dimmed, and her shoulders sagged. "I want that for Betsy too, but I have to make a living, and the rodeo is all I know."

He ran through all she'd said in his mind. "Do they know you've come here?"

She shook her head. "I didn't tell anyone where I was going—not even my best friend."

He forced out a question he didn't want her to answer. "What is it you want me to do?"

She spread out her hands. "I didn't know where else to turn. I thought I could hide out here, and just maybe Elijah could help Betsy the way he's helped other kids. I can't lose Betsy. I've lost everything else, but I can't lose her. But they might find me here too. I thought maybe with your contacts, you could make sure they can't get custody. I can't let them have her."

"That's true," he agreed. "Jon wouldn't want that."

She had put more faith in his ability than he possessed. He didn't have the kind of contacts that could save her from a custody suit. He stood and went to look out the window. An idea presented itself, a crazy idea. Not even Jon would expect him to go so far to help his wife and kid. His gaze lit on her old rattletrap truck. Both front tires were flat this morning.

He owed Jon his life.

No, he couldn't do it. There had to be another way. His thoughts raced, looking for a way out. A good lawyer could help. He had some cash saved. Turning, he looked at her and saw what a judge would see. A young woman with no steady means of support, dragging a kid all around the country. Put that up against two stable parents with plenty of money and a nice home, and Allie would lose.

He'd promised.

It wouldn't be forever. If he clung to that, maybe he could do it. What right did he have not to? Jon had counted on him. And, really, what would this cost him? Nothing in money. Only some time and a little inconvenience.

He went back to the table. "I made him a promise I've been too chicken to keep."

"A promise?"

"To take care of you and Betsy. I only know of one way to ensure Betsy isn't taken away from you." He hitched his thumbs into the pockets of his jeans. "If you're married and your husband adopts Betsy, his parents won't be able to touch her."

The soft pink drained from her cheeks, and her blue eyes grew enormous. "Marriage? To who?" she whispered. "Are you crazy?"

"To me. You'll have a stable home, insurance for her care, a father to replace the one she lost." He finally found the courage to look her in the eye. "I'll probably be a lousy husband, but I think I could be a good dad. A stepfather would have no trouble adopting Betsy."

She swung her head from side to side. "I can't marry you. I don't know you. Neither does Betsy."

"Think of it as a temporary thing. Once the adoption is final, we can wait a few months, then get a divorce."

"Marriage should be more than a convenient arrangement."

"Do you have a better idea?" He waited until she looked away. "I didn't think so."

She held up her hand. "Just be quiet a minute. Let me think. There has to be some other way."

He pressed his lips together and prayed she'd think of something. But he knew she wouldn't. Sometimes only the hard way worked.

ALLIE COULDN'T THINK, COULDN'T GET HER MIND AROUND RICK'S OUT-landish proposal. The silence had gone on between them long enough that she managed to force down her breakfast, but it was as dry as the sand outside.

She couldn't marry him. Maybe she should just run back to El Paso and take her chances. He was the exact opposite of the type of man who attracted her. The Neanderthal type was too overpowering for her taste. She liked long, slim limbs and someone who didn't tower over her like a ponderosa pine.

Even more importantly, she couldn't run the risk of anyone taking Jon's place with Betsy. The little girl was already warming up to the big man. How well did she remember her daddy? The thought of her forgetting Jon broke Allie's heart. Jon deserved whatever it took to keep his memory alive in his daughter's heart.

Elijah stepped into the room.

"Breakfast, *mujercita?*" Elijah's dark eyes drooped with fatigue, but his step was spry.

Allie pinned a smile in place. At least she and Rick didn't have to discuss it now. "Good morning, Elijah. I hope you're hungry."

"I could eat Roscoe, the big bull in the back pasture," Elijah said. He took the plate of food. His gaze swept the kitchen. "You worked hard this morning," he said. "Thank you for taking care of us bachelors. I think we would win a title for biggest slobs, *sí?*"

"My bedroom is neat," Rick said. "Too much military in me for me not to make my bed."

Allie avoided looking at Rick. "Is there anything else I can do for you today, Elijah? I thought I might clean the house if that's all right."

"I'm in need of a housekeeper since my Rosa retired," Elijah said. "Would you want the position?"

"Of course!" There. She didn't have to marry Rick. There were surely other options.

"The housekeeper takes care of the accounts too. Are you trained in this area as well perhaps?"

"I—I—no. But if you showed me, maybe I could do it." She'd always had trouble with numbers. Her eyes jumbled them up as badly as letters. But she had to try for Betsy's sake. She *would* master it. If all went well, she could save enough to replace her lost glasses.

He nodded. "Rosa lives on the other side of the ranch. You might speak with her about the duties. I must warn you, the pay is not so much. You will get room and board for you and the *niña,* and a little besides for incidentals."

"I don't care about money," Allie said. "I just want Betsy to get better."

Elijah's dark eyes touched Betsy's head. "I want this too, *mujercita.*" He glanced at Rick. "Would you object to giving us references, Allie?"

She bit her lip. If she gave references, her stalker might find out where she was. "I have good references, bu-but it would be better to keep my whereabouts quiet. Can you ask questions without identifying where the ranch is located?"

"I'll be careful with the questions," Rick said.

She would have no trouble getting a recommendation from the

rodeo. She was careful to keep her gaze averted from Rick's. "Where will Betsy and I stay? In the bunkhouse?"

"No, you may take the small suite at the top of the stairs. There are two beds in it, and it has its own bathroom. I'm afraid we have no chaperone, but with the *niña* in the same room and an old man like me in the house, no tongues should wag in town."

Gossip was the least of Allie's worries. "Could you explain to me how the ranch operates? What you do here?"

Elijah cocked a gray eyebrow. "Rick, if you would be so kind?"

Rick shrugged. "Bluebird Youth Ranch encompasses nine hundred and fifty-three acres. Elijah started with rescuing abused and neglected horses."

Allie shuddered. "I've seen some of that in the rodeo. Breaks your heart."

Rick's gaze softened. "It happens more than anyone realizes. Owners turn the horses out to pasture and abandon them. A drought comes along, and the horses starve. They suffer mostly from neglect, not mean-spiritedness. But the end result is the same."

"Do you see abused horses too?"

"Yeah. I wish we didn't, but it happens. An owner gets mad when the horse doesn't turn out to be a Flicka. Or an abuser takes his rage out on his animal rather than his wife or kids."

"Go on with the story of the ranch. Sorry I interrupted," Allie said.

"It's important to know the background. Elijah took in some foster kids back in the sixties. Some of them had been abused by their parents, and he found that the horses and children bonded in some amazing ways. They helped one another heal from past traumas. Bluebird was born out of his passion to help kids and horses."

Allie glanced at the old man. She didn't get him, not at all. How could he have such passion for this work, yet turn his own child out onto the streets? Unless her mother had lied to her.

"Who runs the ranch?"

"I'm the foreman, but I talk everything over with Elijah. We've got three hands who live in the bunkhouse. They care for the horses and cattle that roam the ranch." He nodded at Elijah. "The boss has a group counseling session with the kids every day. I take care of the interaction between the kids and horses."

"What training do you have for that?" She didn't mean to challenge him, but it sounded like some pretty troubled kids came through here.

He didn't look at her. "I was one of those kids once. I've got a degree in social welfare."

"And I have a degree in psychology," Elijah put in. "The children are safe here."

Allie couldn't figure Rick out. She moved toward the doorway. "Thanks for the information. If you don't mind, I'll clean the house before we move our things in."

Elijah chuckled. "Mind? Rick and I will help. Right, Rick?"

Allie finally dared to look at Jon's best friend. They were going to have to talk about his proposal, but not yet.

"I'll clean the bathroom," he said.

Allie wanted to laugh, but she bit it back. The idea of the big guy on his knees, cleaning the porcelain throne, was ludicrous. But she might actually pay good money—if she had it—to see a sight like that.

5

THE BLOATED MOON SHONE IN THE WINDOW AND MADE MONSTERS OUT OF the dresser and nightstand in Allie's room. She closed her eyes against the images. There were enough monsters in her life. With all she had to do today, she'd managed to avoid considering Rick's proposal—but now that darkness had fallen, it was all she could think about.

What if he had a temper or was some kind of pervert? The possibilities of danger were enormous. He could be a serial killer for all she knew. She thumped the pillow like it was the obnoxious man's head. Okay, maybe not a serial killer. Everyone said serial killers seemed *nice,* and Rick Bailey would never answer to that description. Rude and opinionated, but not nice.

What on earth had Jon seen in Rick to recommend him so highly?

All she saw was a muscle-bound jerk who looked at her like she was a cow patty under his boots.

Still, it took guts to make an offer like that.

His solution hung out there, tantalizing and repelling at the same time. It would work, there was no doubt in her mind. Betsy would be safe from any custody suit. But what a price to pay. Allie didn't know if she had it in her to make that kind of sacrifice, even for Betsy.

There had to be another way.

She rolled onto her side and stared at the hump in the bed next to hers. Her daughter enjoyed the sleep of the innocent. Betsy's deep, easy breathing should have eased the tension humming along Allie's veins, but something was off. She strained to hear the sounds outside: the crunch of horse hooves in the paddock outside, the shuffle of cattle in the pasture, the wind chimes tinkling in the night breeze.

He couldn't have found her already. The sense of something lurking outside was her imagination. Rick's preposterous suggestion had put her out of kilter.

Though all the sounds were normal, she swung her feet out of bed and moved to the window. The breeze lifted the gauzy curtains and brushed them against her cheek with a touch as light as spiderwebs. She shivered and pushed the fabric away, but the wind blew it right back against her. Moving them out of her way, she stepped to the screen and looked down on the bucolic scene, illuminated by the moon and the security lights.

The remuda of horses stood in a corral west of the barn. Huddled together against the chill that had swept down off the mountain with the setting of the sun, they dozed on their feet. A few head of cattle lay nestled on the other side of the fence. The two trucks sat silent and empty on the far side of the barn.

Nothing stirred but the wind.

Then why did the hair on the back of Allie's neck stand out? Why did she feel if she breathed someone would hear? Something had awakened her, but nothing in the barnyard below gave any cause for concern.

Then she heard a sound that stole the oxygen from her lungs. The bloodcurdling scream pierced her eardrums.

Someone was in trouble.

In her bare feet, she leaped for the door and threw it open. The tile chilled her toes. Her feet pounded down the steps, then she was at the front door. She threw it open and stepped out onto the porch. The scream came again, and she shuddered. The poor woman was in deadly peril. Did no one else hear? Why wasn't Rick out here too? Or Elijah?

"Rick, Elijah, help!" she yelled up the steps.

Maybe they were exhausted from lack of sleep tonight. She needed a gun. Whirling, she dashed back inside and grabbed the key from the top of the gun cabinet. Twisting it in the lock, she threw open the cabinet and lifted out a shotgun. The shells were on the top shelf. She grabbed a handful, jammed two into the gun, then relocked the cabinet.

The moon illuminated the outdoor scene. The horses moved restlessly in their paddock. Their skittishness spooked her even more. The scream didn't come again, but Allie had localized it just past the big rock at the edge of the piñon grove. She stepped off the porch. Her toe slammed against a rock, and she winced.

Jem, the ranch border collie, whined and touched his nose to her hand. The warm contact strengthened her. "Come with me, Jem," she whispered, slipping her fingers under his collar. Limping, she picked up the pace. At the grove, the trees blocked out the moonlight, and she hesitated before stepping into the darkness. She should have brought a flashlight. Maybe she should wait for the men.

The unearthly scream came again. Were there ghosts in these mountains? She'd heard of the Marfa lights, the centuries-old unexplained phenomenon of lights with no apparent origin.

The men were slow. Some protectors they were.

She pointed the gun and sidled toward the trees, inhaling the scents of vegetation. "Where are you? Are you hurt?" The trees bounced her voice back in her face. There was no other sound beyond normal night noises. She stepped cautiously away from the safety of the clearing and farther into the darkness. Her own breathing sounded harsh and fast.

A twig snapped behind her. The sound of rushing steps came toward her, and she whirled to run. Before she made it two steps, someone grabbed her. In several quick moves, hard hands flipped her around, yanked the gun from her hand, and pinned her against the bark of a pine tree.

It was too dark to make out more than a hulking shape. "Let go of me," she said, jerking her arm in the man's grip.

"What do you think you're doing?" Rick's voice was a low growl.

She should have been relieved it was only him, but her terror fueled anger instead. "Get your hands off me."

His big hands lifted from her shoulders. "What in the sam hill are you doing wandering outside with a mountain lion on the prowl?"

"Mountain lion?" She clutched the fabric of her shirt in her fists. "I—I heard what I thought was a woman screaming."

"Oh brother." He grabbed her arm and hustled her back toward the porch. "You don't have any shoes on either. You want to get snake bit or stung by a scorpion?"

"Wrong time of year," she said, dragging up a bit of defiance. How stupid of her. A mountain lion. She glanced over her shoulder, expecting to see yellow eyes or a large cat springing toward them, but there was only darkness. "Wait, what about the rifle?"

"Leave it."

"We can't leave it. Betsy might find it." She jerked her arm out of his grip. "You threw it down. Where is it?"

"Feel free to get it. I don't carry a firearm. Not for any reason."

A cowboy that didn't carry a rifle? What did he do about snakes and other varmints? If only the moonlight were brighter here in the trees. She'd like to study his expression and try to determine what was behind his odd statement. His voice was as prickly as a cactus too.

She retraced their few steps and felt around on the ground for the rifle. Her hand touched stiff grass, rocks, and sand. Then her fingers settled on cold steel. She picked up the rifle and hurried back out of the tree cover, all the while expecting to feel the teeth and claws of an angry panther. When she started back to the clearing, she realized he'd followed her. At least he hadn't left her at the lion's mercy.

It was probably long gone by now, and she was being skittish for no reason. She nearly ran from the trees into the warm wash of moonlight and Rick's solid presence.

"The least you could have done was come with me," she said.

"You made enough noise to scare away a pride of lions. The cougar was long gone."

"Do you have mountain lions here often?" she asked him. The breeze, laden with the scent of pine from the piñons, touched her face.

Rick didn't reply. They stepped into the moonlight, and he stopped for a second, then took off running for the barn.

Allie darted after him. "What's wrong?" Then she saw. The gate gaped open, and the horses were out. She put on another spurt of speed, ignoring the rocks that poked her feet. A rope, she needed to help lasso them. Dodging Rick, she stepped into the barn, grabbed two ropes from the hook, and rejoined him in the paddock.

She handed him one of the ropes. "It wasn't open a little while ago. I looked down from my window and watched the horses before the scream came. The gate was closed. I'm sure of it."

"I'll check it out. But first, we'd better get those horses back." Uncoiling the rope, he walked away.

Allie followed. There were four horses out. At least she could show him she knew how to rope and ride. While she might not have a lot of skills, she'd be an asset to any ranch.

He called out the name Moonbeam, and a black horse with a gleaming white blaze turned its head to stare at him. Rick approached, and the horse snorted and backed away. The coil of rope he threw missed Moonbeam's neck, and the horse whirled to bolt.

Running her hands over the rough rope, Allie twirled it and let it go. The rope burned her palm as the loop on the end sailed through the air and settled around the horse's neck. She braced her feet, digging her bare toes into the sandy soil. Moonbeam's head came up and he snorted, but she had him.

"Come here, boy," she coaxed, pulling on the rope.

"Nice," Rick said, his voice grudging. "Where'd you learn to rope like that?"

"Rodeo. I could rope a calf by the time I was five." She ran her hands over the horse's gaunt frame. She winced at the bones poking through his rough coat. "He's so thin."

"You should have seen him when we rescued him. I didn't think he'd make it." Rick grabbed Moonbeam's rope halter when the gelding neared. "I'll put him in the barn while you lasso the next one."

Some men would have been intimidated by her superior skill. Score one for the cowboy. She spared a glance after him. He was powerfully built, with broad shoulders and muscular thighs. Very different from Jon. Maybe that was a good thing. It would ensure that she and Betsy wouldn't put him in Jon's place.

Her thoughts danced away from his preposterous suggestion again. Marriage to him terrified her.

She lassoed the next horse, Cupcake. The mare came willingly with her colt following after. They were probably skittish after hearing the mountain lion. If the big cat had gotten hold of little Frost . . . Allie shuddered.

Once all the horses were secured, she and Rick walked the fence line. "Maybe the gate failed to latch, and one of the horses pushed it open," she suggested.

"It's got a chain on it." He secured the chain and latched the padlock. "It couldn't have been accidental."

The stalker had found her. No. No, she was sure no one knew where she'd gone.

"Could Betsy have come out to see Frost?" Rick asked.

"I had trouble sleeping, and she's been asleep since her head hit the pillow." Allie followed him toward the porch.

"I'd guess it was kids, but we're so remote out here they'd have to come from Alpine or Marathon."

The explanations all fell flat. Why come here?

"Maybe campers from the Big Bend." He stretched his big frame, then folded his arms across his chest. "We didn't get a chance to finish our discussion."

She took a step back. "I—I don't know what to say. I appreciate the offer, but I just can't marry someone I don't know." The night air held a chill, and Allie told herself she was shaking only because of the temperature.

He didn't answer right away. Rick leaned his shoulder against a porch post and looked out into the star-filled sky. "Jon saw this coming," he said finally. "He said if anything happened to him that his parents would try to get Betsy. He made me promise if it happened that I'd marry you and adopt her. I guess his childhood was bad."

"I know," Allie said. The cold penetrated her bones, and her teeth began to stutter together. "Always drinking and fighting. They've got several foster kids too, so they'll look good to a judge with their pseudo-Christian mask. They go to church all the time and quote all kinds of rules, but it's all for show. They don't possess an ounce of real faith."

"Didn't Jon ever tell you what he'd asked me? He said he would."

Allie shook her head. "He only said if I was ever in trouble to come to you. Maybe he didn't want to worry me. I—I think it seems a little extreme, his solution, I mean. You've been in special ops. Surely you can pull some strings and make the problem go away."

He smiled, his white teeth catching a glint of moonlight. "No strings that could alter a custody battle. They'll find you eventually, but there would be nothing they could do if we were married and I adopted Betsy."

She studied his face, the strong planes and angles, the determined jaw. Jon said Rick was one in a million, but she couldn't imagine being tied to him for the rest of her life. Maybe it wouldn't have to be that way. "W—we would divorce once Betsy was secure?"

"If that's what you want."

Was that relief she heard in his voice? He probably didn't want this any more than she did. Maybe she wasn't his type any more than he was hers. "I'll think about it," she said, turning to flee to the safety of her room.

Rick dismounted Gunner and scanned the faint marks in the dust. Two people, one smaller than the other, had left their tracks in the pasture behind the barn. Maybe a man and a woman or a man and a youth. Or the tracks could have been made before last night. He was too tired to tell.

He shaded his eyes with his hand and let his gaze wander over the hills around the ranch. There was no movement other than a jackrabbit darting from shrub to shrub.

"Anything, Cowboy?" Charlie asked.

"Nope." Rick dropped his hand back to his side. His gaze lingered on Charlie's new saddle. "Nice chrome. You must have spent a year's pay on that."

Charlie grinned. "It was worth it."

"Did you hear anything last night?"

Charlie shook his head. "I fell asleep with the TV on. The volume was kind of high." He gestured to the tracks. "Could be illegals. I'd guess a couple wandered through here and tried to catch a ride. Maybe the big cat scared them off."

"Maybe." Rick wasn't buying it. "You go to rodeos. You ever see her?"

"Allie? She was working the rodeo in El Paso I went to last month. I told her Elijah might be able to help Betsy."

"What do you know about her?"

Charlie mounted his roan mare, Freckles. "Her parents were killed in a small plane crash about a year ago. Her mom was Anna Morgan."

Rick whistled. "I heard about that crash. It will probably be a long time before anyone breaks Anna's record. Most barrel racing wins. She was a phenomenal rider."

"Word was Allie had a good shot at it. I saw her in one event. She's fast. She had a great horse. I wonder what happened to the mare?"

The men turned their horses' heads to the trail that rambled to the top of the butte. A good barrel-racing horse was worth as much as forty thousand dollars. Plus whatever she got from her parents' estate.

"So the poverty act is just that—all show." His lip curled at the memory of the way she'd wolfed down the sandwich. And he'd fallen for the act. What a sap.

Charlie shook his head. "Not according to the chute boss who told me about it. Her dad liked toys: his own plane, the best of everything. Wasn't much left after everything was sold, and she sold the horse to pay for trying to fix Betsy's problem."

Rick regretted his cynicism. Okay, maybe she wasn't just a good actress. He eyed Charlie. "You sure know a lot about it."

The kid flashed a grin toward Rick. "She's a hottie, man, in case you didn't notice. So, yeah, I watched her."

"She's a little long in the tooth for you."

"Only ten years or so. Her sister was a real looker too."

"Was?" Though Rick knew she was dead, he wanted to probe a little. Maybe Charlie had heard some rumors.

"She was murdered—about a month ago, I think. What a waste."

Rick pulled up on the reins and stopped in the trail. "What happened?" Maybe Charlie could add to what Allie had told him.

"Talk around the rodeo was it was someone who was after Allie. Hey, race you to the top." Charlie shook the reins, and Freckles leaped forward at the jingle of tack.

Rick let Charlie beat him while he pondered the information. Parents and a sister, all killed—just like she'd said, though she'd said the sister walked in on a burglar. Why would rumors be flying that the killer was after Allie? She'd said nothing about that.

But it didn't matter. He saw no way out of fulfilling his promise to

Jon. He'd been as surprised as Allie when he blurted out that marriage proposal, and ever since the words left his mouth, he'd been looking for a way to take them back.

His contacts in special ops might be able to shed some light on her situation.

Charlie turned in the saddle to look at him, and Rick waved him on. He pulled out his cell phone. Coverage was spotty on the ranch, but he'd always found good reception on this hill. Reining Gunner to a stop, Rick called up the number and waited for Brendan to answer on the other end.

"Waddell." Brendan's curt voice came over the line.

"It's Rick. You got a minute?"

"Hey, Cowboy. It depends. I've got a situation here I need you for. Tit for tat. I do your favor, you come back to work."

"You know I can't do that." Rick let the grin filter through the phone to his friend. He and Brendan never had a conversation without his ex-partner grinding that old ax. By now Brendan should know it was a lost cause.

The sound of Brendan closing a door came through the phone. "You know you miss it."

Sometimes Rick longed for the days of never knowing what country he'd be in come nightfall, but if he showed a sliver of weakness, Brendan would be all over him.

He forced derision into his voice. "What's to miss? Hard beds, crappy food, a bullet around every corner."

"It's paradise, I know. I can hear your voice break." Brendan laughed, and his voice sobered. "What can I do for you, buddy? Got cattle rustlers bothering you? Illegal drugs being smuggled across the desert?"

"Nothing so exciting. A woman and kid showed up here, Jon

Siderses widow and daughter. Her parents died in a plane crash, then her sister was murdered. Now she's asking for my help because Jon's parents are suing for custody of the daughter."

"Jon was a good man. I always wondered what happened to his family." Brendan's voice fell, and the hiss of a bad connection filled the phone line. "You going to do something about it?"

"Something like that."

"What's her name?"

"Allie. Little girl's name is Betsy." Rick debated about telling Brendan the little girl was mute. Nah, it wasn't an important detail. The names would be enough. "She seems to be in some kind of trouble. Won't talk about it. Can you see what you can find out?"

"Sure. Let me check it out. I'll get back to you by tomorrow. You sure you don't want to get in on the rescue of some hijacked tourists in Baghdad?"

"I think you can handle it by yourself," Rick said, his grin widening. "Thanks, Brendan. I owe you." He closed his phone, then called up directory assistance and had the woman dial the rodeo where Allie said she worked. Rick gave his name but was careful not to say where he was calling from. The man he talked to there told him she'd been one of his best employees for eight years, and he hated to lose her. He'd said she might have won the national barrel-racing competition as well, if she hadn't taken off.

Rick put his phone away and urged his horse on up the slope. Had he been hoping it was all a scam—that she really wasn't Jon's widow? How could he? One look at Betsy spoke a world of truth. He saw Jon in the little girl's eyes.

He had to honor his promise, but all he wanted to do was bail.

6

ALLIE STOOD ON THE PORCH AND RUBBED LOTION SMELLING OF LAVENDER into her chapped hands. The Chisos Mountains were called "sky islands" by the locals, and she'd already fallen in love with their brooding presence. They held up the sky in the distance as the cold night gave way to sunshine, warming the rocks and vegetation.

So far she'd avoided Rick this morning. She still couldn't believe she'd been stupid enough to mistake a mountain lion for a woman in trouble. What should she do about Rick's suggestion? Part of her wanted to let someone else shoulder her burdens for a little while, but they'd been with her so long, they'd become part of her. She didn't know if she could even let them go.

Through the open window she could hear Charlie talking to himself as he tried to figure out how to catch a calf that had slipped through the gate.

The door opened behind her, and Elijah stepped out. "There you are, *mujercita*. I have time to show you the books now. To my office, if you would be so kind."

The books. A ball of dread coiled in her throat. While bluffing it came easily to her, this might be more than she could fake her way through. "I should probably check on Betsy."

"The *niña* is on the back porch playing with the kittens. This will not take long. They are not difficult." Elijah beckoned her with a brown finger.

Allie swallowed her excuses and followed the old man to the office off the living room. A large, high-ceilinged space, the pale yellow walls were further warmed by the sunlight streaming in the four large windows. An oak desk dominated the center of the room. The chair's back was to the window, and the light fell on the vast expanse of the desk.

Her eyes were drawn to the ledger in the middle of the desk. It lay open, the squiggly black lines of letters and numbers crawling across its pages like scorpions. Such small text would make the job even more difficult. She'd hoped for a computer that let her make the fonts larger.

Elijah swept his arm over the chair. "Be seated, please."

Allie went around the desk and sank onto the cracked leather desk chair. She stared at the ledger. Clasping her hands in her lap, she told herself the nursery rhyme that usually calmed her:

Once I saw a little bird

Go hop, hop, hop.

So I cried, little bird,

Will you stop, stop, stop?

And I was going to the window
To say, how do you do?
When he shook his little tail
And away he flew.

Something about the cadence stole her flustered feelings away. She eased back in the chair and listened to the singsong in her head until her confidence surged again.

It was only numbers in a book. She would work hard and learn.

Elijah stood beside her. A stack of bills lay in a wire tray on the desk, and he took the first one. "This is the electric bill." He ran a gnarled finger down the rows to stop on the third line down. "You find the month by going across." He moved his finger in a vertical direction to the third column. "This is the February bill, so it is to be written down here. Very easy, much as you have likely done in your private affairs."

Allie clamped her teeth against the hysterical laughter rising in her throat. If he only knew what a mess her private affairs were.

When she didn't pick up the pencil, Elijah did it. "I'll show you." He carefully inscribed the date and some numbers in the boxes.

She forced herself to look at the page, trying not to feel sick at the way the black text jiggled on the white paper. She squinted and managed to make out one entry. "Your electric bill is over five hundred dollars?"

"It costs money to run the pumps for water for the livestock, for showers when we have a bunkhouse full of children."

"How do you pay for all this?"

He smiled. "I made much money in my younger days as a child psychologist in Houston. The ranch, we bought when our daughter was a baby, but we did not come to live here until she was a teenager."

His face grew pensive. "This was maybe not so good a choice. My wife, she was very frugal. I have enough for many years to come. The agencies who send the children, they also provide some income."

"When is our next group coming? How does it all work?"

"Sometimes we have a group come for a month or two, sometimes a larger group for just a day. Right now, the crew is remodeling the bunkhouse, so we have none. But a few rooms are done, and we will take a handful later today." He went toward the door. "You look, *sí*? I will get us coffee."

The stack of bills seemed huge. Her head already ached from looking at just one page of the black numbers on white paper. She should confess her condition and get it over with. Sitting back in the chair, she glanced around the room until her gaze settled on the picture of a young woman.

It almost could have been her.

She stood and picked it up, running her fingers over the cool glass. The woman was younger than Allie, and her eyes were brown instead of blue, but she had the same high cheekbones and full lips. The same dark hair. Who was she?

She heard Elijah coming and put the picture back on the bookshelf. He arrived at the doorway as she turned around. Caught.

"That was my granddaughter, Maria."

"Was?"

"Ten years now she has been in her grave. A riding accident when she was twenty-five."

"I'm sorry."

"You have the look of her, *sí*?"

"I noticed. Was that why you stared when you first saw me?"

"It is so." He turned to the door. "I will leave you to your work."

"Could I use the phone to call my friend in El Paso and let her know I arrived safely?"

"*Sí*, of course. Anytime you wish." He closed the door behind him.

Allie looked at the picture again. Maria would have been her cousin. Her mother had always told Allie she was an only child. So who were Maria's parents? The thought she might still have family filled her with a sense of purpose and rightness about coming here.

Allie went back to the chair, picked up the phone, and dialed Yo's cell phone number. Her friend answered almost at once. "Yo, it's me."

"Allie, I've been so worried. Are you okay, girl?"

The chair squeaked as Allie leaned back, glancing at her nails. She'd managed not to bite them for three days, but the polish looked terrible. "I'm fine. Got here in one piece. How's everything? How are you riding today?"

"I am all that, girlfriend," Yo crowed. "Ran just over 14.7 seconds today."

"Oh great, Yo. You're going to win this year!" Allie pulled polish remover from her purse and began to remove the chipped polish. The pungent sting of the chemical reminded her that her chance at the title was a thing of the past.

"As long as I don't bite it."

"You won't. You'll do great."

"I miss you, girl."

Allie closed her eyes and wished she could be back where she belonged. "I miss you too, Yo. Listen, I need your advice." She started to bite her nails, then yanked her fingers from her mouth. Her mother always used to say a lady didn't bite her nails.

"Like I'm the one to ask." Yo's voice held a smile. "What's up?"

"I've had someone offer to help me make sure I don't lose Betsy.

It's a friend of Jon's. He says if I'm married and he adopts Betsy, she'll be safe from Jon's parents."

"Uh-uh, no way, girl. You don't go marrying no stranger." Yo's voice rose.

"He was Jon's best friend. I—I think I trust him, Yo. And it would only be for a year or so. Just until Betsy is safe." Was she actually arguing *for* the idea?

"What kind of lesson is that teaching Betsy? You marrying then divorcing for convenience's sake. And she'll be yanked from pillar to post."

Allie winced. "I'll take care of her."

Yolanda sighed. "Allie, you don't know this guy. He could be an ax murderer or something."

Allie grinned, remembering how Rick had said he wasn't an ax murderer when she'd been afraid to get in the truck. "He's not like that, Yo."

"Hmm, do I hear some interest, girl?"

"Not hardly. He's a big guy, all muscle and testosterone. Not at all like Jon."

"That's not a bad thing. It's not good to try to find a Jon look-alike."

"Now who's pulling for the idea? Not interested."

"Because he's not like Jon? Honey, you've got to let him go sometime. He's dead. I know it's harsh to say it, but you've got to face it. You're still young. I want you to find someone else and love again."

"I'll never love anyone like I loved Jon. And I don't want Betsy to put someone else in her daddy's place."

Yo sighed. "Girl, she can't remember him by now. Kids forget."

"She *won't* forget," Allie said fiercely. "I won't let her."

"Time has a way of smoothing out the bumps. You wouldn't want

Betsy to grieve forever. I don't want you to, either. You've got to trust again, Allie. Let go of that ironclad control."

Allie pressed her lips together. Yo didn't understand. She hadn't gone through the losses Allie had suffered. She turned to glance out the window. "I've got a job, Yo. Doing bookwork and housekeeping."

"Bookwork? Your specialty." Yolanda's chuckle lightened her poke at Allie's problem.

"Ironic, isn't it?"

"So why marry this dude? You've got a job, a place to stay."

"I thought about that. But it's a room in a ranch, not a home of our own. That won't look good to a judge. It won't appear we're any better off than when we were living in a travel trailer." She heard footsteps outside the door. "Listen, I have to go. I'll call in a few days. Pray for me, Yo, that I'll know what to do."

"You got it, girlfriend. Love you."

"Love you too." Allie clicked off the phone and put it down as Elijah stepped back into the office.

"Do you have any questions before I go outside?"

"No, I was on the phone. I'll start work now."

He tipped his head to one side and listened. "We have visitors."

Allie heard it then too, the distant growl of an engine.

"Set that aside for now. You shall find out what the ranch is all about. The group I mentioned is coming. We go meet them, *sí?*" He held out his hand for her.

She put her fingers on his forearm and rose, allowing him to escort her to the door. The rough-and-ready rodeo riders she knew never acted so courtly. She could get used to this treatment.

There was something about Elijah that comforted her. What would her life have been like if she'd had a relationship with him

growing up? She'd always wanted grandparents. Rattling around the
rodeo all her life, she never experienced the stability of deep family
roots. Her parents loved her, but they were often busy.

The ranch was a world apart, a place where she longed to scrape
away the hard surface soil and peer underneath to the reality. She was
certain she would discover something beautiful. She longed to ask
Elijah a million questions. Like did she have any other living relatives?
An aunt or uncle?

Elijah opened the front door for her and followed her to the porch.

A van appeared on the road between the rocky outcroppings on
each side. Dust billowed from its tires, and its engine revved up for the
final approach to the house. The vehicle stopped, and the back door
opened. Several teenagers emerged, blinking in the bright sunlight.

Allie counted four—two boys and two girls. A man exited the front
of the van and corralled the teens. She could hear him directing the kids
to get their luggage. The group moved en masse toward the porch.

"Hello, are you the lady of the house?" the man asked, his dark eyes
sizing her up.

"I'm the housekeeper," she said. "Allie Siders."

In his forties, the man's eyes peered through metal-rimmed
glasses. His black hair lay in a sleek cap on his head, and he wore a gray
suit and black shoes that were already picking up traces of red dust.

He shook her hand. "Emilio Valdez. You must be Elijah," he said,
glancing at the old man.

"*Sí.* You are new."

Emilio nodded. "Yeah, they sent me since this bunch is a little hard
to handle. I'll ride shotgun over them and do schoolwork with them
as well. Where do you want them?"

"Take the boys to the bunkhouse, out behind the barn. The girls have rooms inside the house on the second floor. If you'll show the boys to their bunks, Allie will take the girls inside."

"*Gracias*." Emilio turned to the huddled teens who were trying to look bored. "You heard the boss man. Boys, come with me."

"Why do the Betties get to stay in the house?" The boy who objected looked like he'd seen one too many tattoo parlors. Skulls and crossbones covered both arms, and he had rings in his ears, eyebrows, and lower lip.

The bright red hair matched his eyebrows, so Allie decided it must be natural.

The other boy shoved him. "To save them from dudes like you." Thin to the point of emaciation, the second boy picked up his backpack and turned to go.

"Are you going to introduce us?" Allie asked.

Emilio took a tighter grip on his briefcase. "Tattoo boy is Devin." He pointed to the skinny boy. "Leon. The girls are Latoya and Fern." He nodded toward Allie. "Go with the lady, girls. We'll be back as soon as we get things stowed, and you can see the ranch."

"Peachy," Devin said in a mocking voice. His untied shoelaces dragged in the red dirt as he slumped after Emilio and Leon.

Elijah went down the steps. "I will check on Cupcake. You can handle this, Allie."

Allie forced a smile. She wasn't used to being around teenagers much. "You both share a room beside mine." The girls followed her into the house.

Were these kids part of the foster care system? She'd heard Elijah had great success with troubled kids and had headed here without knowing more than that.

"Wow," Latoya breathed. "Cool digs."

Shapely with perfect dark skin, Latoya held her head high and sur-
veyed her new domain. Allie could see she'd have her hands full with
the young woman. Fern kept her head down, and only the pink of her
scalp showed in the part between two yellow braids.

Why were they here? Drugs? Prostitution? For the first time, Allie
realized she might have brought Betsy into contact with characters
who might not be the best influences. She'd assumed the kids would
all be younger, with problems similar to Betsy's. When she thought
about it, though, she realized internal scars were the most profound.

She showed the girls their room and pointed to the dresser. "You
can put your things away there."

The girls began to unload their backpacks. Latoya brought out a
delicious color of hot-pink nail polish.

"Ooh, that's pretty." Allie picked it up. "Sparkles." She glanced at
her bare nails. It had been all she could do not to bite them with no
polish on them.

"Try it." Latoya put her hand over her mouth and exhaled. "Girl,
I've got the dragon. My teeth feel like slime. Where's the bathroom?"

"At the end of the hall." Allie picked up the bottle of polish when
Latoya went out. Why not? She sat on the edge of the bed and uncapped it, then slicked a thin coat over her nails. Holding out her left
hand, she showed Fern. "What do you think?"

Fern barely glanced at her hand, but her head bobbed. "Pretty."

Latoya came back in with gloss on her lips. She pooched her lip out
at Allie. "Minty fresh." She peeked at Allie's nails. "That's so you, girl."

"It's fresh," Allie said. "I like it."

"It's yours." Latoya leaned over and pressed the bottle into Allie's
hands.

"Oh no, I can't take it." Was the girl trying to bribe her? Allie stared hard at Latoya, but the teenager just smiled back. "I'll borrow it sometime." She put the bottle back on the dresser. "Let's go find the guys." They all trooped back downstairs. She was careful with her wet nails when she peeked out the back door to check on Betsy. Her daughter lay in a hammock on the back porch with three kittens snuggled around her. They were all sleeping.

She and the girls tiptoed past the little girl into the backyard and headed toward the barn. Rick's familiar battered cowboy hat moved into her line of vision. He stood by the paddock with one boot on the bottom rail and his hands gripping the top. Funny how the same pose she'd seen Charlie take looked so much better on Rick.

Emilio and the boys clustered around the paddock with him.

"Who's that?" Latoya asked, her voice vibrating with awe.

"Rick Bailey, the foreman."

"He's gorgeous. Puts me in mind of a young Arnold Schwarzenegger with all those muscles." Latoya's hips took on an exaggerated sway as she made a beeline to join the guys.

Allie grinned, imagining the way Rick would put the girl in her place. Latoya didn't realize she was up against Prince Charmless, as Allie had dubbed him in her mind.

About to become her rescuer Prince Charming.

The thought shocked her.

"Want to see the horses?" she asked Fern. Her eyes still downcast, the girl nodded. "Do you have any brothers or sisters?" Allie asked.

"A brother," Fern said, her words so soft Allie had to strain to hear them.

It was going to take time to get through the wall Fern had built around her. Maybe the horses would be a good start. "Come with me," Allie said.

Cupcake's winter coat was a little rough and ragged, but she was still a beautiful mare. With little Frost following at her heels, she pranced around the paddock with her tail out and her head up.

Fern peeked at the horses, a smile starting across her pinched face. "A colt," she breathed.

"He's only two days old," Allie said. They had reached the rest of the group, and she saw Rick stiffen at the sound of her voice.

What a way to start a marriage.

Her assumptions had altered. His offer was a way out. Maybe the only way.

She focused on the needy teenager beside her. "Cupcake is a good mother. See how she keeps her body between us and her colt?"

Fern nodded. "She's beautiful."

The boys were hanging on the fence, watching the mare gallop past. "Hey, check out the rides," Devin said. "I wanna try."

"Nope, can't ride Cupcake," Rick said. "And Frost is way too young. He'll need to be at least two or three. But there are other horses you can ride." He glanced at Allie. "Would you help me saddle up enough horses for all of them?"

She went past him into the barn. The tack room door to her right stood ajar, and she pushed it open to glance around. The scent of the new stacks of hay in the corner made her sneeze.

She felt rather than saw Rick enter the room. His presence made her feel claustrophobic, which made no sense. She was used to being around overwhelmingly masculine men. But then, she'd never thought about *marrying* one of them. Grabbing a saddle, she turned to push past him and found his broad shoulders blocking the doorway.

"Stand aside, please," she said. He didn't move, and the way he stared made her cheeks grow hot. "I thought you wanted to saddle the horses."

"Have you thought about what I said? Jon's parents will find you soon."

"I know, I know," she muttered. "Let's not talk about it now." She moved to go around him, but he still blocked the doorway. "What?"

"Be careful with Elijah. Don't hurt him."

"What are you talking about?"

"Just back off, okay? Don't be so helpless and appealing. His family is all gone now. The daughter ran off when she was seventeen and abandoned a granddaughter she never saw again. Now Elijah doesn't even have her."

Allie opened her mouth, then closed it again. Could he be talking about her mother? She never left behind a grandchild. She set the saddle down a minute. "I thought the daughter left when she was pregnant. Did he have more than one?"

He gave her a curious look but didn't ask where she'd heard the story. "Just the one girl. Selena. She left when she was about eight months pregnant, but Elijah tracked down the baby and brought her here to live."

Her mother had abandoned Allie's sister?

Allie wanted to sit down. Her mother had told her the baby died.

Rick didn't seem to notice her shock. "He poured all his love into his granddaughter, but she died when she was twenty-five. She looked a lot like you, and I think that's why he's taken to you so much. But you're not his Maria."

Allie scrambled to recover her senses. "I saw her picture today."

"So you understand the resemblance. You could twist him around your finger, but if you try, I'll break it off."

She managed a smile, trying not to show her shock. "I'm attached to my fingers, so don't worry. I'm not here to get anything out of Elijah."

"No, just out of me. You made a decision yet?"

Was that dismay in his voice? She studied his features but couldn't penetrate his impassive expression. "It would save Betsy."

"It's the only way to be sure." Resignation settled over his mouth.

"I want to get one thing clear right up front. You are not Betsy's father." Her voice trembled just a little. "I will have the say over what's best for her."

His blue eyes narrowed. "Nope. Won't work, lady. This is a partnership. I'm doing this for Jon and for Betsy, not for you. She'll never talk with the way you're smothering her."

Allie gasped and took a step back. Her knees trembled, and she curled her fingers into her palms so she wouldn't hit him. "A mother protects her child."

"A mother's job is to teach her child to stand on her own."

"She's only five!"

"Old enough to be tying her own shoes, to make her bed. I saw you making it for her this morning while she colored on the floor. You have to teach her some responsibility."

Allie didn't trust herself to speak. Luckily, he took a saddle and went back outside. Maybe all men didn't get how important it was to protect children from the bumps of life. Jon thought she coddled Betsy too. She whisked a tear from her lashes. Rick wasn't a father and didn't understand.

She wasn't going to let him bully her or Betsy. Talk about a throwback to pioneer days! Here she was about to enter into a marriage of convenience. And really, it would have been impossible if he actually *wanted* to marry her. If he touched her . . . She suppressed a shudder. He didn't attract her *that way* at all.

This way they could both keep their distance.

She picked up the saddle and bridle and went out to the corral. Rick was on his cell phone, and she almost expected him to snarl like the cougar over whatever he'd been told. He snapped his phone shut and beckoned to her. Dropping the saddle over the fence post, she joined him at the gate.

"We need to rescue a horse, and I may need help catching it. Charlie is gone, and the other two hands need to stay here and take care of these kids. You'll have to do."

"What about Betsy?"

"She can hang out with the kids."

"Not a chance."

"Then bring her. But be quick about it."

The prospect of letting her daughter see how some people treated horses called her hasty decision into question. Still, she couldn't let a horse die because she was squeamish. "I'll get her."

Allie found her daughter still asleep in the hammock with the kittens lying on top of her.

"Betsy," she called in a soft voice.

Her daughter's eyes popped open. She sat up and rubbed her eyes, then rolled out of the hammock with a kitten in her arms.

"Rick needs us to go help a horse." Allie held out her hand, and Betsy ran to grasp it. She put down the kitten before taking her mother's hand. "Can you be big and brave? Some people aren't nice to their horses."

Betsy nodded, and the two of them went around the front of the house to where Rick sat waiting in his truck. Betsy climbed in next to Rick, and Allie fastened her daughter's seat belt and her own.

"How far?" she asked Rick.

"About ten miles."

"Who called you?"

"A neighbor saw the horse staggering across the desert."

"Owner?"

His mouth took on a grim slant. "I think I know. I've been keeping an eye on them for a few weeks. The owner is a city dude who thinks it's fun to fly out here three or four times a year."

"Can we do anything if he refuses to let us take the horse?"

"The sheriff will cite him for neglect. But it won't come to that. I'm taking him home with us, and we'll deal with what we have to later. He's not a bad guy, just stupid."

From the way he clamped his lips shut, Allie knew he didn't want to talk. Good thing, because she didn't want to either. She stared out the window.

The golden stipa grass mingled with the cactus and sage from horizon to horizon. It was a harsh land but beautiful. The purple haze of the mountains climbed to the sky in the distance, and the blue bowl overhead added to the isolation. The air smelled hot and dusty even though it was only March.

The thought of staying in this sanctuary comforted her. She and Betsy were safe here. They'd see anyone dangerous coming from miles away. A stranger would stick out like water in the desert.

Rick braked hard, and the truck slewed in the road before coming to rest near the ditch. "There she is!" He opened the door and grabbed a saddlebag from behind his seat. "Come on."

Allie unlatched her seat belt and got Betsy free as well. "Stay close to me," she told her daughter.

She nearly stepped on a tarantula lumbering across the road.

Withdrawing her foot, she let the arachnid have the road until it disappeared on the other side. Creepy things. With Betsy in her arms, she hopped a yucca plant and headed after Rick, who was disappearing behind thick brush.

If she saw another tarantula, she might scream.

At least she wore boots. She put Betsy down and took her hand. "Let's run to catch up."

The hot, dusty wind blew in her face, and her feet slipped so much on the thin soil that it took much longer to catch up with Rick than she'd imagined. She thought about calling for him to wait, but he was too far ahead. Besides, he was a man on a mission, and she doubted he'd listen.

Betsy tugged at her hand and pointed to their right. Allie stopped and stared at the pitiful sight. A blue roan mare stood outlined against a rocky hillside. Her bones stood out in stark relief through her ragged coat. She tried to move away from them, but she staggered as she walked.

When was the last time the mare had food or water? Allie feared they were too late to save her. "Let's see if we can get close, Betsy."

Betsy tugged her hand out of Allie's and ran toward the horse. Allie tried to grab her and grasped only air. "No, Betsy, you'll scare her." When Allie leaped after her daughter, her foot slipped, and she sprawled onto the ground. Her hand dove into a cactus. She scrambled up again, but Betsy was out of reach by then.

Rick's head turned at her shout, and he put out his hand as though to catch the little girl, but Betsy veered around him and continued on her course to the animal. When she got about ten feet away, she stopped.

Allie ran to catch up with her daughter. "Don't get any closer,

Bets," she called, still several feet from her daughter. "She might be dangerous." Though the poor horse looked like she didn't have the energy to walk, much less kick.

Betsy put her hand out and walked closer to the mare. "No, Betsy!" Allie put on an extra burst of speed, but she felt she was moving through air as thick as quicksand. Betsy would reach the horse before Allie could stop her.

But the mare put her head down, and her nose touched Betsy's outstretched hand. The shudders wracking the horse's body stopped, and she stood quietly as the little girl rubbed the white blaze on her head.

"Well, I'll be," Rick said softly as Allie fell into step beside him. "Keep her here. I'll go get the truck."

"It's not safe." Allie scooped her daughter into her arms.

Rick rolled his eyes. "She's fine. There's an affinity between them."

The horse stepped closer to where Allie stood with Betsy. The little girl put her hand out, and the horse nuzzled it. Hope shimmered in Allie's heart. Maybe he was right. Maybe this horse was the key to unlocking Betsy's heart.

7

RICK WASN'T SURE THE HORSE WOULD EVEN SURVIVE THE TRIP. TRYING TO avoid the bumps in the road, he drove slowly back to the ranch, but the trip took its toll on the mare. Her legs trembled as he opened the tailgate and prepared to lead her into the holding pen by the smaller of the two barns.

"What do you want me to do?" Allie asked him.

"Just stand out of the way while I get her out."

The mare kicked at him when he stepped up into the truck, and he darted away from her wicked hooves. He hadn't thought she had that much fight in her. "Come on, girl, you need some food and water."

Betsy climbed onto the wheel well of the trailer and put her hand out.

"No, Betsy!" Allie sprang toward her daughter.

Rick grabbed her arm. "The mare can't hurt her from there." The mare nuzzled the small hand, and the little girl smiled. It was the first smile Rick had seen on her.

He scooped her up and deposited her by the gate. "Betsy, call to her. See if she'll come to you."

"She won't talk," Allie whispered.

Rick glowered at her. "Give her a chance, woman. You're smothering her."

Sparks that could have electrocuted him flashed from her blue eyes. She opened her mouth to speak, but he turned his back on her. "Call to her, Bets."

Betsy looked down and shook her head. She started back toward the truck, but he stopped her. "Wait a minute. Let me get some sweet feed. She might come to you if you have food."

He ran to the small barn and scooped up a bucket of sweet feed. He stopped to grab some electrolytes and the stainless hand pump. The mare needed fluid fast. When he went back to the yard, he found Allie leading the horse out of the truck.

"I think she's afraid of men," Allie said.

Rick's elation faded. "You just spoiled the perfect opportunity for Betsy to bond with the mare," he said under his breath. "Cut me some slack here."

"She's my daughter. I know what's best for her." Allie's chin grew more determined. She led the horse toward the corral.

Too late to cry over spilt milk. "Looks like she's been beaten." Rick pointed to the stripes on the mare's flank.

"I noticed." Allie neared her daughter. "Stand back, Betsy. I don't

79

want her to kick you." Betsy stood out of the way, and her mother led the mare through the gate.

"I want to tube her first. She needs water the most."

"She won't let you. I'll do it," Allie said.

"You know how?"

"I've done it before." She held out her hand for the tube.

Rick handed it over and watched her approach the mare. Allie stuck her fingers on each side of the animal's mouth, forcing her to open. Then she massaged the mare's esophagus, and the mare swallowed. As the horse swallowed, the tube advanced down her throat.

"Slick," he said. "I couldn't do it that well. Make sure it's in her stomach. If you get it in the lungs, she'll drown."

Allie shot him a look, and he shut up. She said she'd done it before, and he couldn't fault her technique.

She stepped back and nodded to him. "The lady is ready for a drink."

He dumped the powdered electrolytes into a bucket and turned the hose on. "Ready when you are."

Allie took the bucket he handed over, dropped the pump into the bucket, and began to pump the fluid into the mare's stomach.

"Take it slow," he warned, ignoring the way she rolled her eyes. He didn't want to lose this animal.

Allie pumped slowly, pausing often. Finally, the bucket emptied. The mare seemed to be stronger already.

"Try some feed," he said, handing her the feed bucket after she'd pulled the tube out. "See if she'll eat, Bets. I'd better stay away for now until she knows she can trust me."

He'd like to get his hands on the man who mistreated this animal. She'd been badly beaten, and maggots infested the cuts on her legs. He'd have to spend some time getting them out as soon as possible.

He seldom saw true meanness. Generally, neglect was the killer, but this wounding was deliberate.

Betsy climbed over the fence with the bucket and approached the mare. The old girl snorted and stepped closer to the child. Then the mare thrust her lips into Betsy's outstretched palm and delicately ate the nuggets of feed.

"Good girl," Rick said. "I'll be back in a minute to take care of her wounds."

"She won't let you," Allie said. "I'll do it."

"It's nasty," he warned.

"I see the maggots," she said in a soft voice. "I've handled things like this before."

So far all he'd felt toward her was guilt and obligation, and the admiration that welled at her competence with the horses surprised him. "I'll get the tweezers and antiseptic."

Once he brought her what she needed, he went to find Elijah. Last time he'd seen the old man, he was heading to the big barn. On the way, Rick's cell phone rang, and he saw Brendan's name flash on his caller ID. "That was fast," he said when he answered it.

"You're not going to like this."

Rick's earlier admiration spiraled down like a dust devil. "What is it?"

Brendan's sigh came loud through the phone. "You think this woman is capable of trafficking in Mexican illegals?"

"No way," he said with more conviction than he felt. Rick didn't want to believe Jon's widow would be involved in anything like that.

"The Border Patrol had some pretty strong evidence, and they have questions for her."

"That's not what I wanted to hear, Brendan. She said nothing about any trouble with the law."

"Of course not. I'd think she'd be afraid to tell you the whole truth for fear of you turning her in."

"If she goes to jail, Betsy will go to Jon's parents for sure. I can't let that happen." Had Jon known what his wife was up to? Was that why he made Rick promise not to let his parents get Betsy?

Brendan cleared his throat. "There's more. Jon's parents have charged her with kidnapping."

"What?"

"They'd filed for custody. She can't just up and disappear."

"So the FBI is looking for her?"

"Yep. I should tell them, but I'm not going to."

"Thanks, buddy." Rick ran his hand through his hair. Time was running out.

"What are you going to do?"

"I'm going to marry her," Rick said, his voice wobbling a little. He'd hoped to find a way out.

"You kidding me, man? Even Jon wouldn't expect you to go that far."

"He's tapping my shoulder even now," Rick said. "Thanks for checking it out, Brendan. If you find out any more, let me know."

"I will. But think before you leap, buddy."

"I already have." Rick shut his phone. Man, he wanted a shot of whiskey. Everything in him recoiled at the thought of marrying a woman he didn't know, but he'd promised Jon. Maybe if he followed through, the monkey of guilt on his back would go away.

Rick opened the barn door and stepped inside. Elijah sat on a bale of straw, watching Cupcake and her foal in the stall. The curry brush and comb lay abandoned on the floor beside him.

Rick could have sworn there were tears on Elijah's cheeks, but the old man bent his head and swiped at his face.

When Elijah turned to face him, the brown wrinkles were dry. "The new campers are settled?"

"Yeah, and I found that old mare of Allbright's half-dead and wandering the desert. I brought her home."

"Ah, that is what the commotion was about, *sí*? She will live?"

"I think so."

"Allbright may come by to get her."

"Over my dead body." Rick propped his boot on the lowest rail of the stall. "You okay?"

Elijah stared at the mare and colt. "Did you request Allie's references yet?"

"I talked to the rodeo boss, and he told me she was a great worker, and he hated to lose her."

Elijah nodded, his face without expression.

"Are you having second thoughts about hiring her?"

"Not at all. I was going to tell you not to bother with the references." Elijah seemed to snap back from whatever place he'd gone. "You've called your contacts about her, haven't you?"

"Yep."

The old man took a stogie out of his pocket and chewed on it before taking out a match. "Any word?"

"Some." Rick told Elijah what he'd found out. The boss would have to know. The Bluebird Ranch was prime land for carting Mexicans across the border. They'd have to watch Allie.

"I do not hear you calling for me to throw her off the ranch."

Rick settled onto a hay bale. "I'm going to marry her, Elijah."

Through the swirl of smoke, Elijah's dark eyes studied him. "Why would you do this?"

Staring into Elijah's dark eyes, Rick could smell the sharp, stinging odor of gunpowder, the underlying stench of raw sewage in the streets, and the stink of fear. Taking a deep breath, he began to recount to Elijah the promise he'd made to Jon.

RICK SAT ON A FOLDING CHAIR WITH A MAKESHIFT TABLE MADE FROM A cardboard box between him and his bunkmate Jon Siders. Rick glanced at the cards in his hand. A full house. Jon was toast.

He shoved an empty Tabasco bottle to join an assortment of Q-Tips and candy wrappers. "I'll see your dime and raise you a quarter." They'd had to improvise to play poker, but it helped the time pass.

Jon frowned at his hand, but his gaze wandered back to the letter in his lap. All he'd done since he got it was brood.

"Are you going to play?" Rick said, not bothering to hide his impatience.

"I need to get home."

"Don't we all."

Jon frowned and threw his cards to the table. "My parents are badgering Allie again."

"Man, just call them and tell them to lay off." It was a familiar discussion. While Rick had suffered from lack of parental care, Jon's parents had been the interfering type.

"I've done that. You don't know my parents." Jon pushed back from the table. "I'm afraid of what they might do if I don't come back."

If Rick had been a religious man, he would have crossed himself. "Don't give fate any ideas," he said. He wished he had a drink. A little Jack Daniels might help him bear this discussion.

"God's got my fate in his hands." Jon smiled. "Thanks for that reminder."

Rick shifted uncomfortably. Jon's only failing as a friend was how often he brought God into the conversation. Sometimes Rick almost expected to see the Big Guy sitting across from Jon, talking with him.

"What are they doing now?" he asked, more to change the subject than because he was interested. He'd never met the wife and kid. He was stationed in Europe by the time Jon married her.

"Telling her if she respects them, she'll change churches and start coming with them." Jon's eyes took on an uncharacteristically hard glint. "Over my dead body."

"What's so wrong with that? I thought you were all about family."

"Their church is practically a cult. At the very least it's a toxic environment. They won't even talk to people who leave it. It's all about the letter of the law and nothing about love. My parents believed mightily in the old adage 'spare the rod and spoil the child.' At church they were always smiling and sweet, but at home I rarely got more than a nod of recognition. I'm not having my family exposed to that."

The type of church Jon described was how Rick thought they all were, but he decided to keep this appraisal to himself. "Allie can just say no."

"And she has." Jon's gaze fixed on Rick's face. "We've gone to the wall together, buddy. You're the only one I'd trust to take care of things if I don't get home."

Death was not on Rick's agenda. Not his and not his best friend's. "Don't change the subject just because you're losing." He tapped his cards against the box. "You folding?"

Jon grinned, but his eyes held a trace of sadness. "And let you win? Not on your life." He shoved a handful of gum wrappers into the center. "I call. Show me what you've got."

Rick laid out his cards with a flourish. "Read 'em and weep, my friend." Even as he raked in his winnings, his thoughts danced away from Jon's words.

RICK SHUDDERED AND CAME BACK TO THE PRESENT. "JON TOOK A BULLET meant for me. I have to take care of his family," he told Elijah.

"He has been gone two years, *sí*? Why only now are you looking to help them?"

Rick winced at the blunt words. "I could make an excuse and tell you I couldn't find her, but the truth is, I didn't look very hard. I was wallowing under a mountain of guilt and just wanted peace. So I came here." He still couldn't tell Elijah the full truth of why he would carry that guilt all his life.

"And how did the child's death fit in with this?" Elijah asked.

Heat swept up Rick's neck. "That was a separate incident." But interconnected more than he wanted to face. He could still see the eight-year-old's face in his mind, the wide dark eyes, the fear. Until the gun barked in his hand and obliterated the boy.

The fact that it was an accident failed to expunge his guilt.

Elijah nodded, his dark eyes still studying Rick's face. "I have kept quiet to let you heal, but the time for silence is past. Sweeping your guilt under the straw will only make it stink. Better to bring it to the sunshine. Is this your penance, Rick? Coming here to *El Despoblado*?"

"I believe in this place just as much as you. Have you forgotten I was a throwaway kid myself once? If not for the Bluebird Ranch, I'd be in prison somewhere. The woman may not have been worthy of Jon, but she's still his wife. And I have to help her and the kid."

"You seem to have forgotten what it means to be desperate," Elijah said softly. "Could desperation be Allie's sin? I am content that you are to help her. But do not assume too much about her guilt and shut yourself off from a true marriage with her."

A true marriage? That was not the plan.

THE AROMA OF ENCHILADAS FILLED THE KITCHEN WITH WARMTH. ALLIE had the teenage girls help her prepare supper. They grumbled about it, but she held firm, and they'd fallen into line. The boys went out with the ranch hands to feed and water the stock. They were all too tired to talk much during supper.

The girls kept stealing glances at the black night devoid of street-lights. The barns' security lights provided the only illumination, and the darkness swallowed their beams only a few feet out.

"What do you do all evening?" Latoya asked after the dishes were done. "Let's hop in the whip and see some action."

"The whip?" Allie dried her hands.

"Some wheels," Devin said. "I'm with the Betty. This place is whacked."

"We've got board games," Allie said. She tried to hide her smile, but it came breaking through. "Monopoly, chess. Check out the game cabinet."

"Video games?" Devon asked, fingering the ring on his lip.

"They belong to Rick. You'll have to ask his permission," she said.

Leon fixed a stare on Rick. "What games you got?"

"Video games are a privilege. Once you earn the right to play, we'll scrounge up a game on Saturday night," Rick said.

"Earn 'em? Oh man, you talkin' smack!"

"You'll get points for grooming horses, feeding them, cleaning the pens. When you get enough points, you can take me on in Pac-Man."

"Pac-Man," Leon said. "Man, don't you got no Tomb Raider or Madden football?"

Rick shrugged. "Take it or leave it."

"Like we got a choice," Leon grumbled.

"Grow up," Rick said. "There are always choices in life. People are going to pull you in all directions. Where you end up is a direct result of how wise your decisions are."

Allie wondered if he really believed that. Did he own every wrong decision he'd made? It wasn't through any decision of hers that her parents were dead and that Jon had left her to raise Betsy alone.

Betsy rubbed her eyes, and Allie read the fatigue on her face. "Let's get you to bed, Bets. You've had a long day."

Betsy tugged on her hand and pointed to the door.

"You want to go tell the horse good night?" Rick asked.

"I'll take her," Allie said when he moved toward the door. She should have guessed what Betsy wanted before Rick had.

"I'll go with you. That cougar might still be prowling around."

Allie wanted to object, but maybe he wouldn't insist on talking in front of Betsy. She took Betsy's hand, and they stepped out into the moonlight.

"I can't get over how black it is here when night falls," Allie said, giving Betsy's hand a comforting squeeze. The new dew on the ground smelled fresh.

They reached the barn, and he shoved open the sliding door. Allie and Betsy went through first. Allie watched as her daughter ran to the stall holding the newest addition to the ranch. The sores on the mare's withers were crusty, and the harsh glare from the bare bulb overhead showed every bone through her rough coat. Rick scooped some sweet feed into a bucket and offered it to the mare. She nosed the bucket and began to eat.

"Do they always make it?" Allie asked. The guy had some good qualities, even if she hated to admit it.

"Not all." His gaze met hers. "We try our best, just like we do with the kids."

"How'd you end up here, Rick?" Allie wanted to know, but she wasn't sure he'd talk about it. He seemed different tonight. More wary, and she wasn't sure why.

He leaned on the rail and watched the mare eat. "Like most of the others. I'd been in trouble—shoplifting, a stolen-car spree, fights at school. A teacher who took an interest in me heard about Elijah's ranch and talked Child Protective Services into sending me and a few other kids here. I wanted nothing to do with Elijah, but I couldn't resist a horse that he'd rescued two months before." He smiled. "Whiskers was his name, and he was five. His owner had raised him to buck in the rodeo, but he beat Whiskers to get him to do it."

Allie winced. "The rodeo where I worked was always careful not to mistreat the animals. No rodeo boss would stand for that."

He nodded. "The chute boss saw lacerations on Whiskers and disqualified him. The owner was going to sell him to the pet-food factory, but Elijah got wind of it and bought him instead. But Whiskers wouldn't let anyone near him. The day I arrived, he looked in my eyes, and I looked in his, and we each saw a soul mate. He wouldn't let me ride him that day, but by the time my time here was over, I was riding him all over the ranch. I came back every summer until I joined the army."

"And then when you got out?"

He nodded. "Elijah wrote me all ten years I was in, then offered me a job when I told him I was resigning. He needed help, and I needed a sanctuary."

Sanctuary. The word made a warm sensation well up inside Allie. That's what she and Betsy needed—a safe haven where they could grow and put down roots. Elijah seemed all about helping other kids. Why had he never sought out Allie's mom? He'd been content to take his granddaughter and let his own daughter disappear into the underbelly of the city.

She'd come here expecting some kind of ogre and discovered a man who cared about kids. The dichotomy between what he professed and how he'd acted with his own child left her shaking her head and wondering who was the real Elijah.

Maybe when he found out who she really was, he'd throw her out the way he'd tossed her mother onto the street.

8

THE OFFICE HAD THE APPEAL OF A BEAUTIFUL SNAKE. LOVELY COLORS AND form, but inspiring the same dread in Allie as coming face-to-face with a rattlesnake. She looked forward to her time in the big, comfortable room with the tin ceiling until she looked down at the way the black marks jittered their way across the ledger page.

The last two days had been placid, and she began to relax—until she realized the work she had to do. Leaving Betsy napping on her bed, she entered the office prepared to do battle but was already mentally waving a white flag.

She dropped into the cracked leather chair and squinted at the new stack of receipts in the tray. These files wouldn't be easy to whip into shape. The sun was too bright in here. She closed the blinds, but her eyes weren't ready to deal with this yet.

She pulled open the lap drawer and glanced through it. Paper clips, rubber bands, a couple of erasers and mechanical pencils, a pack of gum, and a few keys. Nothing really interesting.

Allie tried the drawer on her right and found it full of file folders. The soft gold of the manila folders made it easier to read the tabs. Glancing through them, she found them labeled with different categories of bills like electricity, food, and maintenance. The next drawer held blank envelopes and postage stamps. The top drawer on her left contained cleared check stubs and blank checks.

She moved to the last drawer and tugged on it. It refused to budge. Maybe it was stuck. Yanking on it, she could feel the lock that held it in place. Why would Elijah have a locked drawer?

The keys in the lap drawer. She pulled it open again and glanced at the keys. They all looked like door keys until she moved them around and found a smaller key hiding under a large one. It might fit. Fingering it, she thought about whether she had the right to invade a place Elijah obviously wanted to keep hidden.

Maybe she didn't have the right, but she was going to take it anyway. She wanted to get at the truth behind all her mother had told her. Selena had told at least some lies. Fitting the key into the lock, she twisted it and heard it click. The drawer slid open with a gentle tug.

Several picture albums lay in the drawer. Cracks radiated across the leather cover of the top one, and the texture was worn smooth along the opening edges. Allie lifted it out and ran her hand across it. Maybe it was a record of the kids who had passed through this place over the years.

But if it was, why lock it up?

She lifted the top cover and peeked at the first page. Old black-and-white pictures with labels under them crowded the black paper. The first picture of a little girl looked a lot like Betsy. It had to be Allie's mother.

She flipped the pages and peered into a world fifty years in the past. Her mother looked so happy and carefree sitting on the fence rail with the horses in the pasture behind her. By her late teens, the smile changed to a deadpan scowl.

The last few pages were empty and appeared to have had pictures removed. Allie started to go to the next album when she heard the front door slam and boot heels clatter along the wooden floor. She dropped the album back into the drawer. Noiselessly sliding the drawer shut, she locked it and returned the key to its place just as Rick came through the door.

Her face felt hot and moist, and when he stared at her for an extra beat, she wondered if guilt stamped her features. "Everything okay?" she asked.

He had a rope in his hand, and dust streaked his face. "Peachy. The bull got out and is chasing the horses. Any chance you could help me get him? You've got a good arm."

Pleasure surged through her at his words. Better to do something she was good at than to sit here staring at words and numbers jumping across the page. She rose and grabbed her cowboy hat. "Where is he?"

"Back pasture." He led the way out the back door.

The sunlight pierced her eyes, and she lowered her hat on her forehead. Squinting against the dust and glare, she saw the big bull on the other side of the fence. Tossing his head with its sharp horns, he pranced around the field, looking as mean as any she'd seen in the ring.

"Whooee, what a brute. You ever take him to the rodeo?" she asked.

"Nope. I wouldn't want to be responsible for him killing someone.

I told Elijah we needed to get rid of him, but he won't hear of it. The old man loves Roscoe for some reason."

"Roscoe. He seems too big and mean for a Roscoe," she said, approaching the fence.

The bull quit his posturing and erupted into action. Dirt clods flew from under his sharp hooves as he chased the mares from corner to corner. Good thing Betsy wasn't out here to see him cornering her little mare. The poor thing barely had the strength to outrun the beast. How'd he get out anyway?

She took the rope from Rick and started to climb over the fence.

"No, stay on this side of the fence," he said, reaching for her arm.

She dodged his hand and vaulted. The bull hadn't seen her yet. Looping the rope, she waited for the bovine to get closer.

"Allie, he's dangerous!" Rick climbed the fence and came to stand beside her. "Let me get us some horses, and we'll rope him from horseback."

She shook her head. "He's about to catch up with Betsy's mare." She twirled the loop through the air as she waited for the right moment. The bull moved a few steps closer, and she waited. Missing at this close range would be dangerous.

"Let me get another rope then. We need to grab him from two directions so he doesn't trample you." Rick ran off toward the barn.

Allie wasn't worried. Animals usually tried to pull away from the rope, not run toward it. The bull's head jerked toward Rick as he jogged toward the barn. He snorted and pawed the ground, then charged toward Rick. Allie shouted a warning. Rick put on a spurt of speed and dived through the barn door, and the bull followed.

"Oh no," Allie whispered. She darted toward the barn as the beast erupted from the door. Skidding to a halt, she began to back away from the snorting animal. At least the bull hadn't been inside long enough to do much damage to Rick.

The bull's head swung away from her, and she spared a glance to her right to see what had attracted its attention.

Betsy.

Betsy was in the paddock, walking toward the animal with flowers in her hands. She seemed oblivious to the danger.

Allie's muscles felt rusty and slow as she tried to run toward her daughter. Time slowed as Allie saw Betsy's dark curls bounce with each step. The sunlight gleamed on the little girl's hair, and she wore a serene smile.

"Betsy, run!" Allie had lost the loop on her rope. Coiling it again, she screamed and shouted at the bull, but the animal fixated on her daughter. Her best chance was to rope the creature before it got any closer. She'd never be able to get to Betsy before the bull did.

The beast snorted and pawed the ground, but Betsy stood still with her eyes wide. The fear cleared from her face.

Allie became aware of a faint humming sound and realized it was coming from her child. Whipping the rope around her head, Allie tossed it through the air toward the bull. In her agitation, her aim was off, and the loop fell to the ground.

The animal ignored the rope and began to trot toward Betsy.

"No!" Allie jerked the rope back toward her and began to run toward her daughter. She was too far. Her mind noticed every detail of the way Roscoe was moving, the way he tossed his horns, the way his tail switched along his back.

Betsy looked so small and defenseless. The bull would get to her first. Allie had to try the rope again.

She stopped and twirled the rope over her head. *Please Lord, make my aim true.* She barely breathed as the rope sang through the air. It didn't even touch the animal's ears as it settled over his head. She dug her boot heels into the dirt and prepared for the animal to charge away.

Then another rope dropped over the bull's neck from the other direction, and Allie saw Rick winding the rope around his palms. The animal stopped but didn't try to get away. It did nothing but stand and breathe heavily.

Still humming, Betsy put her hand out toward the beast.

"Betsy, stay away!" Allie's gaze locked with Rick's. "Help," she mouthed.

He glanced behind him at the barn door, then stepped to it and looped the rope through the door handle. "Betsy, turn and walk toward me," he said in a deep, authoritative voice.

Betsy seemed lost in her own world. Her blue eyes stayed locked on the bull's. Rick was running toward her, and her steps quickened toward the animal.

Before Rick could grab her, Betsy was directly in front of Roscoe. The animal snuffled into her small, outstretched hand. She rubbed her fingers along its head.

Then Rick had her little girl in his arms. The rope burned into Allie's palms with the force of her grip. She was afraid to relax her hold on the big bull, though it seemed to have no inclination to attack the two, who were still within reach of the sharp horns.

Holding Betsy against his chest, Rick turned and raced away. Only when they were far enough away that Roscoe couldn't reach them did Allie relax her death grip on the rope. She let it fall into the red dirt and ran toward her daughter. All she wanted was to bury her face in Betsy's hair and assure herself that the little girl was all right.

"Allie, look out!" Rick was on the other side of the fence by now with Betsy. He was gesturing at something behind her.

Allie didn't have to turn around and look to know that Roscoe had managed to free himself from Rick's rope. She ran for the fence, but she didn't think she was going to make it. Even as her hand slapped the top rail and a splinter stabbed her palm, she felt the animal's hot breath on her neck. Any minute now, she would feel his sharp horns striking her back.

Praying for speed and strength, she gripped the railing and began to scramble over. Rick shouted again. She heard her jeans tear and felt a stab against her skin, then the hot spurt of blood on her thigh, but there was no pain yet.

Then she was falling on the ground with the smell of manure in her nose and the hard taste of dirt in her mouth. Rolling onto her back, she looked up into blue sky. Her hat was gone, and the pain started, first in her thigh and then in her shoulder.

Still trying to get to her, the bull was battering at the fence and snorting. She rose up on her elbows, then sat up. "Calm down," she said. She got up and dusted off her jeans. Blood had soaked her thigh, and standing made her feel dizzy.

"Are you okay?" Rick was still carrying Betsy as he came toward her. A red stain darkened his jeans below his right knee.

Allie tried to move toward them as her knees buckled and she sank to the ground.

RICK WAS STILL SHAKING BY THE TIME ALLIE CAME AROUND. WORRY wrinkling her brow, Betsy hovered over her mother's bed, and he kept watching the little girl. She'd calmed the bull with a song.

Any other person approaching the animal like that would have been trampled.

Betsy had a touch with the beasts. Had she always been that way? He'd have to ask Allie.

Elijah came to the bedroom door. "She will be all right, *sí?*"

"I think she'll be fine," the doctor said, moving away from the bed. "She's lost a little blood, but I think it was probably more shock that made her lose consciousness. She's coming around now." He left the room, and Rick and Elijah moved to stand beside the bed.

Allie moaned and moved her head. Her eyes opened, and Rick stared down into their blue depths. Her hand went to her head, and she tried to sit up.

"Don't move," Elijah said, putting a brown, wrinkled hand on her shoulder.

"Betsy," Allie whispered.

"She's right here," Rick said, putting Betsy closer to the bed.

Allie touched Betsy's face, and the little girl climbed into the bed with her mother. Allie snuggled her close, and Betsy's eyes closed.

"The bull?" Allie asked.

"Safe in the paddock," Elijah said in a clipped voice.

Rick had carried Allie in, then went out with the stock hands to capture the bull before coming back to check on Allie. He motioned to Elijah when Allie's eyes closed again. The two men stepped into the hall. "The door to Roscoe's stall was standing open. I think someone let him out. Any idea who would do that?" he asked Elijah.

The old man hesitated. "I have not wanted to worry you, but I have had an offer for the ranch—a good offer that I turned down."

"Who would want to buy clear out here in the middle of nowhere?"

"You have heard of Stuart Ifera, *sí*? He wants to put up a fancy resort much like Lajitos."

"How would releasing the bull force you to sell?"

Elijah shrugged. "He thought the animal worth more than it is, *sí*? But perhaps it was not this man." He nodded toward Allie. "Could it be something to do with Allie?"

"I don't see how."

Elijah shrugged. "If you will keep watch over her, I will get us some coffee and return."

Rick needed to talk to her anyway. Right now might not be the best time, but it would have to do. Maybe she'd be truthful in a weakened state. He stepped back into the room. Allie was studying a picture on the wall, with a sleeping Betsy curled beside her.

"You doing okay?"

"Fine." She shifted in the bed. "I should get up."

"I wanted to ask you about something." He let his gaze bore into her like an interrogator. "Are you moving illegal Mexicans around with the rodeo, Allie?"

Her eyes widened, and her lips parted. She started to sit up but Betsy stirred, and Allie subsided against the pillow. "That's ridiculous," she said. The blue of her eyes was as cold as an ice storm. "Why would you even ask me that?"

"So you didn't know the border patrol is looking for you with questions?"

"Border patrol? Are you serious?"

Unless he was a bad judge of character, he'd swear she had no idea about this. But he'd never been able to read women. His mother could look like an angel, then grab up a razor strap and lay his back open. "So you know nothing about it?"

"No," She shook her head violently, dark curls whipping against her cheeks. "I can't believe they would suspect me."

"They're going to come looking for you. If they take you away, Betsy will have no choice but to go to your in-laws. We need to get moving on protecting her." He needed to tell her all of it. "There's more bad news, Allie."

She swallowed hard. "Okay, give it to me."

"Jon's parents have charged you with kidnapping."

Her cheeks reddened. "They can't do that!"

"Evidently because they'd sued for custody, they were able to make a case for it. We have to get married right away."

She opened her mouth, then closed it again. Swallowing, she tried again. "Thank you, Rick." The words seemed pulled out of her.

Her obvious struggle to take it all in touched him. He shrugged. "You might not thank me after you've had to live with me for a few months."

"How—how long will this marriage need to last?"

"Probably at least a year. It will take time for the adoption to go through."

Her teeth bit into her colorless lower lip. "I'm worried about Betsy. First she has a new stepdad and then she doesn't? What will that do to her?"

"What will Jon's parents do to her?" he said bluntly.

She nodded. "It's the lesser of two evils, I guess."

She looked like she'd been handed a life sentence, and Rick had to admit he felt like he was facing a stint in a Mexican prison.

9

ALLIE WAS TIRED OF LYING IN BED. THE NIGHT HAD BEEN LONG, THOUGH she'd slept fitfully. Judging by the sun, it was nine or so. She eased her arm out from under Betsy's head and sat up. She had to think.

The border patrol was looking for her. The FBI too, if she'd been charged with kidnapping.

It made no sense. How could they think she would be involved in something like trafficking in illegals? Her testimony had sent Jimmy Hernandez to jail, and that should have shown how much she hated that kind of thing. If he hadn't died there, she'd think maybe he had implicated her to take his revenge.

And Jon's parents. She felt even more betrayed. They were family. How could they do this to her?

In an instant, Rick's marriage proposal had become more pressing. Marriage really was her most promising choice. She would make it very clear to him that she would be his wife in *name only*.

She swung her feet to the floor, and her vision began to blank out. She put her head onto her knees. When the fuzziness cleared, she grabbed the bedside table for support and managed to stand. She hurt all over, and her thigh especially pained her with a burning, throbbing persistence. The bull's horns had been sharp.

"You shouldn't be out of bed, *mujercita*." Elijah spoke from the rocking chair in the corner.

Allie hadn't seen him. "Have you been here all night?" She hoped not.

"*Sí*. I wanted to be here if you needed anything."

There was something different about him that Allie couldn't put her finger on. His expression toward her seemed soft and gentle. Maybe it was because she'd been injured.

"I wouldn't turn down a new leg." She smiled then to show she was joking. "I'm fine, really. You've been so kind."

"How could I do less for my own flesh and blood?"

He knew!

The lightheadedness swept over her again, and she sank back onto the bed. "When did you know?" she whispered.

"You think I would not keep track of my daughter? I knew her rodeo name, of course, and her children. I watched her career with pride, even though she excluded me from her life."

"You threw her out!"

The compassion in his eyes didn't change. "She told you this?"

"How could you?" She swept her hand toward the window. "You

have all this and help so many other kids. But you threw your own daughter out like road litter just because she was pregnant." Her conscience smote her. Apparently he'd taken in the baby. She didn't know the whole story, and who was she to judge it?

He rose. "If this is what you believe of me, why did you come?"

"Rick was here," she said. "And I was . . . curious." More than curious, she was driven to find some piece of her family left alive. Some blood connection.

His eyes filled with moisture. "Things are never as simple as they look to the young," he said.

"Rick told me you found the baby and brought her here. M-my mother said the baby died."

"*Sí*, my Maria died. But twenty-five years later." Elijah turned to stare out the window. "My daughter could have come home anytime. I would never turn her away."

"Why did you throw her out in the first place?"

He turned then. "You must discover the truth for yourself about that."

"My mother is dead. If you don't tell me, how can I find out?"

"Listen to your heart," he said softly.

Rick knocked, and they both glanced at the door. He stepped inside. "Your lawyer called. He said he has papers ready for you to sign."

Elijah nodded. "I must go to town." His gaze locked with Allie's. "We will discuss this later, *sí*?" Without waiting for an answer, he went to the door.

Allie watched his stooped shoulders and wanted to call him back. Tell him she forgave him. But she kept her mouth shut. There was so little she knew or understood.

AFTER HE'D TENDED TO ALL THE SICK AND MISTREATED HORSES, RICK made some calls and found out what he and Allie needed to do to get a marriage license. Marriage license. Mention of it was enough to strike fear in his heart. He pocketed his list and went out to feed the livestock. The familiar scent of corn and oats calmed his agitation as the sun sank lower in the sky.

Charlie entered the barn with the other two hands, Buzz and Guinn. The older men had been with Elijah since the days when Rick first came here, and they were both wrinkled as raisins.

"You heard from Elijah? He's still not back from town." Charlie's forehead creased, and he turned to look down the dirt track to the road.

Rick glanced at his watch. "It's nearly five. He's not usually gone this long. He said he'd be back by one."

"He hasn't called either," Guinn said. "I hope the old man is okay."

"Let me call Wally. Elijah went to see him. Did he say anything about another errand?" Rick asked.

"Nope." Guinn's dark eyes held worry.

Rick looked up the lawyer's number in his phone's address book. He talked to the receptionist, then closed his phone. "He left there before lunch. She said he talked about having to get home to tend to the new kids. I'd better go out looking for him. Maybe his Jeep broke down."

"Want me to come too?" Charlie asked.

"You'd better stay with the kids. You have your cell phone on you?"

Charlie nodded. "For all the good it does in the barn. What should I do with the kids?"

"Where are they now?"

"On a hike."

"Get them to curry the horses tonight. Keep them away from the two new mares though. They're fragile, and I'm not sure they're going to make it."

"Sundown will be here in an hour or so," Charlie observed. "You think Elijah is all right?"

"He's probably fine. He should have called though." He tried Elijah's cell number but got voice mail. Not an unusual occurrence with the spotty coverage out here. Even so, Rick had a bad feeling about this. It wasn't like Elijah to be out of touch, and he was rarely gone from the ranch longer than a morning or afternoon. He'd been gone nearly seven hours.

Rick unhitched the trailer, got in his truck, called for Jem, then drove out via the dirt lane. When he turned onto the road, the two-lane highway snaked out ahead and behind him with no other vehicles in sight. Town was only a few miles away. There would be no reason for Elijah to be gone this long.

He drove all the way to town without spotting Elijah's old SUV. There was no familiar Jeep in front of the café. The lot beside the grocery store held only a dirty brown pickup and the faint scent of exhaust. Turning around, he drove back the way he'd come.

About two miles from the ranch, something glinted in the dying sun to his right. Squinting against the glare on the glass, Rick pulled to the side of the road and stuck his head out the window. Was that the tail end of a vehicle? He drove as close as he could to a stand of honey mesquite bushes, then got out with Jem. He jogged the remaining distance. Fighting his way through the thorns, he arrived at the vehicle. The battered white Jeep was Elijah's.

Why would the old man pull his Jeep this far off the road, almost hiding it? The vehicle was empty. Rick cupped his hands around his mouth and shouted Elijah's name, but only a hawk answered him. Poking his head inside the vehicle, he discovered the keys still in the ignition.

Jem whined at his feet. "Find Elijah, boy." The dog barked and trotted off into the scrub. Rick kept shouting for Elijah as he walked farther from the road and followed the dog. There was no telling which direction the old man had gone. His gut told him to walk to the mountain. Elijah loved the high spots. Maybe he'd taken a yen to commune with God out here. It wasn't unheard-of.

Small rocks scattered from under the soles of Rick's boots. Jem trotted ahead like he knew where he was going. Rick walked steadily toward the soaring peaks. Cracks carved by rainwater made the rocks look like soldiers standing at attention. He was so intent on examining the mountaintop that he almost missed the splash of red at the base.

Jem began to bark. He leaped over a mesquite bush and began to sniff and whine at the red object.

Rick leaped forward. Elijah had been wearing a red shirt. As he neared, he saw the old man curled up on his side with his back to the road as if he were sleeping. Rick reached the crumpled form and touched the old man's shoulder.

He was cold, colder than seemed possible. And very dead.

WITH HER CHIN ON BETSY'S HAIR, ALLIE ROCKED ON THE PORCH. HER daughter slept peacefully, unaware of the trauma unfolding. Tears ran down Allie's cheeks, and her nose was stuffed from crying. She'd barely known the old man, but he was her grandfather.

She and Betsy were the only ones left in her family. They were all gone—parents, sister, husband, now grandfather. Clutching Betsy tighter, she struggled to get past the profound isolation. They were still a family, though there were only two.

"You okay?" Rick dropped onto the top step of the porch and leaned against a post. Weary lines radiated from his eyes. He sat still as if surrounded by a close wall that kept everyone out.

Allie wiped her eyes with a tissue. "It's my fault, Rick." She balled up the tissue in her hand. "I shouldn't have come here. I knew someone was after me, but I thought he couldn't find me here. I put Elijah in harm's way."

Rick straightened. "It was an accident," he said gently.

Allie shook her head. "No, no, it wasn't. The man doesn't want me to find sanctuary here. He's cutting off any help."

As soon as she'd heard Elijah had died, she knew his death was about her. How could it not be?

Rick stood and walked to where she sat in the rocker. "What man? You're not making any sense."

Betsy's breathing was still deep. She wouldn't hear. Allie leaned her head against the chair back. She should have been honest right up front. Rick deserved to know why she was really running.

Allie ran her fingers through Betsy's soft hair and inhaled her little girl scent. "Someone killed my parents, sabotaged their plane. That was a year ago. I had no idea it had anything to do with me. Not at first. Then the calls started coming." She stared into the blackness outside the circle of yellow cast by the porch light.

She could still feel the horror of the moment when she realized her parents had died because of her. "The man said he would strip me of everything I loved in life. That I should count each moment a gift, because I wouldn't have many of them."

Rick's stillness shattered when he walked restlessly across the porch. "Why didn't you tell me all this right from the beginning? You're saying the plane crash wasn't accidental?"

She nodded. "That's what the police thought, but it wasn't."

"The guy sounds like a nut case."

"I was afraid you wouldn't help me, that the danger was too great."

"Maybe it was a prank." Rick's voice was gentle.

Allie shook her head. "The calls stopped for six months. I began to relax, to believe they were a bad joke. My sister was murdered a month ago. It seemed a burglary gone bad." She shuddered and hugged herself. "Then he came to my trailer and trapped me in the bathroom, stuck a knife between the door and the jamb. He taunted me, saying he'd killed my sister. I knew he'd hurt Betsy. I'd planned to bring her here anyway, so I packed my suitcase and lit out."

His glance lingered on Betsy's head. "What about Betsy? You've never said why she doesn't talk."

She kissed the top of her sleeping daughter's head. "We were watching the plane take off at the airport. Betsy saw the crash, the fire. She's not talked since. It was a horrific scene." Her voice thickened. "Neither of us will ever forget it."

"I'm sorry."

He actually sounded like he was. For a Neanderthal, he was surprisingly sweet. "Thanks."

"How do you know the plane was sabotaged?"

"He claimed responsibility for it. I told the police, and they investigated."

"Did they find any evidence?"

"They don't tell me anything."

"And your sister? He claimed to have killed her too?"

"Yes."

Rick shook his head. "I don't buy it. How do you know you're not being stalked by some jerk who gets off on trying to scare you? Maybe both events were just tragic accidents. And who is this guy anyway? What's he got against you?"

"I don't *know* who it is! And he's not just trying to scare me. He was sticking a knife through the door when he told me he'd killed Tammy."

He sighed and took out a knife and a small block of wood. "Okay. But I don't see how this relates to Elijah. The guy can't know where you are." Sitting on the porch railing, he began to whittle. "I don't know what's going to happen to the ranch. Elijah didn't have any family." Putting the knife on his knee, he stared at her. "Elijah mentioned that guy who wanted to buy the ranch. I wonder . . ."

"What?"

He looked down at his block of wood and began to work it again. "Maybe it wasn't an accident. Elijah would have had no reason to be climbing that mountain. And the truck was kind of hidden, now that I think about it."

"You just tried to tell me it was an accident." She grabbed hold of the thought though. If only his death had nothing to do with her. If only it really was caused by something else.

"Maybe I was wrong. With no family to inherit, the killer might have assumed the ranch would go to someone more willing to sell."

She should tell him the truth, but she didn't want the ranch anyway. "Betsy loves that new mare," she said. "I had hopes that she'd . . ." She looked off into the darkness where the stars were beginning to wink on.

Rick looked up at her, then back down to the wood in his hand. "That's usually how the healing starts."

"What will happen to the horses here if the ranch is sold?"

"They'd probably go to the glue factory. Or be slaughtered for cat food." His mouth twisted as if he'd bitten into something bitter.

All the horses that had already been mistreated. A sick knot formed and grew. She couldn't bear to think about it. Maybe she could buy the one they rescued. Losing the mare now would crush Betsy.

"Maybe Elijah left the ranch to you."

"I don't know what he'd planned."

Allie squinted through the darkness at his face. "I think you do. He left it to you, didn't he?"

"He'd talked about it." Rick's voice was grudging.

"You'll keep the ranch going, won't you?"

"If it's my choice." He cleared his throat. "I found out about the marriage license today," Rick said. "There's a three-day waiting period."

"Do I have to wait for state residency?" She couldn't keep the hope out of her voice.

"Nope."

There went that idea. She wet her lips. "When do you want to do it?"

"I thought we'd just go get the license tomorrow. The sooner the better, if the Siders are after you. They could come riding up here anytime. We can at least get temporary custody papers drawn up in case the adoption isn't final when they track you down."

She couldn't believe this. Her life was scattering in all directions like sand in a dust storm. The tornado was sweeping her up and plunking her down in a life she didn't recognize.

"What about Elijah? It seems heartless to make these plans before he's even buried," she said finally.

"He'd want you and Betsy taken care of," he said.

Rick was right. If there was one thing she'd recognized in Elijah, it was his great heart. Tears welled in her eyes again. "Okay," she said.

CROSSING THE STREET TO THE COURTROOM, A COLD WIND SNAKED DOWN Rick's back, but he wasn't sure if it was real or the product of his desire to turn tail and run. He'd planned never to stand before a judge like this and tie himself to a woman, not with the way his mother caused him to distrust the gender. He reminded himself that Allie wasn't anything like the woman who put the scars on his back.

He spared a sideways glance at her. She wouldn't do anything to hurt Betsy. At least she had that much going for her.

The events of the past three days had left him numb. They'd had a quiet funeral for Elijah, attended only by a few friends in the area, the ranch hands, and the kids. Tomorrow, the day after the wedding—if you could call this sterile affair a wedding—Elijah's attorney, Wally Tatum, wanted to talk about Elijah's will.

Another issue Rick wasn't looking forward to dealing with. Had Elijah left him the ranch? While he hoped the good they'd done wasn't about to end, he didn't relish the thought of shouldering the burden by himself. But what if Elijah hadn't left him the ranch? He might have willed it to the feds to be part of the national park.

Maybe he could buy it. Rick examined the thought. He'd set by a little money in his savings account. Not enough for a down payment, but the bank manager knew him and trusted him. It might work.

But what about counseling for the kids? Elijah had done most of that, and while Rick had a degree in welfare, he didn't have the experience these kids would need. Devon's face flashed in his mind. The kid was so much like Rick when at that age, it was scary. Rick wanted to do everything possible to save him.

He glanced toward the woman and child beside him. Betsy clung to Allie's hand. She'd explained to the kid that they were getting married, but did Betsy understand how weird it all was?

Rick held open the door to the courthouse, and the Siderses entered ahead of him. They wouldn't have that name much longer. The shock of realizing he would be giving his name and protection to two people he barely knew made him freeze at the door. The wind whipped past him into the building.

He pulled the door shut behind him. His boots clicked along the tile floor, echoing against the high ceiling. The sound belonged to a condemned prisoner going to the gallows. Allie still hadn't said a word. She was probably as appalled by their choice as he was.

Still, Betsy would be safe, and he could dampen some of the guilt he felt about Jon's death.

Thrusting his hand into the pocket of his jeans, he fingered the simple wedding band he'd picked up for Allie after the funeral. Since the marriage wasn't going to last long, he'd hesitated to spend the money, but it didn't seem right not to have her wear a ring.

The registrar greeted them and ushered them into the judge's chambers. The place smelled ancient and musty, though the desk and chairs looked new.

He'd known Judge Julia Thompson for years, and her eyes were bright and curious when she greeted them. "Rick, congratulations." Her gaze turned to Allie. "And this is the lucky woman. Half the gals in town are mad at you, and the rest want to know how you managed to lasso this wily character."

Allie's smile was weak. "I'm very lucky."

"You certainly are," the judge agreed. She pulled a pair of glasses from atop her head and perched them on her nose to read the documents in front of her. "Just a civil ceremony? I must say I'm surprised, Rick. I would have thought you'd be married in the church."

Rick hadn't even told his pastor what he was doing. Grady would try to talk him out of it. "We were in a hurry," he said, ignoring the speculation in her smile. Let her think what she wanted. He didn't owe anyone an explanation.

Her expression sobered. "I'm sorry about Elijah." She riffled through some papers and pulled out a small book. "Let's get on with this, shall we?"

"Fine," Allie said. Her voice trembled, and she swayed on her feet. Her complexion was pasty.

"Are you both entering this agreement of your own free will?"

"Yes," Rick and Allie said in unison.

"Good." The judge turned to Rick first. "Rick, will you have this woman to be your wedded wife, to love her, comfort her, honor and keep her, and forsaking all others, keep you only unto her, for so long as you both shall live?"

He hadn't realized that forever promise would be in a civil ceremony. It felt wrong as a Christian to deliberately lie. If he made this promise, he'd have to keep it. He realized his silence had to look bad, but he needed to think, to decide. Glancing at Allie, he saw her go even paler.

Jon's face came to mind, so earnest and good. The man had believed in Rick even when he had no reason to. How could Rick not give his life for him?

"I will," he said, realizing, with a sick feeling in the pit of his stomach, what he'd just promised.

"Allie, will you have this man to be your wedded husband, to love him, comfort him, honor and keep him, and forsaking all others, keep you only unto him, so long as you both shall live?"

Rick could see the convulsive movement of Allie's throat as she swallowed hard. For just a moment he hoped she'd say she couldn't go through with it. Then he would be relieved of his responsibility.

"I will," she said in a firm voice.

"Rick, take your bride's hand."

When his fingers closed around Allie's hand, his eyebrows went up at how cold it was. He saw the fear in her eyes and gave her hand a reassuring squeeze.

The judge's no-nonsense tone droned on. "Take hands and repeat after me: I, Rick, take you, Allie, to be my wedded wife, to have and to hold, for better for worse, for richer for poorer, to love and to cherish, from this day forward."

To cherish. An old-fashioned word. Rick tried to remember if he'd ever cherished anything. He'd once loved whiskey, and he loved God—but cherish? What did it really mean?

"Rick?" the judge prodded.

"Sorry." Rick repeated the vows. He listened while Allie did the same.

"Do you have a ring for the bride?"

Rick nodded and dug the ring out of his pocket. Allie smiled for the first time since they'd entered the judge's chambers. She held out her hand to Betsy, and the little girl handed her a ring too. When had she gotten it? And how did she get the money?

Her hand had warmed up some, and he slipped the ring past her knuckles. When she tried to do the same to him, the ring got stuck after the first knuckle.

"Sorry," she whispered. "Jon wasn't as big as you."

This had been the ring Jon wore? The magnitude of what Rick was doing nearly made his knees buckle. This was *Jon's* wife he was promising to care for. And his daughter. Rick curled his fingers around the ring to keep it safe. Jon had been like a brother, and Rick remembered something in the Bible about a man's brothers being responsible for his wife.

"I'll get it sized," he said.

She nodded, and tears glimmered in her eyes. Did she remember the ceremony with Jon? She had to feel the lack of this one in comparison. He should have thought about what a woman needed in a wedding. He was an idiot.

"Inasmuch as Rick and Allie have consented together in wedlock and have witnessed the same before this company, and pledged their vows to each other, by the authority vested in me by the State of Texas, I now pronounce you husband and wife." The judge smiled. "You may now kiss your bride."

Rick put his hands on her shoulders and deposited a quick peck on her lips. They felt as soft as they looked. Her breath smelled minty and fresh, and it was with reluctance that he let his hands fall back to his sides.

His wife. He was a married man with all the responsibilities and trials of partnership. Not just for a year or two, but forever.

10

ALLIE FINGERED THE RING ON HER HAND. JON HAD BEEN GONE NEARLY TWO years, and the metal felt strange on a hand she usually kept bare. It had been all she could do to choke out her responses in the ceremony. Memories of her wedding to Jon nearly brought her to tears. For Betsy's sake, she managed to hold it together.

She sat on the porch, watching the glimmer of stars and breathing in the scent of creosote bushes, a pungent fragrance she loved. Betsy sat on her lap. Allie had tried to call Yolanda, but she'd been dumped into her voice mail. Not that Yo would be happy to hear the news, but Allie felt a need to share this event in her life with her best friend.

The kids were playing Yahtzee inside, and the sound of their voices and the rattle of dice on the table comforted her. Life would get back to normal, eventually.

Car lights winked and grew as a vehicle approached the ranch house. The engine cut off, and the interior lights of the car flickered on as a man got out. The bright yard light revealed a young man who looked like a throwback to the days of Jesse James. His thick mustache appeared waxed, and it curled up on the ends. His jeans were pressed, and his boots glinted in the light.

The screen door banged, and Allie jumped. Strangers always made her uneasy, and this guy looked dangerous.

Rick stepped onto the porch. "Wally. I didn't expect you tonight."

"Howdy, Rick," the man said. "I know you were coming in tomorrow, but I'm going to have to leave town for a few days, and I thought maybe we could handle this tonight."

"We can go to the office."

Wally came up the steps and nodded to Allie. "Is this little lady Allie Siders?"

"I'm Allie," she said. Let Rick announce the marriage if he wanted. Who was this guy? Rick was treating him with respect, and he seemed to know something about the ranch.

"Since Rick hasn't introduced us, I'd best do it myself. I'm Wally Tatum, Elijah's attorney. I'm sorry I missed Elijah's funeral. My wife was sick, and I had child-care duty." His smile became fixed. "You'll need to sit in on this meeting too, ma'am."

Allie saw Rick stiffen. "It has nothing to do with me," she said.

"Yes, ma'am, it does. Elijah changed some things in his will the day he died."

"What?" Allie and Rick spoke at the same time.

Wally's white teeth flashed beneath his mustache. "There was no holding Elijah back when he made up his mind about something." He nodded to the swing. "Mind if I sit a spell?"

Rick folded his arms across his chest. "What are you talking about?"

Allie didn't want to know. A vortex yawned above her, like a great Texas twister about to suck her into something deadly. She kept her mouth shut. Get this over with and get to her room. Elijah couldn't have left her much. He didn't even know her.

The swing creaked as Wally settled into it. He opened his briefcase and withdrew a sheaf of papers. "As you know, this ranch and the kids who have come through here have been Elijah's life for the past forty years."

"I know that better than anyone," Rick said. "I was a throwaway kid myself and came here when I was fifteen."

"Elijah could have bust his buttons over you," Wally said. "Until this recent change, he'd left the ranch to you. I'm only mentioning that because he wanted you to know how much he loved you. But he realized he couldn't do that—not when he has family who should rightly inherit."

"Family?" Rick asked slowly. "What family?"

Allie hadn't meant for Rick to find out the truth this way. Not blindsided. He'd poured so much of his life into this place, it didn't seem right to strip it away at the last minute. She'd refuse the bequest, let Rick have it.

Wally's gaze darted between them. "Elijah has left everything he owns to Betsy, his great-granddaughter."

Rick inhaled sharply, but she held her breath. It couldn't be. Why would he do that? Betsy was too young, and the responsibility would fall on Allie, who knew nothing about running a ranch for kids. Horses, she knew, but that was where her work began and ended.

"You're his granddaughter?" Rick turned to look at Allie.

She nodded, but she couldn't push any words past the constriction in her chest. The betrayal on Rick's face wounded her. Did he think she'd done this deliberately?

"I don't want it."

"Yes, ma'am, but he left it to Betsy," Wally pointed out.

"She's too young. I'm refusing it for her."

Rick finally seemed to rouse from his stupor. "You don't have that right."

"I know this is a shock, ma'am. Let it settle a spell. Elijah did the right thing." Wally rose, and his spurs jingled as he walked toward the steps. "I have some documents for you to sign in my office. Stop by at your convenience and my secretary can handle everything. The adoption papers are ready too."

Rick followed him to the edge of the porch. "Thanks for coming out," he said, his voice distant.

Wally touched his hat. "I didn't want there to be any misunderstandings about the future of the ranch. I'll be in touch."

Neither of them spoke as the sound of the car's tires on the dirt and gravel faded away. Allie peeked at Rick's face and gulped when she saw his thunderous expression.

"You liar. You came here knowing Elijah was your grandfather. Why bother with marrying me? You'd have a stable home here for Betsy, and he would have helped you keep custody."

Did he think she would have tied herself to him if she'd had any other choice? "I didn't plan to tell him."

He laughed, a short bark of derision. "Yeah, right. One look at you and he had to know. He kept track of his daughter. Did you really think he wouldn't realize?"

"He guessed," she admitted. "I was surprised at his welcome. I thought he would throw me out." She clutched her cold hands together. Dredging up some anger from the depths, she fired back at him. "Is that why you really married me? Because you knew he'd leave us the ranch? If you knew he kept track of her, you surely knew her name and that I was her daughter."

"I didn't know what he'd planned—or that you were his grand-daughter."

"Really? Then why were you in such a hurry to do this before you talked to the lawyer? Did you think if I had any other way out, I wouldn't do it? And besides, *you* pointed out my resemblance to Maria."

"I was trying to help you—and Elijah."

They were glaring at one another like two kids quarreling over the last piece of candy in the dish. Allie leaned her head against the back of the rocker. The day had sapped every bit of her ability to cope. "I'm sorry I said that," she said. "If there's one thing I know, it's that you loved Elijah like a father. Betsy having the ranch doesn't change much of anything as far as Jon's parents are concerned. They'd want her even more if they knew the ranch came with her."

He pulled out his knife and a piece of wood. The shavings flew as he applied himself to the whittling with a vengeance. "You've kept too many secrets from me, Allie. If we're going to stay married, we have to keep communication open."

Stay married? She eyed him. "It's only for a year or so. We can stand it for that long."

He opened his mouth, then closed it again. She wasn't quite sure what the expression on his face meant, and she was afraid to ask him.

Betsy's dead weight made Allie struggle to stand. "I think I'll put her to bed."

"Let me get the door." He strode to the door and opened it. "She's pretty big for you to carry all the way upstairs. Let me take her." He scooped Betsy out of her arms and went ahead of Allie.

She climbed the steps behind them. Betsy stirred but didn't awaken. It had been a busy day for her too. At the top of the stairs, Allie darted around Rick into the bedroom and pulled back the covers on Betsy's bed. He laid her gently on the mattress and pulled the covers around her. They both stood looking down at the little girl as the moon gilded her hair and illuminated the sweet curve of her round cheeks.

"She's worth anything we have to do to protect her," Rick said.

He almost sounded like he was trying to convince himself. Allie nodded without saying anything. His masculine presence over-whelmed the room. Her mouth went dry when he turned to her and put his big hands on her shoulders. Surely he didn't expect them to have a normal marriage.

The heat of his hands soaked through her blouse, and she couldn't look away from the intensity of his gaze. The howl of a coyote echoed from the hills, and the sound broke the magnetic pull of his eyes.

She stepped away, and his hands fell to his sides. "Thanks for bringing her up to bed."

He cleared his throat but didn't move away. "I just wanted to tell you I meant what I promised in the judge's chambers."

Which part? Allie's thoughts flew back to what Rick had said on the porch. That whole thing about staying married. "Thank you," she managed lamely. She didn't want to explore that subject, especially not here in her bedroom. His gaze still mesmerized her, and she forced herself to look away. "Good night."

"'Night." He moved to the door and pulled it shut behind him.

The strength ran out of her legs, and she sat heavily on her bed.

Did he mean their plan to divorce in a year was off? He couldn't just make that determination without her agreement. She didn't want to live her life with a man who despised her. Good thing she could divorce him even if he didn't want it.

Her hands shook.

Why did he unnerve her? He was just a stranger. But he didn't feel like it. She believed his eyes could see right inside her soul. And the way he cared for her and Betsy was like coming home. How could her life have spiraled so far out of control? Her identity as Jon's wife seemed to be slipping away right now. She was living someone else's life.

She stood and went to the door. Peeking out, she listened to the sounds of the kids downstairs playing card games. She could probably slip down the stairs and get to the library without being seen. She needed to hear Yo's voice.

She was so alone here. No one else knew everything she'd gone through. Rick still looked at her with suspicious eyes, and she felt like an outsider. Scrubbing the moisture from her cheeks, she lifted her head. Whining wasn't allowed in her life. She could handle this, especially if she could talk to Yo.

Easing through the door, she tiptoed to the stairs and moved noiselessly down to the first floor. Darting toward the library, she caught a glimpse of Rick's back, where he stood watching the kids. Emilio slapped his hand on the table and crowed his delight about winning. In the bedlam, she hoped no one heard the squeak of the door opening.

She just couldn't face Rick right now.

The lock snicked home, and she went to the phone. Listening to the dial tone, she wondered how upset Yolanda would be to hear she'd married a stranger. The phone seemed to ring forever. It was Yo's cell number, so maybe she was in a mall or something. Glancing at the clock on the desk, Allie realized it was too late for shopping. Maybe she'd left it at home.

Then a click came finally. "Hello." It wasn't Yolanda's voice.

"Oh, I'm sorry. I must have the wrong number."

"Allie, that you?"

Allie realized the voice was that of Yolanda's mother. "Mrs. Fleming? Yes, it's me. Is Yo around?"

A long pause hissed back at her. "You don't know?"

"Know what?" Something in the woman's voice made Allie clutch the phone and sink into the chair.

"My Yo, he killed her. She's dead, Allie." The woman's voice rose in a sob.

Allie's hand spasmed around the phone. "What are you saying?" she whispered. Dead? Yo couldn't be dead.

"Stabbed, she was stabbed." The woman's cries grew louder, near hysteria.

Not Yo, oh please God, not Yo.

Allie closed her eyes. She couldn't force any words past her frozen lips. Yo's laughing face flashed through her memory. She was going to win the barrel race this year. It wasn't fair.

"She called me, said the man said she was next. He say that you love her too much for him to let her live. I send her father to her house, but it is too late. The man, he get there first." Mrs. Fleming was wailing, her sobs piercing Allie's heart as well as her ears.

Allie's tears felt hot with guilt. "I'm so sorry," she whispered. "When did this happen?"

Mrs. Fleming's sobs tapered off. "Last night. Wait, wait, my husband, he want to talk to you."

Mr. Fleming was a big African-American truck driver who had met the pretty Mexican waitress and married her thirty-eight years ago. He'd always made Allie feel like part of the family. He probably hated her now.

"Allie? Stay there, girl. Don't come home."

"Mr. Fleming," she choked. "I'm so sorry. I loved Yo so much."

"I know, Allie, I know. And she loved you. This is not your fault, you hear? Don't try making it about you. Whoever he is, it was his evil that killed my baby, not you." His voice thickened and broke. "You stay put. Don't make Yo die in vain."

"I—I can't talk. I'll call you tomorrow." Allie clicked off the phone and buried her face in her hands. No matter what Mr. Fleming said, Yo wouldn't have died if it wasn't for Allie. He had taken everyone she loved.

Everyone but Betsy.

Allie shuddered, then jumped when someone rattled at the door.

Rick's voice came from the other side. "Allie, are you in there?"

She scrubbed at her face and rushed to unlock the door. It opened as soon as she clicked the lock, and she hurtled into Rick's arms, not stopping to question why she needed his comfort, his strength.

"She's dead," she sobbed against his denim shirt.

His arms came around her, and a big hand smoothed the back of her head. "Who's dead?"

His shirt muffled her words. "My friend Yolanda. He's taking everyone I love." She clutched his shirt in both fists. "She can't be gone."

The scent of creosote clung to his clothing. He must have been clearing some of the bush out of the yard this afternoon. She hadn't been close enough to him to smell it before this. The aroma always made her think of summer rides across the desert with Jon, and the spring rains in El Paso that brought the pungent scent to life. It reminded her of sage and cactus, roasted marshmallows around the campfire.

And love later in the tent. But now there was only death all around her.

The thought made her cheeks burn, and she pulled away, swiping the back of her hand across her cheeks. "Sorry," she gulped.

Rick's hands moved to her shoulders, and he didn't let go. "So he doesn't know where you are. That should set your mind at ease that Elijah wasn't killed by him."

Allie hadn't thought of Elijah. "Then who killed him?"

"I'm going to check out this developer guy, the one who wanted to buy the ranch." He finally dropped his hands. "But we might be barking up the wrong tree. It might have been an accident."

"Maybe." Allie had found that most things in her life were inter-connected. This probably was too, once they figured it out. "I should call the police in El Paso, tell them what Yo's dad said."

"I'm sure he's already talked to them. They'll be looking for you and might make you go back as a material witness. We can't risk that. You and Betsy are safe here." His eyes narrowed, and his mouth took on a determined pinch.

Allie was suddenly very glad he was on her side. Rick wouldn't let anything happen to her or Betsy.

Fatigue and grief weighed her down. This day seemed like it would never end. She told Rick good night and headed to her room. Walking back upstairs, she twisted the ring on her finger. She was a married woman.

One in name only. Was there anything more pathetic?

11

THE HOUSE WAS QUIET EXCEPT FOR THE TICKING OF THE GRANDFATHER clock in the hall. Rick sat in the leather desk chair with his feet propped on the desk. He still hadn't been able to take in the reality that Allie was Elijah's granddaughter. Elijah hadn't trusted him with the information, and the betrayal left some cuts that would take time to heal.

And Allie. Rick should have put two and two together when he saw the resemblance between her and Maria. Had she always planned to come in here and worm her way into Elijah's graces?

He decided to call Brendan again. His friend might have found some new information. The stakes had just escalated. If someone was coming after Allie and Betsy, he couldn't wait for the guy to show up.

It was after midnight on the East Coast, but he knew Brendan would be up working anyway. He listened to the ringing with one ear and to the noises outside with the other. Nothing stirred, a good sign.

There was a click on the line, then Brendan's voice. "Rick, you know how late it is? What if I were all toasty in bed?"

"You never get to bed before two," Rick said. He was in no mood for small talk. "Anything new about Allie?"

"Oh yeah, I meant to call you. We had a crisis pop up that we've been scrambling to fix."

The old familiar tug of interest waylaid Rick, but he squelched it. "Spill it."

"The crisis or the information about your woman?"

"She's not my woman. She's my . . . wife."

Brendan whistled. "Talk about a whirlwind courtship."

If Brendan only knew. Rick could hardly believe it himself. "Look, things are happening here. Elijah is dead, and someone is out to get Allie and Betsy."

"The FBI is looking at her now, buddy, and not just for kidnapping. They suspect her of being the ringleader of the immigrant smuggling ring."

The ringleader? Rick pinched the bridge of his nose. "It's a crock, buddy. No way." He told Brendan about the man who had killed Yolanda Fleming, and the calls Allie had gotten. "Could this guy have planted evidence?"

"Maybe. According to my sources, immigration was tipped off about the ring using the rodeo for a front. And here's the funny thing. Your woman testified against someone doing this about a year and a half ago. Because of her testimony, he got sent to jail. Then here we find she was involved all along. I gotta say, I wonder if they were lovers or something. Maybe he dumped her and she turned him in."

"She's not the type," Rick said. He hoped that was true, but what did he really know of her? "How'd they become suspicious of Allie now?"

"Someone faxed pictures of a bunch of Mexicans climbing out of the back of a pickup. The license plates were Allie's. Does she have an old Ford truck—green?"

"Yeah. Could the pictures be doctored? Don't you think this sounds suspicious, Brendan? Maybe it's revenge for sending the king-pin to jail."

"I thought that too. But the guy who went to prison—Jimmy Hernandez—is dead. He got caught up in a prison riot about a year ago and was stabbed."

"So it couldn't be him. Anything else?"

"The other thing they have on her is that bank account records show deposits of money in and out of her account. Like a quarter of a million dollars."

Rick leaned back and rubbed his eyes, his stomach taking a nose-dive. He should have known not to trust her. He was such a patsy. "She showed up here penniless."

"I'm just saying. You check out her purse to see if she really had no money? Women can lie while they're seducing you, buddy. I gotta say I'm shocked you fell for her line."

"She's Jon's widow."

"Look, when are you going to let go of that guilt?"

Rick's jaw clenched down in a painful spasm. "I killed him, Brendan. If I hadn't been drunk . . . I rushed in when I should have known better, and he came in after me. I think he knew how unlikely it was that he'd walk out again." Brendan was the only one who knew, and only because he'd been there.

"When was the last time you took a drink?" Brendan's voice was soft.

"Two years." Rick clipped his words. What difference did it make? All the sobriety in the world couldn't restore Jon to life.

"So live your life in the present. It's easier that way."

Rick knew better than to try to argue with Brendan. "Thanks for the help. You'd better get to bed."

"I've got hours of paperwork ahead of me yet."

Rick closed his phone. The most damning evidence would be money in her account. How did he check that out? If she hadn't just been through such a trauma, he'd march upstairs and drag her from her bed to question her.

Had he been completely duped?

A sound caught his ear, and he stood to look out the window. A pinprick of light danced and bobbed through the trees. Someone was out there. As far as he knew, everyone who belonged on the ranch was tucked inside.

Rick rushed to the door, grabbing a flashlight on his way. Jem met him on the porch and whined. "Quiet, boy," he whispered. "Come with me." He went across the yard and stepped into the coolness of the trees.

A twig snapped somewhere to his right, and he followed the faint noise. Creeping through the dark, he didn't dare flip on the light. That would only alert whoever it was to being spotted. He knew this ranch like the back of his hand, though, and didn't really need the light.

He skirted a big boulder and looked around to see a line of dark shapes moving low and fast toward the top of the hill. Now was the time to flip on his light. He aimed the flashlight at the nearest figure and pressed the soft button. The beam of light zeroed in on the face of a Hispanic man. He shouted in Spanish, and the rest of the people turned to run. He saw three men and two women carrying children. They streamed up the hill and disappeared.

Illegal immigrants, he was sure of it. And the first he'd seen since coming to work here. He didn't want to believe Allie had anything to do with this, but it sure fit.

It was too late and too dark to catch those poor souls tonight. He'd put in a call to the border patrol, but that was the best he could do.

And tomorrow he and Allie would have a talk.

ALLIE'S EYES WERE BLURRY, AND HER HEAD ACHED. SHE STOOD ON THE first rung of the corral fence and watched Emilio direct the teenagers on how to groom the horses. A dust storm was supposed to hit late today, but right now only a light breeze lifted her hair away from her face and filled her nose with the good fragrances of horse and hay.

Rick had been acting weird all morning, and she was tired of dancing around his strange glances. What was bothering him? At first she thought he'd been wondering how she was reacting to the news of Yolanda's death, but it wasn't that. There was no sympathy in his eyes, only speculation, and maybe even a pointed suspicion.

She'd been careful not to be alone with him. Finding out what was biting him was less urgent than avoiding any discussion of a real marriage. Surely he couldn't think she was keeping anything from him. Everything was out in the open now.

Emilio approached the fence, pushed his hat back off his forehead, then leaned against a post. "The kids are doing a pretty good job," he said. "I'm amazed at how well they've taken to ranch life."

Allie nodded. "Even Latoya is acting like a normal kid. She hasn't even been wearing makeup, let alone unbuttoning her blouse to the navel."

Emilio's eyes sobered. "She had a pretty rough go of it. Her mother sold her to the first man when she was ten."

Allie put her hand over her mouth. "I had no idea. That poor kid." Her gaze traveled to the other girl. "What about Fern?"

"Her parents and younger brother were killed in a boating accident in the Gulf. She's been in foster care for three years. She and her mother were really close, and the trauma of her whole family being wiped out about destroyed her." He gestured to the horses and kids. "She's really taken to that colt. I've seen a few smiles."

Fern and Allie shared the same heartache. If Allie had been that young, maybe she'd be as downtrodden as the girl. Allie vowed to do whatever she could to help the teenager regain goals and focus.

Allie was sure the boys' stories were equally horrific, but she couldn't face hearing them right now. Not with her own life weighing her down. "How'd you get into working with these kids?" she asked. "Have you done it long?"

His dark eyes flickered, then danced away, but not before she saw a shutter come down. "Just happened to fall into it," he said. "I'm big enough to scare some sense into them. No big story." He nodded toward the Rio Grande. "I thought I saw some guys on top of the hill. You ever get illegal aliens coming across?"

"Not while I've been here. I imagine it could be a problem though. I haven't even seen any border patrol around. Immigrants from Mexico could get on a boat and float down the river until they found a good landing spot."

"There aren't that many good places to land. A lot of the way is

blocked by sheer cliffs that are impossible to climb. The patrol probably chooses to focus on the easiest spots."

His tone was full of assurance, and she gave him a curious stare.
"You seem to know a lot about it."

Taking a tin from his pocket, he took out a pinch of snuff and
stuffed it in his cheek. "Makes sense."

He must not want to talk about his past at all. Maybe it was too
painful. The sun glared down from the sky, and she adjusted her
cowboy hat to shade her eyes. "Betsy loves that new horse. We
haven't named her. I keep hoping she'll start talking and name the
mare herself."

"Don't give up on that idea. She just might. I saw her come out
first thing this morning to feed her. She's hardly left the mare's side."

Allie nodded, her gaze on her daughter. Betsy was blooming here.
Even though she still wasn't talking, she was smiling more as she ran
and played in the barnyard. The animals flocked around her, from the
kittens to Jem and the horses. Even the cattle watched her when she
climbed up to sit on the fence.

A shadow blocked the sun from her eyes, and she squinted up into
Rick's face.

"I thought we might run to town and file those adoption papers,"
he said.

She straightened. "Let me get Betsy." Without waiting for his
answer, she climbed the fence and went to where her daughter stood
currying the mangy mare. Fern was helping.

Poor thing. The mare's cuts were starting to heal, but all the bones
still stuck out under the rough coat. "Betsy, let's go to town for a while."

Betsy thrust out her lower lip, and she fingered the buttons on her
blue blouse.

"I'll watch her, Mrs. Bailey." Fern's voice was almost inaudible, and she ducked her head without looking Allie in the eye. "I like Betsy. She's the age of my little brother . . ."

"I'd rather she come with me." Panic dried into a bad taste in her mouth. Someone had killed Yolanda. That same someone might find them here.

Betsy tugged on her mother's arm and shook her head, tears filling her eyes. She pointed to the horse and then to Fern.

Allie was such a sucker for Betsy's entreaties. Rick assured her they were safe here. How could anyone find them clear out here? She'd left no trail. Still, someone had killed Elijah, even though the sheriff seemed to think it was an accident. "She'd better come with me. Why don't you come too, Fern?"

The girl's face lit with pleasure. "To town with you?"

"Sure. We'll stop and get an ice cream soda at the drugstore. We won't be gone long."

Fern took Betsy's hand, and the girls followed Allie. Sorrow welled in her throat, choking her. If only she'd let Yolanda come with her.

She rejoined Rick and Emilio. "Betsy wants to stay with Fern, but I don't think it's safe to leave her. I thought she could come with us."

"Sure," Emilio said. "Fern is good with kids."

His gaze toward Allie was intense and probing. Surely he wasn't interested in her, was he? She was a married woman now. Reaching up to tuck a strand of hair behind her ear, she made sure to turn toward him so he would see her new ring.

Rick still hadn't spoken. He headed toward the truck, and Allie followed with the girls. At the cab's door, she stopped and spoke too softly for the girls to hear. "Marriage must not agree with you. You're a bear this morning." She flashed her most winning smile, hoping to coax him out of whatever had brought this on.

He gave her a cold glare. "Let's not talk about it now. I want to get this adoption paperwork done first. We can sign the papers for the ranch, too."

Allie tried to think of anything she'd done to warrant this gruff treatment, but came up blank. He'd been so solicitous and caring last night when he heard the news about Yolanda. Let him stew. She'd done nothing to incur his wrath. And even if she had, what right did he have to act like an enraged rattlesnake?

She let the girls sit between them. They made the trip to town in a silence that seemed to thicken with every passing mile. Allie tried to distract herself with praying for Yolanda's family, but she found it hard to focus when every time she glanced Rick's way he was still glowering.

It was going to be a long year.

The attorney's secretary had the papers ready for them to sign. Allie's signature looked a little shaky, but Rick scrawled his name in bold, confident strokes. His determination to help her daughter made her more willing to overlook his bad mood.

The wind had picked up by the time they stepped back out into the sunshine. A few tumbleweeds lay nestled against the truck tires, and tiny bits of sand stung Allie's cheeks as the two of them hurried to the shelter of the drugstore. Rick had her by the arm to steady her. He opened the door, then shut it behind her.

The aroma of cheeseburgers and French fries, of sock hops and high school dates, washed over her. Black-and-white tiles on the floor and red vinyl booths made the place look like a set from the movie *Grease*. Rick led the way to the booth at the back.

"A jukebox," Fern breathed in a reverent tone.

"Here. Pick out some music." Rick dug a handful of coins from his pocket and dropped them into her cupped palms.

Fern and Betsy went to pick out the music. Allie folded her hands together to keep them from shaking. "Okay, let's have it. I'm tired of tiptoeing around your mood. If you've got a complaint, spill it."

Rick's icy and appraising eyes belonged to a stranger. Where was the warmth that he showed last night? For a few moments she thought he might refuse to speak.

Then he leaned against the seat. "I talked to my friend yesterday, the one who's in intelligence."

"So? I have nothing to hide."

"He had more details about your part in the moving of illegal aliens."

"I didn't have any part in that other than testifying."

"Then where did you get all the money?"

"What money?" Allie's gaze went to her bag containing exactly ten dollars and fifteen cents.

"A quarter of a million dollars has moved through your account in the last six months."

Allie gasped and put her hand over her mouth. "That's impossible." But was it? She never looked at her bank statements. They were too hard to make out. The only way she knew what she had in the bank at any given time was to run through the ATM and check her balance.

"I see you're suddenly remembering," Rick said. "Your face says it all."

"No, you don't understand," she protested. "I never know what's in my account. I—I can't read the statements."

He frowned then. "What are you talking about?"

She looked away from his intense gaze. "I have Scotopic Sensitivity

135

Syndrome. Some people call it Irlen Syndrome. It's really hard for me to read things on white paper. The letters jump and move around. So I don't read my statement."

"I've never heard of it."

From his tone, she guessed he thought she was lying. "Look it up," she snapped. "That's why I have to make sure I wear sunglasses in the glare, or a hat. My eyes can't handle glare."

The ice in his eyes thawed slightly. "I still find it hard to believe you don't know what's in your account."

She kept her gaze focused on her hands, tightly clenched in her lap. "Jon always handled the banking. Since his death, everything like that has been . . . difficult."

"Why didn't you ask Yolanda for help?"

She bristled at his persistent skepticism. "I wanted to stand on my own two feet. If Yo knew how tight things were, she'd insist on helping me. I couldn't accept that."

"Can you explain how so much money could be in your account? Did anyone else have access to it?"

She grabbed her purse and upended it. A bottle of nail polish rolled out, a comb, a lipstick clattered to the table, then her wallet plopped on the surface. Picking it up, she threw it at him. "Take a look. Ten dollars and some change."

He recoiled, but she dug in her purse again and brought out her checkbook. "Here, you want to see how incompetent I am? Make sure I'm a loser?" Her voice rose, and she saw the girls look toward her, so she gathered her self-control. "Here, take a look."

She knew what he would see. Chicken scratches scrawling their way across the page, strikeouts, messy entries that made no sense. Falling silent, sadness replaced the anger. "I'm not a criminal, Rick."

His hand closed around the checkbook. "I'm sorry, Allie. I believe you. If someone's messing with your account, we need to find out who."

Her gaze came up at the softening of his voice. Maybe he recognized the ring of truth. "I've never given anyone the number. Unless it's the guy who killed Yo and my family. Maybe he's trying to make me look guilty of something. That smuggling thing, maybe."

"He's doing a pretty good job of it." Rick laid the checkbook next to her other things. "The FBI will track you down in short order."

"I didn't leave a trail," she said. "No credit cards, nothing."

"Did you know you were under suspicion when you left El Paso?"

"I had no idea." She began to return the items to her purse.

"What about this Jimmy Hernandez that you testified against? How did that happen?"

Allie sighed. It was an old story, and she was sick of it. Everyone seemed to think it had some bearing on her present circumstances, and she knew it didn't. "He worked with me. He was in charge of getting stock handlers. I noticed he seemed to have a lot of men milling around who couldn't speak English, but I didn't think much about it at first. It's not unusual, you know? I was on my way to the grocery store one night and noticed him pull off onto a deserted road in front of me. He had a load of workers in his truck. It was long after hours, so I decided to circle back and see what he was doing. I parked my pickup along the road and walked back. The workers were all transferring to a van. The next day I started paying attention and noticed none of the workers Jimmy used were the same day to day. I got suspicious and told the police. A couple of months later he was arrested, and I was called to testify when the trial came up."

Rick's scowl turned thoughtful. "So he could be behind it if you sent him to prison."

"They had a lot more on him than my testimony."

"But you turned him in."

She held out her hands, palms up. "They were already suspicious."

"He might not know that."

This was getting them nowhere. Allie shook her head. "Look, he died in prison during a riot. It's not him."

"If you had nothing to do with any illegal alien traffic, then some-one is out to get you."

Allie wanted to slap her forehead. "That's what I've been trying to tell you. You're not listening."

"I'm listening now," he said. "Who hates you?"

Allie sighed. "Everyone asks that, and I just don't know." She could see he didn't believe she didn't know who was after her. But she could feel a noose tightening around her neck.

12

THE WIND HOWLED AND RAGED OUTSIDE THE WINDOW LIKE A PACK OF wolves baying for entrance. Allie stirred the pot of chili and watched the eddies of sand dance in the glow of sunset.

"Smells good." Charlie stood with his thumbs hooked in his pockets. The expression in his eyes said he was talking about her and not the chili. He looked washed-out.

Allie hid her smile. Rick seemed to barely notice how she looked, let alone how she smelled. "It'll be ready in a few minutes. You okay? You look a little pale."

He rubbed his forehead. "Just a headache." He smiled and held out a small, velvet box.

"What's this?" Allie took the box and opened it. A diamond eternity necklace lay nestled on the satin. The diamonds circling the pendant made her blink. "Charlie, it's beautiful. Who's it for?"

"You." His smile was shy.

Allie caught her breath. "Oh no, Charlie, I can't accept something so expensive." In her hand, the little box closed with a snap. She pressed it back into his hand. "I'm sorry."

"It's true, isn't it?"

"What is?"

He stuffed the box into the pocket of his jeans. "Someone in town said you and Rick got hitched."

"It's true."

He blinked rapidly, and his eyes looked moist. "You married Rick? You just got here."

"He knew my first husband." She knew it sounded lame.

"That's no reason to get married." Charlie's lips trembled like he wanted to cry. He pressed them together like he suddenly remembered he was a grown-up.

"Well, we did." She clamped her teeth against any explanation. It wasn't like Charlie was a good friend or anything. He was just disappointed not to make his conquest. He was on his way to growing up, and she'd just given him a valuable lesson in not counting chickens.

"Probably for Betsy," he mumbled, then turned and shuffled away.

If only she had someone she could really talk to here. Or anywhere, for that matter. There was no one left to her now, no one to help her see the path through the trees. Had she even done the right thing? But Jon had trusted Rick. Surely she could do the same.

Rick just seemed so sure of himself. She was anything but. Part of her insecurity came from the trouble she had with light, and part of it was the life she'd led—that of a nomad. The rodeo was her family, but the personnel often changed with every event. She'd learned to hide behind a smile and her work.

The thump of Rick's boots on the floor had become familiar, and she glanced up as he came into the kitchen. The expression on his face told her he had more questions.

"I've been thinking about who could be targeting you," he said, pulling out a chair from the table and sitting down. "I wonder if it could be someone who has something against Jon."

"Against Jon?" Allie shook her head. "Everyone liked him."

"Not everyone," Rick said.

Allie joined him at the table. "What do you mean? He was like a pied piper. At the sound of his voice, people flocked to him. He had that certain something that made people instantly warm to him."

"I know. But some people resented that. We had a colonel who couldn't stand him. He thought Jon was a fake who used his charisma to advance himself."

Allie stared at him. "Jon was genuine."

"I know. I'm just saying not everyone liked him."

"He's dead," she pointed out. "This stalker keeps saying he's going to strip me of everything I love. So it's personal and targeted at me."

"Yeah, that's true. Shoot, I thought maybe I was on to something." He stared at her. "Tell me about your life with Jon. About the rodeo. Maybe we'll see something you've missed."

"It was a fairy tale," she said softly.

"How'd you meet him?"

"He was on leave, and his buddy talked him into going to the rodeo. He hated it, you know. The dust, the smells. I was moving horses from one corral to the other, and he stepped into some horse dung. He was so mad. I laughed, and he looked up. Our eyes met and it was . . . magic. He asked me out, we saw each other every night for a week, and he asked me to marry him. I said yes."

"He moved fast."

"You moved faster." They locked gazes, and Allie laughed. No magic there, though Rick's steadiness drew her.

It was just as well. Loving Rick would be like trying to ride a horse that had never been broken. The flight into the air might be high, but the jarring when she came back down could crush her bones.

"We married right away, against the advice of his parents. They never really accepted me. He found a house off base, and we settled in. Betsy was born about ten months later. Life was perfect for three years." The few years she'd spent with Jon had been the best of her life—a home, a neighborhood, a church. Bliss.

"Then he was sent to Iraq."

"Yes." She looked down at her hands. "A few months later I got the news. I had no choice but to go back to the rodeo. I had to support Betsy, and it was the only way I knew how."

"Jon's insurance?"

"Only a little left over after the burial costs. He meant to get more," she added when she saw his frown.

"Anyone at the base you might have had a run-in with?"

She thought back. In her memory, the days spent with Jon at Fort Irwin, California were filled with sunshine and laughter. No darkness marred the halcyon days. She shook her head. "There was nothing."

"And the rodeo?"

She shrugged. "You get a lot of transients. People who think the rodeo is glamorous until they are faced with the reality of dust, sweat, and cow patties. Some hate being told what to do and walk off. I've had the usual rounds of misunderstandings, minor arguments. Nothing that stands out."

"What about competitors? Any sore losers?"

A face leaped to mind. "I just thought of someone," she said slowly. "There was a stock contractor we used for about five years. Ted Rediger. I found him injecting some bulls with something to make them buck harder. That's a big no-no. I turned him in, and he lost the contract with the rodeo."

"Did he know you were the reason he lost the contract?"

"I don't know. Maybe." She hadn't even thought about the incident until now. It had seemed so minor.

"He never confronted you?"

"No, I never saw him after that."

"I'll have Brendan check it out." Rick leaned back, and his un-blinking eyes focused on her. "Are you afraid?"

Allie shuddered. "Wouldn't you be? Some faceless person wants to hurt me, and I don't even know why. It would help if I knew the reason."

"Did you date anyone before Jon? With looks like yours, you could break someone's heart."

Was that a flicker of awareness in his eyes? Allie wanted to look away and couldn't. His gaze bore into her, and she realized she liked Rick. And was drawn to him as well. He was steady and strong, and those broad shoulders could weather any storm. She felt so battered by life. The thought of a port in her storm was attractive. But maybe only because he was a link to Jon, and she was so lonely.

She'd have to be careful or she'd find herself in love with him, and that would be disastrous. Their goal was to help Betsy. Nothing more. She wanted to smile at her rationalizations.

The chili. Glad to tear her gaze away, she rose and went to stir the pot. "Jon was the only man I ever loved."

"But not the only man who ever loved you?" he persisted.

"There was a rodeo clown who asked me out a few times, and I went. He was . . . strange." She heard his chair scrape, and she tensed when he came up behind her. His proximity set her nerves tingling.

"Strange how?"

"Intense. A little too attentive. It was more than I was interested in, and I kept turning down his invitations. He didn't give up for six months or so."

"What happened to him?"

She turned and found Rick standing inside her personal space. With the stove behind her, there was nowhere to back up. "I don't know. He quit, and I never heard from him again."

"What was his name?" He took out his phone and starting inputting letters.

"Mark Haskell." She watched his focused, efficient movements. "You must be used to interrogating people. I've wracked my brain trying to remember anyone who might be behind this and came up blank. Not that I think either of these men is guilty, but at least we have a place to start. Somewhere to look."

Even though she believed her memories would only lead to dead ends, it felt good to be doing something. To hang a possible name on the faceless enemy. In a few days they'd be back to square one with no idea who her enemy could be, but right this minute, she felt hope—a foreign emotion that had vanished when the soldier showed up on her doorstep to tell her the love of her life had given his.

"Why didn't you come?" she said abruptly. "When Jon died. Why didn't you come to tell me instead of letting a stranger do it?"

He took a step back, and his gaze iced over. "I was a stranger too."

"Not really. You were Jon's friend, so I considered you one too. If you'd come to tell me—" She tore her gaze away and turned her back to him. Stirring the pot, she waited to see if he'd lie to her, deny the way he looked at her.

"I—I couldn't," he said.

Her hand with the wooden spoon in it paused above the steaming pot. "Were you injured?"

"No, I didn't have a scratch." His tone sharpened with an edge of bitterness. "Jon died, and I didn't have a bruise."

She put the spoon down on the stove and turned to face him again. "I'd like to know about that day. How Jon died. If he said anything."

"Now's not the time." He backed away. "I'll call the rest for dinner."

Watching him retreat—he was running away for sure—Allie began to wonder if there was more to Jon's death than she'd realized.

She would swear she saw guilt on Rick's face.

THE WHISKEY GLOWED GOLDEN IN THE GLASS. RICK COULD SEE IT IN HIS mind, taste the hot, smoky taste on his tongue. He hadn't wanted a drink this bad in two years. Seeing Allie's trusting blue eyes on him, knowing she thought he could fix everything, made him feel like a scorpion hiding under a rock.

She had no idea he'd cost her the perfect life she'd loved.

The story would come out sooner or later. He hadn't lived thirty-four years without seeing how wrongs never stayed hidden. What kind of friend was he that he'd kill his best friend and then take his wife? When he'd been doing it for Betsy and Jon's memory, Rick felt less confused. But standing in the kitchen, he realized he wanted Allie. Wanted her for his own, not to make amends.

He couldn't betray Jon like that. It would be as bad as King David killing Uriah so he could have Bathsheba. Somehow he had to find the courage to keep the wall up between them, to keep her from creeping into his heart.

Betsy and Fern were playing with the kittens on the back porch. He stepped through the screen door, and the two girls were so engrossed with the antics of the cats that they didn't look up.

"Supper, girls," he said. Betsy got up and ran to hug his leg. He lifted her in his arms. "You hungry?"

She nodded.

"How about after dinner we go check on your horse? She was moving around better today."

Betsy's brilliant smile was her answer. Watching her expressive face, Rick wondered if there was more to the story behind her silence. Could she have seen or heard something besides the plane crash that caused her to retreat?

He lifted Betsy to his shoulders and opened the door for Fern. "You liking it here, Fern?"

"Yes sir," she said in her soft, nearly inaudible voice.

"You're doing a good job with the horses. And with Betsy."

She peeked up at him through her lank bangs. A tremulous smile flashed across her face before it disappeared. "Thanks," she whispered. She went through the doorway ahead of him.

He bent his knees so he didn't bang Betsy's head on the doorframe and followed the others to the kitchen. Food covered the table, and the aroma of chili mingled with the scent of the apple dumplings she'd put on the windowsill to cool.

"Hey, man, I ain't eatin' no chili." Leon dropped into a chair and stretched out his long legs.

"You chicken, Leon?" Rick asked, lifting Betsy and depositing her in the chair beside Fern. "Can't handle the spice?"

Leon glowered at him. "Get off my grill. I can handle anything, man."

"Bet I can eat it hotter than you." Rick grinned and sat beside the boy. "Let's have a chili face-off. You game, Devon?"

The boy shook his head. "Dude, that's seriously messed up. Chili makes you fart. I want to be able to breathe tonight."

The girls snickered. Latoya ruffled Devon's red hair as she passed. "You don't need no help. You smelled yourself lately?"

The rest of the kids hooted with laughter. Rick grabbed the ladle. "Want some chili, Betsy?"

The little girl nodded, her smile breaking out.

"Then tell me. Say yes." He waited, but the little girl ducked her head. "Come on, Betsy, you can do it. You're a big girl."

Allie grabbed the ladle from his hand. "She already said she wanted the chili." Moments later a big spoonful of chili was steaming in Betsy's bowl. Allie crumpled crackers into it and blew on it before lifting a spoonful to Betsy's lips.

"Oh for Pete's sake! She's not a baby, Allie. She can talk, and she can feed herself if you'll let her."

Allie flushed and glanced around at the others listening to their conversation. She sat down, but Rick knew she would let him have it in private. Their minor spat squashed any banter, and the staff and the kids vanished as soon as they gulped down their supper.

Fern took Betsy up for her bath, and Rick leaned back in his chair. "I shouldn't have said anything in front of the others," he said, when she opened her mouth. "But Allie, you've got to quit babying her. It's not helping Betsy grow up."

Allie banged a pot down into the sink. "She is *my* daughter, Rick. Mine and Jon's, not yours."

"She's going to be mine shortly," he pointed out. "Legally and in every way."

"I think I know what's best for my daughter. You don't understand how fragile she is, Rick."

"I know what it's like to grow up too fast. I don't want that for her, but I *do* want her to grow up eventually. Yes, she's got a problem, but the way you coddle her, she's never going to talk. Quit answering for her, and start putting her in positions where she has to speak."

"I don't want to hurt her."

"She's already been hurt. Your job is to help her get past it, not wallow in it."

Allie's face reddened. "You're such a—a male!"

"I don't know how to be anything else."

"I love her. She's just a little girl."

"But growing up fast. We've got to get her past this no-talking thing before she goes to school. I've got a lot of experience here with kids. Trust me a little."

The expression in her eyes left no doubt that he was asking the impossible. She began to put the leftover chili away with jerky movements. She wasn't done with this argument, not judging by the tense set of her shoulders. When she finally whirled to face him, he was ready.

"Let's get something straight right now. I'm not going to have my parenting questioned at every turn. Betsy will always be my little girl. A piece of paper doesn't make her yours. You're only going to be in her life a year, and I don't want her confused about who her father really is. Jon is her daddy, and he'll always be her daddy. I don't want you mucking up her memories."

Like he'd do anything to hurt Jon's memory. "Where'd you learn to grip the people you love in such a stranglehold?" he asked softly.

She flushed nearly the color of the chili, but she didn't answer. It might take more patience than he had to get past her defenses.

13

THAT COUGAR'S LONELY CRY SENT GOOSE BUMPS UP HER BACK. ALLIE LAY ON the sagging mattress and listened to the animal's wail. Even though she knew what it was, the moan made her shudder. Betsy slept peacefully.

Allie rubbed her burning eyes. Yo's death still weighed heavily on her. The reality was impossible to wrap her mind around. She peered at the clock on the bed stand. It was after midnight, and the moon cast a soft wash of light through the curtains. She sat up and untangled her legs from the sheet before swinging them to the floor. On nights like this, she wished she didn't struggle so much to read.

She stood and walked to the window. Nothing moved tonight but the wind. The dust storm had descended with a vengeance after dinner, and drifts of dust piled against the porch, the barn, and the pump house. The howl of the wind had become more muted in the past hour, and she thought the storm had about blown itself out.

Her argument with Rick was another reason for her sleeplessness. Did she really have a stranglehold on Betsy? Her gaze touched her sleeping daughter. She wanted only the best for her baby girl. Rick didn't understand how important it was to keep Jon's memory alive. Maybe the most important thing in her life, other than Betsy herself.

A whisper of sound came from behind her, and she turned to see a white square of paper on the floor, highlighted in the glow of moonlight. Someone had slipped it under her door. Rick maybe? Allie stepped to the door and picked up the note, then carried it back to the window to look at it in the moonlight.

She laughed softly at the way her pulse raced. A midnight tryst with her husband. *Husband.* She'd never thought to experience marriage again. But why hadn't he knocked and asked her to talk?

Maybe it was an apology.

She unfolded the note. Holding it up to the light, she tried to make out the words, but her eyes refused to cooperate. Glare bothered her, but this small bit of light wasn't enough either.

Glancing at Betsy, she saw her daughter was still sound asleep. Allie grabbed her robe, stuffed her feet into slippers and tiptoed out of the room. She could use some company. Jem was outside, and the porch light might be enough to read by.

Padding noiselessly through the quiet house, she slipped out onto the front porch. The dog wasn't around, so she whistled for him, a light sound that seemed unduly loud in the night.

After a few minutes, she saw him coming over the hillside. The porch light illuminated the yard enough that she could see him do his little excited dance in the air before he joined her, but he didn't make any noise.

She patted his head, and he settled at her feet. "I could use some company," she told the dog in a soft voice. He wagged his tail and licked her hand. She slipped to the porch floor and wrapped her arms around him, relishing his warm fur and his happy tongue.

Yo was dead. The realization kept surprising her, then grief would well afresh. Tears slipped down her face, and she buried her face in Jem's fur.

He whined and nuzzled her neck. She let him comfort her until the pain eased, then pushed him away and got up. The forgotten note fell to the ground. She grabbed it from the floor, settled on the swing, then held the note under the wash of light, which was soft enough not to cast a glare on the page. Still, the black typewritten letters jumped around on the white paper. If only she had the money to replace her pink glasses.

Maybe someday.

She blinked and squinted and managed to make out the letters.

I've found you. Tag, I'm it. Your worst nightmare.

The blood congealed in her head, and she felt faint. "No," she whispered.

Jem whined, and she rubbed his ears, clinging to the contact with another living thing.

He couldn't have found her. It was impossible. She was misreading this. Squinting, she reread the note, but the words remained the same. Ominous words full of menace.

She gasped, her hand going to her throat. How had the guy gotten in? He was out there somewhere, maybe standing in the shadows.

Betsy!

Allie sprang to her feet and threw open the door. Rushing pell-mell up the steps, she bolted into the bedroom and ran to Betsy's bed. Her daughter was still sleeping, but a lingering scent of some kind of men's cologne made Allie whirl and flip on the light. She blinked at the bright light and stared hard into the shadows.

She and Betsy were alone.

Could it be one of the teenagers' idea of a joke? Maybe one of them had overheard her telling Rick about the stalker. They'd been up the night she found out about Yolanda's murder. She didn't want to believe they'd be so cruel, but they might not realize how hurtful it was.

Allie hugged herself. She had to tell Rick about this, but she didn't want to leave Betsy alone. Better to wake her daughter up than to have some madman take her. Allie scooped Betsy up in her arms, grunting softly with the little girl's weight as she headed down the hall to Rick's room.

Leaning against the doorframe, she supported Betsy with one arm and rapped on the door with her other hand. "Rick?" she called softly.

The silence of the house set Allie on edge. She wanted to turn her head and look behind her, but she was almost afraid to find out if *he* was watching her. "Rick," she called louder. A muffled click came through the door, then a light shone out from under the crack. Relief flooded her.

Rick could handle anything.

The door swung open, and she nearly fell into the room. Rick's hair stood on end. Dressed in pajama shorts and no shirt, he leaned on the doorframe and blinked the sleep from his eyes. "Allie? What's wrong?"

Allie's fears left her as soon as she saw him. She wanted to walk into his arms, let him wrap her in safety. How did he do it? She could be a bundle of terror, but one moment in his presence and she felt safe.

He lifted Betsy from her arms. "Is she sick?" His voice, roughed with sleep, held concern.

"No, no, she's fine." Allie walked past him into the bedroom. She'd been in here to clean, but it looked different at night with Rick's presence filling the room. His jeans lay atop his boots at the foot of the bed, and the rumpled covers lay in a heap.

Rick stepped past her to the bed and laid Betsy on it, then drew the covers around her before turning back to Allie. "You look scared. Did someone call?"

"Worse." She handed him the note.

He frowned and held it out to read it. His expression changed from bewilderment to anger. "Where was this?"

"Under my door." Allie cinched the belt on her robe tighter. "I was awake and heard him slip it into the room."

"Did you try to see who it was?"

She shook her head. "I—I thought it might be a note from you, so I wasn't concerned at first. I tried to read it in my room and couldn't, so I went to the porch. I didn't see anyone."

"The house wasn't locked. We never lock it in case one of the hands or the kids need something in the night. Anyone could have gotten in."

"How did he find me so fast?" Had it really been less than two weeks since she drove the long, lonely stretch of I-10 from El Paso? Life here at the ranch seemed so normal, so right.

"I don't know." Rick put the paper down on the bed and came to her. His hands dropped onto her shoulders. "I'll protect you, Allie. Don't look so afraid."

"I'm afraid for Betsy," she admitted.

He pulled her against his chest, and she inhaled the musky male scent of him. It had been so long since she'd relaxed in a man's arms.

His arms and chest were hard with muscle, and the hairs on his chest tickled her cheek. For the muscle-bound type, he was pretty nice.

She wasn't attracted to him, but to the safety he offered.

No!

She drew away and stepped back. Rick wasn't Jon. She was just lonely. It would be easy to forget herself in his arms, and she couldn't let that happen. The year would be up before she knew it, and her heart couldn't stand being broken again.

Besides, falling in love with anyone would be a betrayal of Jon. Jon had been an easygoing guy, content to let her do what she liked. She sensed controlling Rick would be like lassoing the wind. There were few things she still controlled in her life—Betsy and her heart—and Allie planned to keep a tight grip on both.

Rick's hands dropped away. "I'll find him, Allie. I promise." His gaze held hers. "I'm going to go search the house. Prop a chair against the door. I'll call to you when I come back. Don't go outside of this room until I tell you it's safe, okay?"

"Okay." He bent over his shirt and jeans, and Allie gasped. "Your back."

Thick scars crisscrossed his back. Someone had beat him badly, or cut him with something. Allie reached out and touched the worst one, and Rick flinched away.

"Old story," he said shortly. He jerked a T-shirt on over his bare chest and yanked on his jeans over his shorts. She followed him to the door and clicked it shut behind him. Dragging the ladder-back chair from the corner, she propped it under the doorknob and crawled into bed with Betsy.

The pillow smelled of Rick. She told herself not to be a fool, but she buried her face in the pillow anyway and pulled the covers around her neck as if she were enveloped in Rick's arms.

Stupid, stupid. She wasn't so naive that she didn't recognize how she was beginning to fall for her new husband. She kicked off the sheets. Betsy shuffled and rolled away from her. Maybe someday he'd tell her who had made those scars. And why.

THE HOUSE BLAZED WITH LIGHT. RICK HAD LOOKED IN EVERY CLOSET, behind every curtain in the empty bedrooms and in the downstairs. He hadn't wanted to awaken the teenage girls, but when he didn't find an intruder, he rapped on their door and had them come out while he searched their room.

Their hair a mess and dragging their sheets, they'd congregated in the hall while he poked around their room. It stank of cheap perfume and nail polish.

"If you want to hook up, just say so," Latoya said, batting her lashes. "You don't have to make no excuses to visit my bedroom."

Rick was in no mood for her antics. "You've got sleep in the corners of your eyes," he told her.

Her coy smile faded, and she cleaned the gunk out of her eyes. "Thanks," she said sullenly.

"Is there an intruder?" Fern asked, her voice barely audible but shaking.

"Yep. But he seems to be gone. Did either of you hear anything?"

Latoya tossed her rumpled head. "You mean other than you hollering at us to drag our booties out of bed? Not a thing."

"How about you?" he asked Fern.

She hesitated. "I thought I heard someone in the hall a while ago. But I was half-asleep."

It could have been him or Allie. "What did it sound like?"

"It sounded like someone opened the door, then closed it again. But like I said, I was half-asleep and didn't look up."

"Wishful thinking," Latoya scoffed. "She's got a crush on Charlie."

Fern flushed and looked down at her bare feet.

Rick stepped back into the hallway. "Go back to bed. There's no one in the house, and I locked the doors."

The girls shuffled back into their bedroom and shut the door. He could hear Latoya haranguing Fern about her ridiculous crush on Charlie. Poor kid. After running back downstairs to double-check the doors, he went back up the stairs and started toward his room. As he passed Allie's room, he decided to take one more look at the hall outside her door. The guy had slipped the paper under the door. If his aim was to hurt Allie, he could have just as easily gone into the bedroom.

Why hadn't he?

Rick didn't know what the guy's game was, but the thought that he'd waltzed in here and back out without detection really steamed him. He'd have to ask Brendan for help. Running his hand over Allie's doorjamb, he felt every nick and scratch. The guy wouldn't have had to pick a lock because there were none in this old house other than the outside door locks and the office.

He knelt on the rug and lifted the edge of it. Nothing there. Rising, he stepped into the room and glanced around again. Everything was neat and in its place. A few cosmetics lined the dresser. Before he realized it, he'd picked up the gaudy nail polish and turned it in his hand. She was such a contradiction—all cowgirl and competent—then very feminine with bright nail polish and sleek hair.

He put the bottle back, then picked up her cologne and brought it to his nose. It smelled sweet and dainty, just like Allie. He put the bottle back hastily.

Don't go there. She'd chew his heart up for breakfast and spit it out. Backing away as if a rattlesnake lay coiled on the dresser, he turned to the closet. He'd checked it once, but he wasn't ready to give up finding whoever was behind this. Opening the door, he swept his hand through the hanging clothes, and the sweet scent drifted out again. Her shoes, two pair, were lined up evenly in the bottom of the closet. Betsy's shoes were just as precisely placed.

She didn't seem the type to want everything so ordered. Maybe it was a way of controlling the things she *could* control when there was so much she couldn't. What was that eye problem she'd mentioned? Something about Irlen. He'd have to look it up. Maybe there was something he could do to help her.

Shutting the closet door, he went down the hall to his bedroom. He tapped on the door. "Allie? It's me."

He heard the bed springs squeak, then a few moments later, the scrape of the chair being removed from the doorknob. The door opened, and she looked up at him, her blue eyes wide with trust. Something shattered in the region of his heart when he saw how completely she believed in him.

Had anyone ever looked at him like that before—like he could conquer the world? Maybe Jon. At the reminder of his friend, he pulled his mental shield back into place. Allie and Betsy were Jon's, not his. He couldn't ever let himself forget he was just a stand-in.

"Everything's okay," he told her. "I'll carry Betsy back to bed for you."

She sighed at his perfunctory tone. "Thanks." She stepped aside to allow him space to enter.

He went to the bed and lifted the little girl. Betsy didn't stir as he carried her back to her bed. "You'll be okay?"

She nodded. "Fine. Thanks for checking." She hesitated. "Maybe we should leave, pack up and run."

"He found you here," Rick pointed out. "Running is never the answer. This guy is tenacious. At least here we can see someone coming from miles away."

"Just like tonight?" Her smile did little to take the sting from her words.

"We know he's found you now. I'll get some friends on it tomorrow. We'll find him."

Her eyes looked sad, but she nodded. "Thank you, Rick. I don't know what we'd have done without your help."

Her words sounded stilted and formal, and he wished she'd look at him with that trust again. He gave a curt nod and backed out of the room. "Put a chair under your door," he said.

She shut the door, and he waited until he heard a chair scrape across the floor and lodge under the knob. Retreating to his bedroom, he listened to the wind howl through the eaves. He used to howl like that when his back was laid bare.

He shut the door, shucked his jeans and shirt, and crawled between the sheets. The sweet scent of her in his sheets filled him with an emotion he couldn't bring himself to name.

14

Everything seemed different by the light of day. Betsy clung to Allie's side all morning. Even though she'd slept through the whole upheaval in the night, she seemed to understand that something had changed.

Her little girl sat by the refrigerator with her doll clutched in her hand and watched Allie slice roast beef and homemade bread for lunch. Allie hadn't seen her daughter have the doll out since they'd come.

"How about if we go out looking for bluebirds after lunch?" she asked Betsy. "We'll see if Rick will go with us."

She needed a distraction as badly as Betsy did. The realization that Yo was gone kept ambushing her.

Betsy looked up and nodded, her smile breaking out of the gloom. Allie's eyes burned as she watched her daughter bend her head until her dark curls touched the golden head of her doll. She wanted so much for her daughter, but it seemed Betsy was living the life of the cinder maid.

The haven they'd found here hadn't lasted nearly long enough. How could Rick protect them from a phantom who slipped in and out of sight like the fog?

The screen door banged, and Latoya strolled into the kitchen, followed by Fern. The two girls were so different. Latoya came in like she owned the world, while Fern slunk in with her head down and her shoulders slumped. Allie wanted to take Fern by the shoulders and tell her to stand up straight, look the world in the eye, and chart her course.

But had Allie done any better with her own life? She'd had big handicaps to overcome, and once upon a time, she thought she had done a pretty good job of scaling the mountains that had once seemed so daunting. But life had a way of dethroning you when you least expected it.

Allie wanted to be more like Latoya, certain of herself and her power over other people. But maybe the teenager was just better at hiding her fears. Maybe people were all the same inside.

"Girl, my stomach is growling like that lion I heard last night," Latoya complained.

"Lunch will be ready in a few minutes," Allie said, snapping out of her reverie and turning back to her task. "Did you get all your chores done?"

"That mare of Betsy's about chewed the bag up and spit it back out. She's one hungry mama. Did you go see her this morning, Bets?" Latoya squatted beside Betsy, who just nodded without looking at her.

Latoya stood and went to the cabinet, where she began to pull down plates and glasses.

Allie wanted to smile but hid it by turning away to get the mayo out of the refrigerator. A week ago, the teen would have sullenly agreed to set the table only after being asked numerous times.

The pottery clattered on the wood table as Latoya carelessly tossed the dishes into place. "That little colt loves me like his mama," she said in a conversational tone. "He followed me all over that corral." She giggled like a five-year-old. "He kept nibbling on my shirt." She sank onto the chair and crossed her legs at the ankles. "I like it here."

"Me too," Fern said, laying out the tableware. "I wish I never had to leave."

Allie felt a pang at the wistful tones of both girls. She might have thought her life was hard, but these girls had even more strikes against them. At least she'd had loving parents. She could see the attraction in helping kids like these.

"We're going to go look for bluebirds after lunch. You girls want to come?" she asked them.

"Bluebirds? What's up with that?" Latoya demanded.

"Betsy loves them. Haven't you ever heard of the bluebird of happiness? Betsy loves the old Shirley Temple movie called *The Blue Bird*. We could watch it tonight after supper if you've never seen it."

"I used to watch Shirley Temple at my grandma's," Fern said in a soft voice. "My brother had a crush on her. He never knew she was old enough now to be his grandma."

"Shirley Temple? She that curly-headed Betty in the old black-and-white movies?" Latoya demanded. "That's kid stuff."

"Aw, come on, Latoya," Fern said with more animation than Allie had ever seen. "It's a really good movie."

Latoya sniffed. "I'll watch it for a while, but if it gets too hokey, I'm outta there."

Allie wanted to gather the girl up in her arms and tell her it wasn't too late to regain her childhood, but she knew the words would seem empty. And maybe they were. Once innocence was lost, she wasn't sure it could ever be regained.

THE SKY HAD CLEARED OF THE SAND THAT YELLOWED THE AIR AND PILED around the foundations of the buildings. Rick and Charlie spent the morning tramping the ranch, looking for any sign of the man who had broken into the house last night.

Rick called the sheriff, and he came out too, but there was nothing to see, no one to interrogate. The two older hands had been here over twenty years, and Rick couldn't see Buzz or Guinn trying to frighten Allie. Charlie was just a kid. None of the help had any reason to terrorize her.

He ruled out Emilio and the kids too. Her stalker must be lurking nearby after tracking her here.

"You want me to stand guard tonight?" Charlie asked, a worried frown settling on his forehead when the men failed to turn up any clues. "Me and the hands could take turns."

"Maybe. I asked the sheriff if he'd give her some police protection."

Charlie snorted. "Good luck with that. I don't think he's got an officer smart enough to find his butt with both hands."

Charlie had a point. The sheriff's good ol' boys weren't capable of anything beyond arresting drunk and disorderly residents. There wasn't much crime here beyond the occasional theft from a tourist's car and the fights that broke out in Long Branch Saloon.

Maybe he should talk to Brendan, but he didn't see what his friend could do about the situation. He likely had his plate full saving the world. Still, maybe Brendan could at least put some feelers out and give him some indication of how the guy might have found Allie.

His wife. The thought still made his stomach plunge. The realization that he was married kept playing hide-and-seek in his mind. Rick couldn't quite grasp the reality of it, even yet.

Charlie was staring at him.

"What?" he asked.

"Allie told me."

"Told you what?"

"That you married her. You could have called dibs on her when she got here, but you kept mum." His glance was full of curiosity.

"She's too old for you anyway."

"I'm only ten years younger," Charlie said, his voice indignant. "Why didn't you say anything about knowing her?"

Rick shrugged. "I didn't know her, Charlie. She was my best friend's wife, and she came to me for help. I told her husband I'd take care of her."

Charlie pulled an aspirin bottle from his jeans and shook out three pills.

"Migraine again?"

"Yeah, my counselor says it's stress." Charlie pulled his canteen from his belt and uncapped it. Throwing back his head, he swallowed the pills and wiped his lips before resealing it and putting it away. "That's a rare brand of loyalty."

"Jon's parents are trying to get custody of Betsy. It seemed the best thing to do to keep Betsy with Allie."

Charlie grinned then. "Anything to get a woman like that in your bed, huh?"

"It wasn't like that." Rick clamped his teeth against any more explanation. "It's about lunchtime. We'd better get back."

Charlie's face took on its hurt expression again, and Rick wondered how the kid could have fallen for Allie so fast.

Who's talking? The voice whispered in his head. *You're just like Charlie.* He shook the thought away. He was just doing his duty. Charlie might succumb to her charms, but he wouldn't.

"I'm heading in," Charlie said.

"Be right there." Rick sat on the back porch step and listened to the cattle low in the back field. He pulled out his cell phone and called Brendan.

"Me again, buddy," he said when his friend answered. "Trouble came calling last night." He told Brendan about the intruder and the note. "How could he have tracked her here?"

"She talk to anyone back in El Paso?"

"No. Oh wait, yeah, she talked to her friend one day, then her friend's parents. The one who was killed."

"Maybe the guy had their phone tapped. You know how easy it is to get hold of a listening device."

"But she didn't tell them where she was."

"She call on the house phone?"

"Yeah," he said, his heart sinking. "Caller ID."

"Yep. Nothing's secret these days. Anything else I can do?"

"Nope, not unless you've got some personnel with nothing to do that you'd like to send me for protection."

"Wish I did, Rick. Sounds like you need some backup."

"I'll manage."

"She couldn't be in better hands." Brendan gave a knowing chuckle. "Pun intended, Mr. Newlywed."

"It's not like that," he said for the second time in five minutes.

"Whatever." Brendan's voice became brusque again. "Listen, I've gotta go. Keep me posted, and call if there's anything I can do."

Rick put his phone away and got up. Protecting Allie and Betsy lay squarely on his shoulders, and he wasn't sure he was up to the task anymore. He'd gotten soft living here on the ranch, where the only danger was from animals and the weather. Humans could be more treacherous and more deadly than any of their counterparts in the animal kingdom.

THEY FOUND TOO MANY BLUEBIRDS TO COUNT. ALLIE'S MUSCLES ACHED IN a pleasant way from the hike as she rested at the bottom of a rock formation Rick called Eye of the Needle. A thin plume of dust billowed up from the car that pitched and rocked its way along the potholes in the lane to the house. She watched it travel toward the buildings. The vehicle looked vaguely familiar, but she couldn't quite determine the make from this far away. Betsy and the girls sat among the bluebonnets, and she turned back to them to take their picture.

Betsy's smile radiated up at her, and Allie smiled back. All seemed right with the world this afternoon, and she wondered how she could feel so happy when she knew her enemy had found her. But he wasn't here today. Today she could lift her face to the hot sun and breathe in the aroma of sage and creosote.

She snapped the picture and put her camera back into her shirt pocket. When she turned to look back at the house, she saw a man step out of the car. The lawyer. Wally Tatum. Maybe he brought news about the adoption.

"I'm ready for some iced tea. How about you?" she called to the girls.

"Ice cream sounds better," Latoya said, getting up and dusting the dirt from her shorts. "With hot fudge."

"I think there's some in the freezer. How about you and Fern go fix it, and I'll be in shortly. I need to talk to the man down there."

"We'll take Betsy," Fern said, clasping the little girl's hand.

"I'll walk you to the house." Allie wasn't about to let Betsy out of her sight until they were safely inside.

As they neared the buildings, she saw Rick step off the front porch to greet Wally, and she quickened her steps. The girls ran ahead of her, and once they were inside, she stopped at Rick's side.

"Mrs. Bailey." Wally tipped his hat.

Mrs. Bailey. She saw the start Rick gave and knew the words had shocked him as much as they did her. She wasn't a Siders anymore, wasn't part of Jon's family. She hadn't even thought about that. Something squeezed in her chest, a sharp pang at just how much her life had changed. She'd thought she would die a Siders, would lay beside Jon in the little cemetery in El Paso.

Her fingers curled into her palms. "Mr. Tatum. Any news?"

"Please, ma'am, if you call me Wally, I'll call you Allie. We don't like formality here." Wally gestured to the rockers on the porch. "How about we set a spell, and I'll bring you up to speed."

Rick took Allie's arm, and they stepped onto the porch. She settled onto the swing while the men took the rockers. "Is it good news?"

Wally smiled broadly. "About as good as you can get. With most adoptions the child needs to reside with the adoptive parent for six months. The judge is waiving that requirement in your case since she knows Rick here. The home study will be done the first of the week if you're agreeable, and we can set the finalization of the adoption at the end of the month."

"You're kidding," Rick said. "I had no idea it would move that fast."

Wally grinned and put his boots on the porch railing. "The judge thinks you're a saint, and she was mighty fond of Elijah. Betsy's his great-granddaughter. Stands to reason the judge would do everything in her power to help out."

Allie could hardly believe it. All the dominoes were falling into place. She was so used to things going wrong that it didn't seem possible the adoption would be this easy. "No problems at all?"

"Nope. The road is clear before us." Wally stretched his arms over his head. "I could go for some iced tea right about now."

"With news like that, you deserve a hot-fudge sundae," Allie said, getting to her feet.

"I wouldn't turn it down," Wally said.

"How about you?" she asked Rick.

"A celebration sounds good," he said.

His eyes were smiling, and he looked as relieved as she felt. Had he thought it wouldn't go through? She knew so little about Rick. Was she doing the right thing? When he adopted Betsy, he would always be in their lives, even after the divorce. What if she found out things about him later when it was too late?

Staring into his face, she searched his gaze until he lifted a brow in question. "Anything wrong?" he asked.

"No, no, nothing," she said hastily.

But how did one ever know what was in the heart of another person? She had to trust that Jon had known him well and said she could rely on Rick. Sometimes you just had to trust.

Trust came hard to Allie anymore. When had that happened? She remembered her younger years, when she believed the best about everyone. Maybe she'd seen too much, lived through too much heartache to think there might not be secrets behind Rick's smile.

Today she would choose to trust though. Trust that God had led her to the right place for help, even when she didn't quite understand the method.

15

THE LANDSCAPE CHANGED FROM EMPTY DESERT TO SIGNS OF HABITATION as the truck neared the city limits of El Paso. Mr. Fleming had said not to come to the funeral, but Allie couldn't sit at the ranch while her best friend was laid to rest. Her beater truck would never make the six-hour trip each way to El Paso, and Rick wanted to take her anyway, so she'd agreed to let him.

She'd passed the drive dozing with her head against the window until about an hour ago. It was better than trying to make conversation when her heart felt as barren as the landscape at the ordeal ahead of her. She'd attended too many funerals the past two years.

Yo was Allie's last link with her old life. Everyone she loved except Betsy was gone now. It wasn't fair. If she'd done something wrong, why did her family have to suffer? She wished she knew what caused the man to fixate on her.

She dug her nail polish out and carefully applied a fresh coat of hot pink.

"Whew, that stuff stinks," Rick said, wrinkling his nose. "Why do you wear it anyway? It doesn't stay on long."

Allie held out a finished hand. "You don't think it looks pretty?"

"It looks fake."

Allie capped the polish and blew on her nails. "Nice nails are the difference between a lady and a woman."

"Who told you that? You're a lady no matter what."

"My mother."

Rick grunted, then shuffled some papers on his lap. "You awake enough to help me navigate?"

"Yes." Allie stretched and looked down at Betsy. "She's still asleep though."

"Can you help me look for the street? You're more familiar with El Paso than me."

Allie nodded and turned to look out the window. "The funeral home is about five lights or so in. You'll turn right, so get in the right-hand lane."

The familiar streets looked alien and dangerous. She'd gotten used to open land and blue skies. It would be hard to ever move back to the city again.

"You doing okay?"

She turned her head to glance at him. "It's going to be a hard day. Yo was the only Fleming kid."

"I still wish you wouldn't go. It's not safe."

She hunched her shoulders and ran her hand over the soft velour of the seat. "It's not safe at the ranch. Nowhere is really safe."

His eyes narrowed. "I won't leave your side. And I'll keep hold of Betsy every minute."

She nodded and turned to look back out the window. They passed Cowtown Boots, and nostalgia swept over her. Yo had bought Allie's boots there just three months ago. They'd mugged it up as they tried on every outlandish pair they saw before settling on something practical.

How could that bright spirit be dead?

Allie reminded herself that Yo wasn't really dead. She'd gone on to a better place. They would be together again someday.

But right now she felt like someone had ripped her heart out.

"Turn here," she said.

Rick slowed the truck and turned at the light. A few intersections later, she pointed out the funeral home, and he parked in the lot.

"I'll carry Betsy," he said. Rick unbuckled the little girl's seat belt and lifted her in his arms.

Allie's hand stayed on the door lever. All she'd done for the past year was stand by the caskets of those she loved.

"You coming?"

"Yes." She pushed open the door and got out, but she might as well have been slogging through knee-high mud. Yo's parents waited inside that building, and she would be expected to offer comfort when she had none.

Rick took her elbow and guided her toward the door. The strength of his fingers was a support she badly needed. He held open the door, and she walked into the crowd milling around the reception hall. A young woman pointed her in the right direction when she asked for the Fleming funeral.

Mr. Fleming spotted her first. His girth strained the buttons of his blue suit. The big lapels looked out-of-date, and Allie wondered if it was the suit he'd worn to his wedding thirty years ago. His kinky black hair was shorter than she'd ever seen it, and the dark face under it had developed new lines.

He enveloped her in a hug. "Told you not to come, girl."

Tears welled at the sorrow in his voice. "I had to say good-bye."

His beefy hands patted her shoulder. "Who's the Paul Bunyan type with Betsy?"

"Oh, I need to introduce you." Allie glanced around and gestured to Rick, who stood a few feet off as if to give her some time alone with the family.

He joined her with Betsy still in his arms. The little girl was awake now, but she clung to Rick like he was her port in the storm. Allie knew the feeling.

"Mr. Fleming, this is m-my husband, Rick Bailey."

The older man's smile seemed to freeze in place. He looked Rick over carefully. "My Yo, did she know of this?" Suspicion coated his words.

"I told her the last time we talked what I planned."

Mr. Fleming and Rick locked gazes, then Yolanda's father nodded. "You take good care of these girls, Mr. Bailey."

Rick shifted Betsy to his other arm. "I intend to."

THE WEEKEND HAD FILLED RICK WITH A STRANGE SENSE OF CONTENTMENT. Attending church with Allie and the kids beside him just like a real family, going bird-watching, watching Allie paint her nails and Betsy's tiny half moons with color. Rick could get used to this.

There had been no more incidents, though Rick watched over the ranch and every person there with a sharp gaze.

The home study on Monday had been a breeze. A form to fill out, a few perfunctory questions, and the woman had smiled and left. Rick didn't anticipate any problems. Everyone in town knew him and his commitment to working with kids.

He and Emilio talked out how to handle the kids with Elijah gone. Rick took over the group talk sessions and found them just like his studies had told him—sometimes frustrating and sometimes rewarding.

Tuesday morning he and Charlie stood at the corral fence and evaluated the condition of the horses. Three of them had been rescued within the last three months, and the latest one, which they'd all come to call Betsy's mare, was showing signs of lethargy—not a good thing when she'd been so perky.

"We can't lose her," he told Charlie. "Betsy would be devastated. Did you call Grady?"

"He's out of town. His assistant is going to come take a look at her this afternoon." Charlie popped a Hershey's kiss in his mouth from a bag he'd nearly emptied in the last fifteen minutes. "We got company."

Rick turned to see a Ford sedan approaching the house. The sedate blue color and tinted windows made his muscles tense, and somehow he knew before the two men stepped out in their navy suits and neat ties that the FBI had found Allie.

"I'll handle this," he told Charlie. "Don't say anything." He strode over to intercept the men who were approaching the porch. "I'm Rick Bailey, the ranch foreman," he said, sticking out his hand.

The closest man shook his hand, then pulled out a badge and flashed it. "FBI. We're looking for Allie Siders."

"No one here by that name." It wasn't exactly a lie. Her name was Allie Bailey now. Rick wanted to head them off long enough for the adoption to take place. "Just me and my wife live here, along with some kids in the foster system who are here temporarily."

The expressionless men didn't move away. "We know she's here," the leader said. "You might have married her, but we still need to talk to her."

He should have known they would know about the marriage. The feds always had their ducks in a row. "Look, she had nothing to do with the illegal aliens. She reported what she saw, that's all."

"Actually, we already know that," the guy said. "We're not here to arrest her. And her in-laws have dropped the kidnapping charge now that they know where she is. They'll be along to sort that issue out shortly."

Rick winced. Trouble was coming. "Then what do you want?"

The man nodded toward the door. "To talk to your wife."

The screen door opened behind him, and Allie stepped out. "I heard my name. Are you looking for me?"

"You're Allie Siders?"

"Yes—I mean no. It's Allie Bailey now." The door closed behind her, and she moved to stand beside Rick. She leaned against him slightly to steady herself. "You're cops?"

"FBI, ma'am. I'm Agent Marshall." He pointed to a blond guy with a crew cut. "Agent Baker. We'd like to talk to you."

Allie took a step back, her shoulders wilting and her head coming up in a defensive posture. "I didn't do anything."

"We know, ma'am. The investigation has turned away from you since Yolanda Fleming's murder in light of this." He handed her a paper. "This was in Ms. Fleming's car, under the seat."

She took it, her pink polish garish against the envelope. It had her name scrawled across it in bold letters.

"You want me to read it first?" he asked when her gaze touched his face.

She shook her head. "What is it?" she asked.

"A letter from the killer."

The envelope wasn't sealed. Allie lifted the flap and pulled out the single sheet of paper.

Rick craned his neck over her shoulder and read the words on the paper.

Doesn't Yolanda look lovely in her casket? But you'll look better.

Allie crumpled the letter in her hand. "He's not going to get away with this," she said. "I'm going to make sure he pays for what he did to Yo." Her voice shook with passion.

"So who hates you?" Agent Marshall asked. "What we want to know is who would want to make you look guilty of trafficking? If we can get some direction on that, we might be able to find the mastermind. Whoever it was tried to make you look like you were involved, but we followed the money trail and your spending habits, and it's clear it was a frame-up."

"But what about Yolanda?" Rick put in. "Was she involved in some way?"

"She seems to have been killed purely to hurt Allie."

Allie clasped her arms around herself. "They accomplished that." She told them about the man who claimed to have killed her family.

"You didn't recognize his voice? Nothing was familiar?" Agent Marshall asked.

"Everyone has asked her that, including me," Rick put in. "And the guy has found her here." He told the agents about the break-in the other night.

"Do you still have the letter?"

"Yes, it's in the office." Rick motioned for them to follow him, and he took them past the living room where Fern and Betsy were playing school. He unlocked the office door and stepped to the desk. He opened the drawer. "That's odd. I left it here." He rummaged through the stacks of papers and bills. "It's gone," he said.

Someone had stolen it. Rick distinctly remembered putting it in the desk drawer. He'd locked the room behind him, and only he and Allie had a key. His gaze tangled with hers, and she looked away. Had she taken it?

"Allie, you have any idea what happened to the letter?" he asked. He didn't want to believe she might have taken it, that she might not want a closer inspection of the letter.

She looked up and shook her head. "I haven't seen it since I gave it to you."

"Can you write down what it said?" Agent Baker asked.

"There wasn't much to it," Rick said, grabbing a blank sheet of paper. "It was typewritten and read, 'I've found you. Tag, I'm it. Your worst nightmare.'"

"Could it have been someone other than the man who killed Ms. Fleming? Maybe someone who knew you were running and thought to tease you?" Agent Baker asked.

"I don't think so," Allie said, shaking her head. "I'd even wondered if one of the teens did it as a joke, but I don't think that's it. I can't explain, but the feel of the words, the way he put them together, sounds like him. I don't believe it's a copycat."

The man handed Rick a card. "If you find it, give us a call." Agent Marshall smiled and went toward the door. The men exited the room.

Rick rummaged around the desk again. "I can't believe this. No one has a key to the office but you and me."

"You suspected me at first, didn't you?" Allie's gaze held steady.

"For a second," he admitted.

"Where's the trust, Rick?" She lifted her hand and flashed the gold ring his way. "Before you put this on my finger, don't you think you should have made sure you believed what I was telling you?"

"The marriage wasn't about you. It was about Jon."

She flinched. "Jon's not here, and I'm the one who has to see the suspicion in your face."

"Fair enough." He'd hurt her, and the thought pained him. More than he wanted to admit. He should tell her that the Siderses had tracked her down too, but he didn't want to see more discouragement in those blue eyes.

THE NEXT FEW DAYS ALLIE FOUND HERSELF CLEANING AN ALREADY SPOT-less bathroom and dusting shining furniture with a lemony wax so she didn't have to think about Yo's death. If the guy thought he'd make her run again, he was wrong. She'd see him brought to justice no matter what it took.

Today she wasn't going to think about it. Rick was taking her and Betsy out to see his bluebird trail. The grassy meadow stretched out under the big sky, brushing the Rio Grande on one side and an escarpment that rose sharply on the other. They rode side by side, Rick and Betsy on Gunner and Allie on Jackson, a six-year-old Appaloosa that she'd been riding since her arrival.

A small cabin sat on the other end of the meadow. "Who lives there?" Allie asked.

"Our former housekeeper, Rosa Garcia. She'd be the one to ask about your mom, but she's visiting her sister right now. She should be back in another few days."

Allie followed Rick as he led the way toward the first birdhouse. Another was planted a few feet away.

"This is called a bluebird trail," Rick told Betsy. They dismounted and tied off the horses at a bar, then Rick lifted Betsy onto his shoulders. "Bluebirds like open, grassy areas. We can't put their houses by the feedlot because there are so many sparrows there eating the grain, and they'd steal the houses from the bluebirds." He hefted her higher and approached the nest. "Look inside, Bets. Are there any eggs?"

Allie stepped between them and the pole. "There might be lice."

"Get a grip," Rick said under his breath. "She's fine."

"She's going to get dirty poking around up there. And one of the birds might attack if she's messing with the nest." Allie shuddered at the thought.

An exasperated huff escaped Rick's mouth. "Look, just be quiet and let me try this, okay? Just let me handle this."

Why didn't he get a mother's concern? "I don't understand. She can watch the birds from down here."

He stared at her without saying another word until she shrugged, and against her better judgment, moved out of the way. She'd about had it with his interference.

He moved closer to the birdhouse. "See any eggs, Bets?"

Betsy peered into the birdhouse. A tiny squeak of excitement came from her throat. Allie's eyes widened, and she and Rick locked gazes. She gave him a tiny nod. Maybe the bluebirds would be a way of getting Betsy to talk.

"How many do you see?" he asked.

Allie forgot to breathe when Betsy opened her mouth. Then her daughter's lips clamped shut again, and she held up three fingers.

"Three, huh? It's called a clutch of eggs. What color are they?" Rick persisted.

Betsy exhaled through parted lips. Allie could almost hear the words wanting to escape, but Betsy ducked her head and didn't reply.

"Are they blue?" Rick asked gently. Betsy nodded. "We have to watch them until they hatch and make sure they're doing okay. When the babies get to be about twelve days old, we'll quit bothering them. We don't want them to get scared and try to fly away too soon."

The meadow stretched out over the hills in all directions. It felt peaceful here, and Allie wished she could let her guard down. It wasn't safe though, not with that man lurking about. He might even now be watching her.

Rick had brought a nightstick with him, and she had no doubt he knew how to use it. She would need every bit of his protection.

"Check this box, Betsy," Rick said, walking to the nearby bird-house. "Any blue eggs in there?"

An iridescent green bird flew from the box. Betsy peered inside and shook her head.

"It's a tree swallow. They like the same type of home as the blue-bird, so we put a house up for them. That way they don't take it away from the bluebird. The tree swallow is a protected species too." Rick lifted Betsy from his shoulders and put her on the grass. "Let's sit and rest awhile. I think your mom brought lunch for us."

Allie went to her horse and got the sandwiches and blanket out of her saddlebag. She spread out the red-and-white checked blanket, and Rick helped her put out the food and bottles of water. They ate in silence as they watched the bluebirds flutter around the pasture. The sun beat down, and she adjusted her hat to block out the glare. She felt relaxed for the first time in days.

Rick lay back with his hands behind his head. "Bets, did you know your daddy could make the most piercing whistle through his teeth? It was enough to break your eardrums."

Betsy giggled, and Allie could have kissed Rick for trying to help keep Jon's memory alive. "Pick me some flowers, Betsy," she said, glancing around at the bright display of bluebonnets and some yellow wildflowers. A roadrunner darted from one rock to another, then ran to the blue ribbon of water. Fragrance filled the air—wildflowers, sage, creosote, and river. She could live here forever.

Betsy smiled and got up from the blanket. She began to pick the three-foot stalks of bluebonnet, but before she got very far, the blue-birds grabbed her attention, and she sat down to watch them.

Allie turned her attention back to Rick. "The adoption hearing is in a couple of days. Are you sure you want to go through with this?"

"You trying to back out?"

"No, just giving you a final window of opportunity." She smiled and plucked a wildflower of her own to keep from touching his face with her fingertips.

"I've already come to care about Betsy," Rick said. "And not just for Jon anymore." He plucked a flower and twirled it in his fingers. "Betsy almost said something at the birdhouse. You've got to back off and let her fly, Allie."

Allie's contentment disappeared like the cottonwood fluff dancing around the meadow. "You're not her father," she said. "You can be her friend, but that's as far as it goes."

"What if I say that's not enough?"

"It has to be. That's all there is. I'm not letting you—or any man—take Jon's place with her."

"Even if it's not what's best for Betsy? Where's your trust, Allie? In me, in God for bringing us together? You going to toss that gift back in his face?" Rick turned his gaze on her. "There's something else I've been meaning to talk to you about," he said.

The solemnity in his face made her want to run. He was going to say he wanted a divorce sooner than a year. She didn't blame him. For a man like him who could have his pick of women, the thought of being saddled to a widow and her kid must be daunting.

"I don't want a divorce," he said. "Did you notice I hesitated before I said my vows?"

She nodded. "I'd wondered if you were about to back out."

"It wasn't that. As a Christian, the thought that we were planning on breaking the vows we took bothered me. Before I said them, I decided I would say them and mean the promise. I'd like us to think about working on making our marriage real. I don't want a divorce in a year."

"Real?" she echoed. Something inside, some last dying bloom of hope, lifted its head.

"I know it's a shock, and maybe I shouldn't have sprung it on you so fast." He took her small hand in his big, warm one. "I'm not saying we move fast, just that we inch along in the right direction."

Allie wasn't sure what to say, how to react. She'd dismissed his strange comment the night of the wedding when he hadn't said any more. And how exactly would they work on it? Wasn't love supposed to bloom by itself without being coaxed? Still, she thought she could learn to love Rick.

And she wanted Rick to love Betsy, to nurture and care for her, but a tiny twinge of longing for the same thing rattled her. If she plucked his other hand from his lap and held it to her lips, what would he do? For a moment she was tempted to find out, but then the cold light of reality washed over her. She wasn't in the market for more pain.

"What do you say?" he prodded, his thumb running in circles against her palm.

She found it hard to think with the way he was looking at her, the plea in his blue eyes. "I—I don't know," she faltered.

The light in his eyes dimmed. "Fair enough. But let's try it out."

Before she could react, he leaned over and took her shoulders in his hands. His head bent down, and he claimed her lips in a gentle kiss. His mouth coaxed her own to respond, and her fingers wrapped themselves in his shirt. She clung to him, and a passion she didn't expect flared between them.

His arm came around her back, and he pulled her closer. She didn't resist. The smell of him, the hard muscles under her fingers, the tenderness of his kiss broke through the defenses she thought she'd reinforced with grief and heartache. Her fingers trailed up to run along his roughened jaw. She cupped his face in her palm and kissed him back with all the loneliness of the past two years.

Dimly, she realized someone was tugging on her shirtsleeve. Betsy. Grasping for some shred of control, Allie pulled away and smoothed her hair. Her hand trembled.

"I think that might be a yes," Rick whispered.

She couldn't look at him. Was he laughing at how easily he'd battered down her walls? Her lips tingled and felt warm. She wanted to touch them but didn't want him to see. Swallowing hard, she gathered Betsy onto her lap.

The thought of sharing a life with this man was an oasis in the desert to her soul thirsting to belong.

16

THE SKY SHONE BLUER AND THE GRASS GLOWED BRIGHTER AS RICK RODE
along the trail back to the ranch, with Betsy on the saddle in front of
him and Allie riding her mare beside them. He hadn't planned on saying anything yet, but her response gave him hope.

And scared him to death.

He'd loved his mother, and she hurt him worse than any enemy.
His back itched with the memories. For two cents, he'd call Brendan
back and tell him he'd changed his mind and would be glad to help
solve the world's problems.

They'd be a lot easier than solving his own.

When they reached the barn, he dismounted, then unsaddled the
horses while Allie went inside with Betsy. She hadn't spoken a word

on the trail. Maybe she was as taken aback by what happened between them as he was. They had a long road to navigate if they were going to stay together.

He poked his head in the house long enough to tell Allie he was going to town for a while. She was sitting at the desk with the bills spread out in front of her. Everything smelled of lemon polish. Betsy was in the big chair by the window and was already asleep. Squinting at the papers, Allie didn't look up when he spoke.

"You okay?" he asked.

"It's just hard to read these things," she said, tucking a lock of hair behind her ear. "I used to have tinted glasses that helped, but they broke."

"So get some more."

She looked up then, and a smile chased away her ferocious expression. "They're expensive. I get by okay. It just takes a little longer."

He heard the forced optimism in her voice. Maybe he could find out something about those glasses while he was in town. "I'll be back in a couple of hours. I've got some errands to run. Anything I can get for you while I'm there?"

"No, we're fine. You'll be back in time for supper?"

"Sure." He grabbed a paper and jotted down his cell number. "You can call me if you need anything."

She took the paper and tucked it into her jeans pocket. "Thanks."

An awkward silence fell between them. The dance of relationship was one Rick had never learned, and the crash course was beginning to wear him out. "Okay then," he said, backing out of the room.

On the way to town, he called Grady. If he wanted this marriage to work, they had to start out right. "Hey, buddy, got a favor," he said when Grady picked up the phone.

"Hey, Cowboy. How did you know I just walked in the door?"

Rick didn't want to even tell his friend he'd entered into a mockery of a marriage. "You got time to do some marriage counseling this week?" he asked, plunging right in.

Grady was an odd combination, a vet who pastored, but the tiny church couldn't support a full-time man, and Grady had stepped into the position with all the accompanying duties.

"But sure, and who is it?"

"Me."

There was silence on the other end of the line. "I'd heard something about this. You really married the woman, Rick?"

"Yep. If we want it to last, we're going to have to figure some things out about each other. I thought the best place to start would be with you. I'm going to adopt Betsy, and we have the hearing a week from tomorrow at nine. Would you have time later in the morning?"

"How about eleven?"

Rick wanted to thank Grady for not launching into a lecture, but he just agreed and marked it down. Time enough later to hear all the reasons he shouldn't have done what he did. It was too late to regret it now. "We'll be there. Oh, did your assistant get a chance to take a look at that new mare?"

"He did. He wormed her and gave her a shot of antibiotic. He thinks she'll be fine, said she looked like she's gaining weight." He cleared his throat. "Rick, you sure you know what you're doing?"

"Nope, but I'm winging it."

Grady sighed. "I'll be praying for you, bucko. Will you be in church this week?"

"We'll be there. And thanks for the prayers. I need them." Rick closed his phone and went to see the sheriff. He slowed and gawked at an accident along Dead Gulch Curve, but the pickup involved wasn't familiar, and an ambulance was already on the scene.

He found Barry Borland in his office. The big man was kneeling in front of a filing cabinet that overflowed with papers. He lumbered to his feet when Rick rapped on the doorjamb.

"Have a seat, Rick." He gestured to the green chair in front of his desk.

Rick dropped into the chair and fished out his notebook. "I need your help, Sheriff."

"You know we don't have the manpower to station someone out there," Borland said.

"No problem, I've got that covered. But could you tell me if there have been any other break-ins in the area? Any reports of illegals being moved through here? Any strangers hanging around town? I reported some suspected illegals to border patrol last week."

The sheriff scratched his huge belly. "Well, now that you mention it, we did get a report of a vanload of Mexicans being detained by the border patrol. Seems a coyote had told them they could slip right through here without a problem. There was another truck seen speeding away when the van broke down. No one got a good make or description, though. And the folks aren't talking about who the coyote is. They were deported pronto."

"Someone recommended this area?"

"Yep."

"Robberies, transients?" Rick asked.

Borland shook his head. "Nothing unusual. Mary Beth Lucas had a window broken by a baseball. A few tourists wandered in and out of town without incident."

"Thanks, I just thought it was worth a shot." Rick hesitated and let his pencil rest against the notebook. "Anything new on Elijah's death?"

The sheriff's expression grew sober. "Sorry, I can't talk about that."

"It was murder?"

"Quit fishing, Rick." The sheriff shot him a long, hard look. "The autopsy report isn't back."

"Have you checked out Stuart Ifera? He was trying to strong-arm Elijah into selling the ranch."

"I've got it covered." Borland shuffled his papers. "Beat it, kid. I've got stuff to do."

"Ifera a friend or something?" Rick shot back.

Borland scowled. "Look, he's my brother-in-law, okay? He had nothing to do with Elijah's death. Now get out of my face."

Rick leaned forward. "Just do your job, Sheriff. Check it out."

"I did! You want me to arrest you, Bailey? I said get out of here." The sheriff looked like he was about to have a stroke.

Rick bolted to his feet and stormed from the room. What a joke the law enforcement was here. The breeze did little to cool his mood. Sitting on a stone wall, he called Brendan. "Hey buddy, did you find out anything on Hernandez's family?"

"Cowboy, you never let up, do you?" Brendan laughed with a trace of annoyance. "That's what made you such a good operative though. And, yeah, I ran a check. It's pretty interesting. You might be onto something with him. He had a brother, Luis. A small-town bully who's been arrested a few times for drunk and disorderly and assault. After Hernandez died in prison, Luis went on a drinking binge. He threatened to get 'the bopper' who killed his brother."

Rick stood and paced along the sidewalk. "So he could be our man. Any idea where he is now?"

"We lost him in Albuquerque. I've got the police keeping a look-out for him there."

"So he's close. He could be in the area. Could you fax me a picture?"

"Sure, no problem."

"I've got two other guys for you to check out. Mark Haskell and Ted Rediger, both from El Paso." Rick gave him the details Allie had given him. "Haskell stalked her once, maybe he's back."

"I'll see what I can find out."

Rick put his phone away. The library was across the street. He dodged the cars and bounded up the steps of the stone building. There were several computers free, so he stopped at the first one and began to look for information on Allie's vision problem. The information astounded him. No wonder she hated doing paperwork. An hour later he'd ordered pinkish lenses and colored overlays for reading.

The thought of her delighted smile when she got them made him grin as he strode back to his truck.

ALLIE SWATTED THE DUST FROM HER JEANS AND SHIRT AS SHE WATCHED the kids ride. Rick should be back from town soon, and she couldn't help glancing toward the lane every few seconds. The realization of how important he was becoming to her scared her.

"Good form, Bets," she called. Her daughter sat with her back straight and her knees hugging the mare's body. Her dark curls flew around her laughing face.

The child could ride anything with four legs. Allie had never seen anything like her daughter's ability with animals.

Allie hadn't been able to think about anything but Rick all afternoon. His desire to stay together had rattled her to the core. Watching her daughter's carefree face, she knew she couldn't take the security Betsy felt here away from her.

And she didn't want to leave either.

The promise of the future was as joy-filled as a glimpse of Betsy's bluebirds. No place had ever been permanent though, and Allie couldn't wrap her mind around the fact that maybe this time could be forever.

What if she fell in love with Rick and he left her too? Jon hadn't wanted to leave, but God had taken him just the same. There were no guarantees in life.

"They're doing good," Charlie said, putting a boot on the fence beside hers.

"I can't believe how well. Look at Fern. She's got her head up and is smiling from ear to ear. And even Latoya doesn't seem to care about getting dirty."

"They go home in another couple of weeks. We'll see if they keep what they've learned."

Allie glanced at him curiously. "You sound a little jaded, Charlie. Don't you think the ranch helps kids?"

"Sure it does. Just not all of them. They have to plant their boots and refuse to be moved."

"Like you did?" She wondered why he never talked about his past.

"Sure, like I did. I figured out my course and stuck to it."

"Were you a foster kid?"

He shook his head. "I had both parents and a brother."

"So you weren't one of Elijah's pet projects." Allie smiled. "He was an interesting guy."

"I was at the rodeo looking for a job, and someone told me about him. The ranch is in the boonies, and not many cowboys want to work out here when it's hot. You wait until summer comes and you may run screaming for the city too."

"I'm from El Paso," she reminded him.

"Another desert jackrabbit," he said, grinning.

Stuck clear out here, he probably had little opportunity to meet young women, but at least he'd taken the hint after her marriage became open knowledge. The campers here were off-limits to staff, and she was too old. And married, to boot. Poor kid couldn't win.

"You still see your parents, your brother?"

"Sure. My brother especially. He's a congressman in northern Texas. He'll be president one day." His voice vibrated with pride.

Allie hid her smile. She guessed he had something to be proud of.

Leon cantered up to them and reined in his horse. "Dude! I wish I could take my horse back with me. The brothers would freak to see this big guy." He patted the black gelding on the neck.

"Scout out the riding stables in San Antonio," Charlie told him. "See if you can get a job there and stay around the horses."

Leon's dark eyes reflected interest. "They probably wouldn't hire me. Too chicken."

"I'll write you a reference," Allie said.

"Way!" Leon urged the horse forward and took off in a canter around the lot.

The sound of an engine made Allie turn, and she saw Rick's truck coming down the driveway.

The way her pulse rattled should have scared the horses.

17

THE MONDAY MORNING ALBUQUERQUE TRAFFIC WAS SNARLED WORSE THAN a mess of baby rattlers. Rick negotiated the rental car through the streets thick with the slush of a late-spring snow. It would take longer to get to his destination than it had taken him to fly the small plane from the ranch. He'd left before daylight this morning, and he hoped to be back by midafternoon, but not if this traffic had its way.

He found a small hole in the line of cars and zipped off the freeway. Glancing at the piece of paper on the passenger seat, he watched for the Raynolds housing addition. Five minutes later he parked at the address.

Trash littered the lawn of the small, southwestern-style apartment building. Gouges marked the front door, and a broken window upstairs blared the details of a knockdown, drag-out fight between a shouting man and a screaming woman.

Rick took another look at the picture Brendan had faxed him, then got out of the car and went to the door. He stepped inside and found the apartment number he was looking for. Doubling his fist, he pounded on the door.

The smell of onions and hamburger hung in the hallway. Behind the door, he could hear a baby crying. He knocked again, his knuckles scraping across the gouged wood. The door finally opened to reveal a young Hispanic woman with a baby on her hip. About twenty, she had the kind of beauty that made any man take a second look. Long black hair swung to her hips, and her skirt barely covered the tops of her thighs.

"I'm looking for Luis Hernandez," he said.

"Luis, a five-o is here for you," she shouted over her shoulder, her gaze never leaving his.

"I'm not a cop," he said quickly.

"No? You look like one." She stepped aside, and he entered the small living room. Everything was in perfect order, and the furniture gleamed.

A young man entered the room. Dressed in jeans and a clean T-shirt, his frown grew more worried when he saw Rick. "You looking for me?"

"If you're Luis Hernandez."

"*Sí*. That's me," he said in a heavy Hispanic accent.

Rick introduced himself. "Do you know Allie Siders?"

"*Sí*. She's the *muchacha* who wasted my brother. Sent him to prison, and he never come out."

"I heard you threatened to get even."

Luis shrugged. "*Sí*, so what? Someone kill her?"

"No, she's fine. I want to make sure she stays that way."

"I don't care about the *muchacha*. My brother, he dead now anyway. I have my own *bebé* to raise. I stay out of trouble."

Looking into the young man's dark, earnest eyes, Rick decided he believed him. He'd come all this way for a dead end. He thanked them both and hurried back to his car.

Once Brendan found out where Mark Haskell was, he'd talk to him too, but Rick was beginning to wonder if he was looking in the wrong direction. Maybe it was just some random nut who'd fixated on Allie.

He drove back to the airport, dropped the rental car, and walked out to the small plane. An hour later, he was back at the ranch with a day wasted and not one iota wiser. He couldn't stand to waste the day. Maybe he'd go to the library and look around on the Internet.

Before he went to his truck, he stopped by the corral and found Allie. She was teaching the kids about horse etiquette.

She joined him at the fence. "How'd it go?"

He shrugged. "It was a washout. I don't think he had anything to do with it." He saw the cloud pass over her face and quickly added, "but I'm going to go into town and try to locate that stock supplier guy, Ted Rediger. You need me for anything?"

"No, we're fine." She put her hand over his. "Thanks for trying, Rick. It means a lot."

"I'll be back in time for dinner." In the car, he realized he hadn't told her what the FBI said about Jon's parents knowing where she was. He made a mental note to talk to her about it once the adoption hearing was over tomorrow. No reason to worry her before then.

He went to his truck and drove to town. As he passed town hall, he saw a man in a suit exit the sheriff's office. Could it be Stuart Ifera?

Taking a chance, Rick pulled his truck to the curb and jumped out. "Mr. Ifera," he called.

The man turned and shaded his eyes from the sun with his hand. "Yes?"

Bingo.

Rick stopped two feet away from the man. Natty dresser. Tie perfectly aligned, pinstriped suit, shoes buffed to a high shine. He could have stepped out of one of those fancy men's magazines.

His high-powered cologne made Rick sneeze. He stuck his hand out. "Rick Bailey."

Ifera shook it. "What can I do for you?"

"I'm foreman out at the Bluebird." Rick watched the man's face change from curiosity to a guarded wariness.

"Terrible about Elijah," Ifera said. "Just terrible."

"You saw him the week before he died. He told me you made an offer on the ranch that he refused."

"What of it?" The man's shrug was delicate. "I make offers on land all the time."

"Were you angry he turned you down?"

Ifera laughed. "Not angry enough to kill him, if that's what you're implying." He swept his hand over the landscape. "Look around you, Mr. Bailey. Land isn't hard to come by out here."

"We're by the river with lush vegetation. I can see where it would be a nice place to set a resort. The park borders us on one side, which would be convenient. Not much available with those amenities."

"Perhaps not," Ifera conceded. "But really, I didn't want it bad enough to kill him. After all, the new owner wouldn't necessarily be ready to sell either."

"She's not. She's my daughter, and I'll make sure it's here for her when she's ready." It was a slightly premature statement since the adoption wouldn't be final until Friday.

"Of course." Ifera's head bobbed in agreement. "If that's all you have, I'm late for an appointment." He turned and scurried away, a rat back to his hole.

Rick's intense dislike of the man didn't keep him from recognizing that everything Ifera had said was true. There was plenty of land to be had in the area. Ifera didn't need the Bluebird.

THE DENIM SKIRT TOUCHED THE TOP OF HER BOOTS, BUT IT WAS LOOSE AT the waist. Allie hadn't realized she'd lost weight since she'd been here. Nearly a month. It was hard to believe how much her life had changed.

She fluffed up her hair in the mirror. Her ruffled white blouse looked pretty and demure, but dark circles marred the pale skin under her eyes.

The judge had to grant the adoption today. Once it was final, Betsy would be safe from Jon's parents.

Her hair refused to be tamed, and she swiped at the tendrils that sprang from her head, trying and failing to tuck them behind her ears. For a dollar, she'd cut it all off.

Her nails shone glossy and perfect. She was ready. Her knees shook as she grabbed her bag and went downstairs to join Rick in the entry. He'd been gone all day yesterday and had returned with a defeated air.

Standing by the front door with Betsy in his arms, he looked uncomfortable in his khakis and starched shirt. They'd explained everything to her last night, and she'd looked at Rick with shining eyes when he told her he would be her new daddy.

He'd wormed his way into Betsy's heart even faster than he got into Allie's.

"Ready?" he asked.

She put her hand on her stomach. "We'd better go."

He held open the door for her to step through, then followed her onto the porch. The sun stabbed knives into Allie's eyes, and she winced. "I should have brought my hat."

"I'll get it." Rick set Betsy on the porch and went back inside.

Allie shaded her eyes with her hand and looked out to the purple cast of hills. A glint of sun on glass made her close her eyes. She slitted them open again and saw a familiar car come careening up the lane.

Everything in her tensed. "Not now," she whispered as the car came to a stop and her in-laws erupted from the vehicle.

"My baby!" Erika Siders ran toward the porch with her arms outstretched.

Allie couldn't remember ever seeing Erika wear anything other than a sensible gray or black dress that came to the bottom curve of her calf, and today was no exception. The thin blond hair was pulled back in a severe bun, and not a stitch of makeup brightened her pale face. Somehow dust found the nerve to settle on the sensible pumps on her mother-in-law's feet.

The controlled appearance was an effort to deny the squalor Erika had grown up in, but Allie knew the effects of that upbringing festered under the pristine surface.

Hugh Siders followed his wife more slowly. A black suit encased his tall, lanky frame. Gold-frame glasses perched on his nose, and he walked with determination toward Allie and Betsy. He could have passed for the most austere of undertakers.

Betsy pressed back against Allie's legs, then attempted to climb her skirt. Allie scooped her up. "Shh, it's okay," she whispered.

"You had no right," Erika said, her initial loud voice modulating to a cultured purr. "How could you disappear without telling us where you'd gone?" She held out her hands. "Come see Grandma, Betsy," she said.

Betsy buried her face in Allie's neck. "You should have called first," Allie said. "We've got an appointment in town."

"Oh, I know all about the appointment." Hugh arrived at the bottom of the porch and shook his finger at her. "It can't be allowed, you know."

"You have no say in it. I'm married now." Exquisite relief flooded her when she heard Rick's boots on the floor behind her.

"What's going on here?" he asked.

"These are Jon's parents," Allie said, hiking Betsy a little higher.

Rick nodded. "Rick Bailey. Your son was like a brother to me," he said. "But we've got an appointment in town. Feel free to wander around the ranch. We'll be back in a couple of hours."

His fingers touched Allie's elbow and helped break her paralysis. They moved to the steps, but Hugh and Erika still blocked the path.

"The appointment will have to be canceled. We dropped the kidnapping charge, but we won't let you adopt our granddaughter."

Rick's jaw flexed. He stepped out a foot ahead of Allie and shouldered through the couple. Hugh reeled back, his face going red. He made a grab for Betsy, who seized Allie's neck in a death grip.

Rick stepped between them. "I don't want to have to get rough, but you're scaring Betsy."

While Rick blocked the Siders couple, Allie ran with Betsy to the truck. She got inside and clicked the lock. The muted sounds of Hugh's raised voice and Rick's quick, commanding tones filtered through the window. What would she have done if Rick wasn't there? The Siderses always made her feel useless and damaged. It was hard to stand up against that kind of mental pressure, though she always managed to survive their insinuations.

Erika went flying back to their car, and Hugh stalked back as well with his fists clenched. Rick slid into the truck and jammed the key into the dash. Allie's hands shook as she fastened Betsy's seat belt.

"Where are they going?" Allie asked as the car peeled away in front of them with dust spuming from under the tires.

"To the courthouse," he said grimly. He tromped on the accelerator, and the truck fishtailed before the tires found purchase.

Out on the open road, he followed close behind the Siderses car, then made a sharp right turn onto a dirt road. "Shortcut," he said, his lips lifting in a grim smile.

"Can they stop us?" she asked.

"I don't think so."

From the way his hands gripped the wheel and the tightness of his jaw, she knew he was worried, in spite of his reassuring words.

She should have known things would go south at the last minute. This time, she'd fight with every ounce of strength she had to protect Betsy.

"They're really something, aren't they?" Rick said after a long pause.

The truck bucked like a wild mustang along the potholes. Allie grabbed the armrest to steady herself. "They've always interfered a lot. It drove Jon crazy."

"He told me about his childhood."

Allie nodded, glancing down to see that Betsy had put her earphones on. Even though he'd probably heard it, she needed to talk it out. "They had eight to ten foster kids at any one time, mostly for the money, Jon always thought. He was pretty much neglected and left to run wild. He never thought they cared about him except as an extension of themselves. He warned me that if anything happened to him, they'd try to get Betsy."

"But why? Sounds like they have plenty of other kids around."

She shrugged. "I think they want to make sure she's raised 'right' by their standards. Their brand of Christianity allows for picking and choosing what they want, like a smorgasbord. Their favorite saying is, 'Spare the rod, spoil the child.' Jon got his share of the razor strap." She looked at him sideways. "You might know something about that." When he didn't answer, she said, "They put on a great show at church and for the court, but at home there was always shouting and fighting."

A quick glance from under his brows at her, then he turned his attention back to the road. "Don't let them shake your confidence, Allie. You're doing a great job with Betsy."

"She still doesn't talk. Maybe it's my fault." She reached out and smoothed Betsy's dark curls.

"We're getting through. She's going to talk a blue streak one of these days. She's so much more animated than she was when she first came. Excitement is going to cause some words to come bubbling out eventually."

"I keep praying that happens."

Another quick glance from Rick. "Speaking of praying, I made an appointment with my pastor for us to have some marriage counseling. We go for our first session after the hearing."

She gulped. "Marriage counseling?"

He nodded without adding anything more.

"The pastor looked familiar, like I'd met him before. He's a nice guy."

"You did meet him, early in the week you came here. He's our vet too."

"Pastor O'Sullivan is a vet?"

"The church is too small to support a full-time pastor. Grady is a real man of God and was called to do both. Counseling with him should be easy."

"I didn't realize we were fighting," she said, sending a teasing smile his way.

He shot an answering grin back. "We want to keep it that way. I thought some counseling might help us learn to know each other a little faster."

Her voice softened. "I—I'm a little scared, Rick."

"Me too," he admitted. "I don't know how to be a husband or a dad. I've got a lot to learn. Getting a solid foundation can't do anything but help us."

Warmth flooded Allie. It took a lot of guts for him to admit his feelings of inadequacy. He felt as unprepared as she did. Maybe together they could bungle along and find their way.

THE COURTROOM FELT COLD AND DRAFTY. RICK HELD ALLIE'S HAND AND stood as the judge entered. So far he'd seen no sign of the Siderses, and he prayed they'd lost their way.

"Good morning," the judge said, adjusting her glasses on the end of her nose. Judge Thompson peered at them over the top of her spectacles. "Rick, you're a good man to be willing to take on this burden."

"It's not a burden, Your Honor. I'm eager to be a permanent part of Betsy's life." Rick felt Allie squeeze his fingers, and he returned the pressure.

"I've reviewed the documents and see no reason not to grant this request." The judge looked down at Betsy standing beside Allie. "Do you want a new daddy, young lady?"

Betsy nodded, and her smile blossomed out. She looked up at Rick with an adoring expression.

The judge laughed. "You always were someone the ladies liked, Rick."

"Stop!" The sound came from the door, and a fresh breeze blew in with the words.

Allie turned to see Hugh and Erika hurry into the courtroom and rush toward the judge's bench. *Oh no.* She wanted to grab her daughter and run from the room.

"What's the meaning of this interruption?" The judge frowned and glared over the top of her glasses at the intruders.

"We're Betsy's grandparents," Hugh said, his voice loud and strident. He pointed a finger at Allie. "She sneaked away when she heard we were suing for custody of Betsy. She's unfit to raise her, Your Honor." He raised a file of papers. "All the evidence is in here."

Allie gripped Rick's hand in a convulsive clutch.

Rick returned the pressure. "Judge Thompson is too smart to fall for this," he whispered to her.

She took courage from his words and tipped her face up to the judge. "That's not true, Your Honor. I'm a good mother."

"Did you know they were filing for custody?"

Allie wanted to look away from the judge's penetrating stare, but she forced herself to look the woman in the eye. "Yes, but I came here for Betsy. I'd heard about the ranch and thought it might be able to help her."

"And she came to be with me, Your Honor," Rick put in.

A smile flitted across the judge's face, then disappeared. "Be that as it may, I'll need time to review the custody suit. If I deem they have a case, I'll order it argued in court."

"But, Your Honor," Rick protested. "We're a family. The uncertainty isn't good for Betsy."

The judge waved her hand. "I'm sure you have nothing to worry about, but I have to review the case. Betsy's future depends on my making the right decision. The court will reconvene in a week, and I'll give you my opinion then." She smacked the gavel down. "Court adjourned."

The triumph on Hugh's face made Rick want to put his fist through it. Silent tears coursed down Betsy's face, and she pressed her cheek against his leg. He swept her into his arms. "It doesn't matter," he whispered into her hair. "The judge will fix things next week. You're not to worry, okay?"

She nodded, her wet cheek brushing his face. His gaze locked with Allie's, and he silently promised her everything would be all right.

18

A FEW CARS ROLLED THROUGH TOWN, THEIR WINDOWS DOWN AND MUSIC blaring from CD players. There was no radio reception out here. Allie stood beside Rick and Betsy on the sidewalk as the few pedestrians walked around them. The Siderses were smiling with triumph.

Allie wanted to hurt them.

All the plans, the excitement of the last few days, blew away like tumbleweeds. She'd tried so hard not to let this happen. The last thing Betsy needed was to be in the middle of this turmoil. She'd made such progress the last month, and Allie couldn't bear to see it slip away.

"We'd like to take Betsy to dinner," Erika said. "Is there any place to eat in this one-horse town?"

"The drugstore has milk shakes and hamburgers," Rick said. "And there's a small café. But we can't let you take Betsy. To tell you the truth, I'm not convinced you wouldn't just get her in the car and keep driving."

Erika's fair skin lit with pink. "Please. What do you think we are?" She held up her hand. "Don't answer that. It's obvious." She turned her gaze on Allie. "Surely you won't deny us the opportunity to spend some time with Betsy."

Allie had never wanted to deny them the right to see their granddaughter. Betsy was all they had left of Jon, but their actions had altered the situation. "I can't let you take her. But you can join us for supper at the ranch."

Erika's brown eyes, so like Jon's, softened as they studied Allie's face. "That will do. Can I bring anything? And what hotel should we stay in?"

"There isn't a hotel in the area," Rick said.

Erika's face clouded. "Where is the nearest?"

"Twenty miles." Rick jabbed his finger to the north. "That way."

Allie's conscience was beginning to bother her. They'd come all this way to fight for Betsy. No child could get too much love. She'd do the best she could to be friendly and encouraging. Maybe they could resolve this out of court.

"You don't need to bring anything," she told Erika.

Hugh took his wife's arm. "We'll go see about that hotel."

His tone had softened too. Now that the urgency of the moment had passed, everyone seemed to be taking a step back and thinking about their reactions. Allie took heart. Maybe they could find their way through this amicably.

Once Jon's parents got in their car and drove away, Rick said, "Our first counseling meeting is in a few minutes. You up for it?"

Not really. Allie just nodded. She felt too upset to deal with anything else, but Rick had gone to all the trouble to set this up, and he
was trying so hard.

"Grady lives just down the street by the church. We can walk."
Rick hefted Betsy to his shoulders.

Allie followed him down the street. The day had turned warm, at
least ninety even though it was late March. Rick turned up the walk
of a two-story stone house that had vines growing up the sides. A welcome wreath decorated the cheery red door, and a scarecrow made
out of the same vines stood beside the entrance.

The scent of honeysuckle wafted their way from somewhere. Rick
pressed the doorbell, and a pretty blond with uncontrollable curls
opened the door.

"Rick! I've missed you." She patted him on the arm and looked up
at Betsy on Rick's shoulders. "You must be Betsy. I've got a little girl
about your age. Her name is Courtney. She's been looking forward to
playing with you."

"Allie, this is Dolly O'Sullivan," Rick said.

Dolly turned her bright smile on Allie, then hugged her. "Don't
stand on the doorstep. I've been dying to meet the woman who managed to snatch Rick from the open market. I'm usually in the church
nursery and don't always get to meet the visitors." She stood aside to
allow them to enter.

A little girl with fiery red hair and big hazel eyes stood in the hallway. Her gaze went to Betsy, and she smiled. Betsy smiled back as
Rick set her on the floor.

"Say hello, Courtney," Dolly said.

"Hi," Courtney said. "I made a fort in my room. You want to see it?"

Betsy nodded, and Courtney took her hand. The two girls went down the hall. Allie stared after them. Betsy hadn't had a friend her own age to play with in ages. Could that make a difference?

She realized with a start that Dolly had been speaking to her. "I'm sorry?"

"I wondered if you'd like some coffee or tea?"

"Tea would be great."

"Iced or hot?"

"Iced today. Can I help you fix it?"

"No, no, come on into the living room." Dolly led the way to a large living room with overstuffed furniture.

Watercolors decorated the walls, and baskets of flowers were on every table, along with small wooden handcrafts. Some held eucalyptus, and the entrancing scent filled the room. The tables were all distressed wood, washed in white. A very country-looking place, warm and inviting.

Allie sank onto a sofa that threatened to swallow her. "This is lovely. I love the pictures."

"She painted them," a man said, stepping into the room through a swinging door that had small handprints painted on the white surface. "She's always dabbling in something." He beamed proudly at his wife, then approached Allie with his hand out. "Hello, Allie. It's good to see you again."

Allie shook his hand. "You did a good job with the mare. I think she's going to make it." The guy exuded confidence. With his help, maybe their marriage would make it too. "And I enjoyed the message last week."

"Thanks. It's good to have you in church." He shook Rick's hand and slapped him on the shoulder. "Cowboy, how could you get married behind my back? You surprised me, bucko." He settled into a recliner. "We can talk in here as easy as my office. It's probably more comfortable."

Rick's bulk sank onto the sofa beside Allie, and the depression rolled her toward him. He put his arm around her shoulders. The warmth of his body soaked into her like sunshine. It felt good to be cared for. She could get used to it.

Grady folded his arms. "We've got a lot to discuss. You two are basically strangers, isn't that right?"

Allie nodded, though Rick felt anything but a stranger now. His presence had quickly grown to be a comfort and a thrill at the same time.

"There are all sorts of potential landmines ahead," Grady said. "You need to work out how you'll handle things like conflicts over money, childrearing, housekeeping, even watching TV." He grinned and nod-ded at Rick. "In case you haven't realized it yet, Cowboy here is a sports nut. He'd watch any sport on TV until he turned into a turnip."

"I've noticed," she said.

Rick grinned. "Hey, she's got her quirks too. I just have to figure out what they are."

"I've got a form for you to fill out. We'll start with that. I want you to list your likes and dislikes, your pet peeves, your faults. There are also some questions for you to answer about how you were raised. We'll identify the trouble spots and talk them out over the next few weeks."

Allie thought she might actually enjoy it until she saw Rick exchange a long look with Grady. She knew so little about her new husband, but it looked like there might be something in his past he didn't want her to know. If it had to do with the scars on his back, she felt only sympathy.

I<small>T WAS ALL GOING TO COME OUT</small>. R<small>ICK KNEW HE DIDN'T HAVE A SNOW</small>-ball's chance of keeping it from her. And even if he could, he knew he shouldn't if he wanted the marriage to work. Still, anticipating having to tell her, he wanted to stop at the Long Branch and get a tall cold one.

Some days he got tired of fighting the desire to drink. He could give in, let the liquor numb the pain and guilt that gnawed at him every day of his life. God had forgiven him, but he couldn't forgive himself, and the whiskey helped him forget it.

He shoved the thoughts away, refusing to entertain them. Staying sober meant keeping his thoughts positive.

Allie didn't have much to say as they started for home. He pointed the truck to the hills between town and the ranch. The truck felt a little sluggish, and he made a mental note to give it a tune-up. It was overdue.

Spring this year had been lush so far. Cactus and wildflowers bloomed along the roadside as far as he could see. The tension eased from his shoulders. He took his right hand off the wheel and stretched it across the seat, his arm brushing the top of Betsy's head, letting his fingers tangle in Allie's hair.

She turned and smiled at him. Then it happened.

The truck lurched to the right, and he saw the front right wheel go rolling off into the ditch. The screech of metal on pavement nearly deafened him. The vehicle careened toward the embankment, and as he fought the wheel, jamming on the brakes to no avail, he heard Allie scream.

The truck tilted to the right, and he prayed that it wouldn't roll. Allie's door would be crushed in. The wheel bucked and jerked in his hands like a wild bull. The scenery rushed past, but he managed to keep the truck on the road as he sent a shout up to God for help.

Dead Gulch Curve was just up ahead. The road tilted to the right, and the vehicle with it. Rick wrenched the truck to the left, then saw an SUV coming toward him in the opposite lane. He veered back to the right, and the vehicle roared toward the ditch.

A large boulder jutted out from the rock face into the drop-off. He wasn't going to be able to miss it.

"Hang on!" With his foot buried in the brake pedal, he aimed for a glancing blow. From the corner of his eye, he saw sparks fly up from the right front end.

The truck slammed into the boulder in what seemed like slow motion. Allie flung out her arm to protect Betsy, and Rick's right arm did the same. Their hands locked across the little girl as the cab crumpled like a candy wrapper and folded in accordion style.

The three of them rocked forward, and he heard Allie's head strike the glass, a sickening sound that made him tighten his fingers on hers.

The silence after the wild ride was eerie. The only sound was the engine ticking as it cooled. Then the horn began to blare in a nightmarish, never-ending alarm.

"Allie? You okay?" Rick's gaze touched Betsy, who was sobbing and touching her mother's arm, trying to shake her. His attention moved on to his wife. His gut clenched when he saw the bright splash of blood on the window, and the way it had shattered to a star.

Her eyes were closed, and blood ran down her face from a cut on her forehead. "Allie?" He reached over Betsy and touched her face. Her eyes still didn't open.

Digging out his cell phone, he dialed 9-1-1, but even as he reported the accident, he knew he'd have to help her now. It would take an ambulance forever to get here.

The SUV in the opposite lane had stopped as well, and a man leaped out and jogged over to Rick's truck. "You okay?"

"My wife is hurt," Rick said through his shattered window. He was trying not to panic and wasn't doing a very good job of it.

"I'm a physician's assistant. Let me take a look at her." The man went around to the other side of the truck and tugged on the door. "It's stuck. I'll have to come in from your side." The man moved back to Rick's door and opened it with Rick's help.

Rick unfastened Betsy's seat belt and pulled her out with him. The other driver crawled inside the truck, and Rick began to pray.

19

Every bone ached like she'd been thrown from a bucking bronco. Allie tried to open her eyes, but they felt glued shut. Her face felt swollen. Had she fallen from a horse?

She tried to move and groaned when the pain intensified. Even the softness of the sheets scraped her wounded face.

"Lie still," Rick's voice spoke in her ear. His hand smoothed her hair.

"Wha-what happened?" She managed to get her eyes open.

"We had an accident."

Her memory flooded back. The wheel coming off, the crash. "Betsy!" She tried to rise up.

"She's fine." His hands pressed her back against the pillow.

She squinted through slitted eyes. The sunlight filtered through blinds in an unfamiliar room. "Where am I?"

"The hospital in Alpine. You've got a concussion."

She managed to focus on Rick's face. Drawn and wearing a worried frown, he sat in a chair pulled up to the side of her bed. "Where's Betsy?"

"Grady and Dolly took her. I told them to be careful to watch her," he said when she frowned.

"I need to get out of here. She needs me." Panic raced across her face again. "Jon's parents. Where are they?"

"I don't know. They probably went to the house for dinner, but we never made it home."

"Make sure Grady knows not to let them have Betsy." She struggled against his hands again. "I've got to get out of here."

"The doctors haven't released you yet," he said.

"I don't care. I want to go home." Strange that she thought of the ranch as home already. She knew she couldn't resist the pressure of his hands. "Could I have some water?"

When he turned to get her water glass, she rose from the pillow and swung her feet to the side of the bed. Her head swam, but she began pulling the needles out of her arms. The blackness receded, and the nausea began to subside. Her head still ached, but it wasn't enough to stop her from getting to her daughter.

"Stop! What are you doing?" Rick sprang toward her, spilling the water in the cup onto her lap.

With all the needles out, she stood, though shaky. "I'm going home. Where are my clothes?" Blood trickled down her arm from the holes left by the IVs.

"Mrs. Bailey, what are you doing?" A nurse's rubber soles squeaked on the floor as she rushed into the room. She grabbed at Allie's arm.

Allie shook her off, practically falling into Rick. She looked up at him, letting him see all her hope and desperation. "I can't stay here. Betsy needs me."

"She's fine, Allie." Rick took her by the shoulders. "I wouldn't let anything happen to her."

"You're here," she pointed out. "Two hours away from her." She pulled away from his grip and nearly fell. "Where are my clothes? I'm checking myself out."

The nurse bit her lip and glanced at Rick. "We don't have the right to keep her," she said, her tone apologetic. "You'll have to sign a paper stating you are leaving against the advice of your doctor," she told Allie. She dug white tape out of the pocket on her smock. "Let me stop the bleeding."

Allie held out her arm. "Hurry, please. My clothes?"

The nurse put a cotton ball and tape over her wrist and pressed it down. "They were cut off you. I'm afraid there's not much left of them." She went to the small closet and drew out a plastic bag full of material. She unzipped it and pulled out the remains of Allie's denim skirt and blouse. "They're not wearable."

"I can't go home naked." For such a small problem, it felt overwhelming, and Allie wanted to sit on the edge of the bed and burst into tears. She gritted her teeth and forced back her emotion.

"I can give you another gown to put on backward," the nurse said. "Just a minute." She disappeared through the door.

"Have a little trust," Rick said. "Grady and Dolly will take care of Betsy."

"She's going to be beside herself, Rick. I'm sure she saw the ambulance cart me off all bloody and unconscious."

"I called and had Grady put her on the phone. I told her you were going to be okay."

"That's not the same as seeing me. I'm fine, it's just a concussion." In truth, her head was hurting more and more, and she felt dizzy and disoriented. But she'd be all right when she got home in her own bed.

"Here, you can talk to her." He pulled out his phone and punched in the number. "Grady? Put Bets on again." He waited a moment, then passed the phone over to her.

"Betsy? It's Mommy. I just wanted you to know I'm okay. I'm coming to get you, okay?" She could hear breathing on the other end and the sound of a sob. "Mommy's okay, sweetie. Don't you worry. You have fun with Courtney."

A moment later Grady came on the line. "She's smiling, Allie. You sure you're okay?"

"Just sore. We're coming after her now."

"You're sure the doctors say you can?"

"The doctors don't know everything. Listen, Grady, if Jon's parents try to take Betsy with them, don't let them have her."

"I won't. She's safe with us, Allie. Rest easy."

"Thanks." She closed the phone and handed it to Rick.

He slipped it into his pocket. "I wish you'd stay. She knows you're okay now."

"I'll be better in my own bed."

And when she held Betsy.

She gave him a curious stare. "How'd you get here with the truck disabled?"

"Charlie came and got me in your pickup. I dropped him at the ranch and came on here."

Allie winced at the thought of a ride back in the old rattletrap truck littered with grain and smelling of horse manure. "What happened? It's all a little fuzzy."

He narrowed his eyes, and his mouth took on a grim slant. "It's pretty strange. The lug nuts didn't break off, which is what I thought at first. But I took a look at the bolts, and they're perfectly fine. I couldn't find any of the lugs laying around in the ditch or the road either."

"A-are you saying someone took the lugs off?"

"I'm suspicious," he said. "That truck's only a year old. I rotated the tires a month ago. Everything was fine. The truck was parked in town for hours. I guess someone could have tampered with it."

All the blood rushed to her feet, and she swayed where she stood. Rick grabbed her arm. "I have to get to Betsy," she said. "She's in danger."

"Grady will take care of her." Though he protested, a worried frown formed between his eyes.

The nurse returned with another gown. "You're making a mistake," she said, holding it out for Allie to slip into.

By the time Allie signed the papers and Rick helped her to the truck, she was shaking with fatigue, and her head felt like it was as big as the boulder they'd hit. It was hard to think past the pain, and she had to keep swallowing down the bile that burned the back of her throat.

She could do this. Betsy had to be protected.

"You can put your head on my lap," Rick said, shooting her a concerned glance.

"Maybe I will." She put on the lap belt, then loosened it enough to crumple onto the seat, her head on the hard muscles of his leg. "Not exactly the softest pillow I've ever laid on," she said, turning her head and smiling up at him.

"Sorry." He drove with one hand on the wheel, and his right hand came down to settle on her shoulder as if to keep her safe.

Even Jon wasn't this protective. Allie had never felt so treasured and cared for. Why did he do it? He couldn't love her, not yet. She didn't quite get it, and though she wanted to ask, the words hid in the back of her throat.

He must have sensed her emotion, because he looked down with his eyebrows winging up. "Something wrong?"

"How can you act this way toward me?" She blurted the words out before she could lose her nerve.

"What way?"

"So sweet—and loving. You don't love me." She watched his face to see if it would give away his emotions. Rick was so hard for her to read. She'd never met anyone like him.

He was silent for so long, she began to think he wasn't going to answer her. Warmth radiated down through his arm and fingers and transferred to her shoulder.

"I haven't had a lot of unconditional love in my life," he said. "Only from God. Grady said something from the pulpit once I've never forgotten. He said, 'Love isn't an emotion, it's an action.' I figure if I *act* with love toward you, I might start feeling it."

Allie had never heard such a thing before. "Not an emotion? What did he mean?"

Rick shrugged. "You should have him tell you. He's better at explaining stuff like that. But I took it to mean that the giddy feelings can come and go. I think he called that infatuation. Real love means I go to work when I'd rather stay home in bed. Real love puts up with burned dinner and no clean underwear." He grinned when she grimaced. "He said love is an action verb. So I decided if we were going to stay married, I'd work out the love and wait for the giddy emotion."

He was basically saying she didn't give him the butterflies she felt even now flying around her insides, and she wasn't sure whether to be offended or to hug him. The thought of steadfast care and support felt like a safety net she'd never had. Her mother had always preferred Allie's sister, who was as good a barrel racer as she'd ever seen. Though she was loved, Allie always felt she came up lacking.

Rick didn't seem to be comparing her against anyone, and she'd been comparing him to Jon constantly. Jon was two years in his grave, and she was still alive. Could it be all right to accept what Rick offered? For the first time, she didn't shudder at the thought of letting down Jon's memory.

"So you're not attracted to me?" She couldn't help but remember the kiss they'd shared in the meadow, a kiss that nearly ignited a prairie fire.

"I didn't say that." His grin widened. "I'm a red-blooded male, you know. And you're a beautiful woman. But real love isn't about chemistry. Or at least not *only* about chemistry. If it were, when I've got a pot belly and you've got a turkey neck, we'll want to go look for someone younger. I want more than that from a marriage."

So did she.

And she was only beginning to realize how much.

RICK SAT IN THE OFFICE WITH HIS FEET ON THE DESK LATE INTO THE night. He hadn't wanted to tell Allie how worried he was about the accident two days ago. It was all he could handle to keep the Siderses from hauling off Betsy, and to get Allie to stay in bed. At least the pain meds had kept her worry at bay.

But not his.

Someone had made a deliberate attempt to harm them and almost succeeded. The doctor told him that if she'd hit her head just a little harder, she would have fractured her skull. He couldn't wait for Brendan or the sheriff to figure out who was behind this. First thing tomorrow he'd go see the border patrol. Maybe they had some new information.

He heard the soft movement of bare feet on the wood floor. Removing his feet from the desk, he stepped to the door and peered through the dark house. A shadowy movement came on the stairs, and he saw Latoya tiptoeing to the landing.

She was fully dressed in jeans and carried her shoes in one hand. She reeked of perfume, some flowery scent that made his eyes water when he got closer.

"What are you doing?" he asked.

She jumped, and her shoes clattered on the floor. Retrieving them, she turned and shook her finger at him. "You scared me out of an inch of nail growth."

"I repeat, what are you doing? If I didn't know better, I'd think you were sneaking out to meet someone."

She tossed her head, and her black cornrows bobbed. "What if I am? Whatcha going to do about it, boss man? Turn me in?"

Rick stepped closer to her. "Nothing," he said. "You're nearly an adult, Latoya. If you're going to make something of your life, you're the only one who can choose your actions. I could make you march back upstairs, but that would just make you resentful. Instead, I want you to think before you walk out that door. The direction of your life hinges on the choices you make."

Her dark eyes never left his face, and he saw the defiance slip out of her tense shoulders and tightly clenched fists.

"You don't know what it's like," she said, plopping down on the bottom step. "To want to *be* someone, to have someone love you."

"Sex isn't love, girl. I think you know that by now. And I *do* know what it's like." He moved to join her. "Move over." She scooted over, and he sat down beside her. "I was where you are once. Only instead of sex, my drug of choice was whiskey. It cost me my best friend and my self-respect. You're young enough to stop that downward spiral. You've got a lot on the ball—you're smart, pretty, enthusiastic. If you want to make people respect you, you've got to respect yourself first."

"Easy for you to say," she said. "My mama brings home her boyfriends. They . . . do things to me."

"You don't live there now. Take back your life, Latoya. Don't let the nightmares of the past destroy it."

She lowered her head, and he caught the glint of a tear on her cheek. Anything he said now would be too much. All he could do is let her think it through.

"You got a way with words," she said grudgingly. "Do you really think I'm smart?"

"I do. And you've got a way with the animals. That shows a lot of heart."

She fell silent again for a few long moments, then she slowly rose with her shoes in hand and turned to go back up the stairs. "Mornin' will be here too soon. I'm going back to bed."

"Good girl. I'm proud of you."

"Whatever. It's just one day."

"It only takes one day at a time. Believe me, I know." He watched her sashay back upstairs. It was so easy to dispense advice and so hard to live by it.

When was he going to let go of his past? All it took was a choice like Latoya had made tonight. God had forgiven him—he had no doubt about that. It was time he forgave himself.

He bowed his head and vowed to make a choice this one day to let go of the guilt.

20

SHE WOULDN'T EVEN NEED MAKEUP TO BE A RODEO CLOWN. ALLIE PEERED
through swollen lids at her reflection in the mirror. Purple dis-
coloration bloomed around her eyes and forehead. Her lips looked
swollen too. A large goose egg jutted from her forehead.

It was enough to frighten little children.

She pulled on her jeans, wincing at the pain the movements
caused. Betsy watched her with big, scared eyes. "It's okay," she told
her daughter. "It looks worse than it is. I'm fine. My muscles are just
sore like when I work hard all day."

After two days, this soreness should have been gone. She should
be moving around by now instead of letting everyone force her to
stay in bed.

She held out her hand to Betsy, and the little girl climbed off the bed and came to her. "Let's go fix breakfast," she told her. "Everyone will be starved, and I need to get everything back to normal. I can't stay in this room another minute. I might scream. Want to hear me scream, Bets?"

Betsy giggled, putting her hand over her mouth. She nodded. Allie smiled back. "Ah!" she screamed.

Betsy giggled again. A giggle was a sound. It was the promise of hope.

When Allie opened her bedroom door, she could smell the aroma of bacon. "Guess they thought they were going to make me stay up here another day," she said. Her head felt clear for the first time in three days, but she took her time getting down the steps to the kitchen.

Rick stood at the stove with a fork in his hand. When the frying bacon popped, he winced and put the back of his hand to his mouth. The bacon was beginning to smell a little burned. Jem sat at his feet with his tongue hanging out.

"You practicing for the fire department?" she asked.

He whipped around and pointed the fork at her. "You're supposed to be resting. I can handle this."

"Uh-huh, I think your bacon is burning."

He turned back around with an exclamation and began to fork up the bacon onto a plate. A few pieces fell to the floor, and Jem gobbled them up.

Allie chuckled to herself and moved to the stove. She bumped him out of the way. "Scoot before you have to break out the big hoses." Plucking the fork from his hand, she turned off the heat and moved the skillet away so she could get the bacon to the plate. Half-cooked scrambled eggs were mounded in a bowl on the counter. The congealed mess looked hardly edible.

Allie got out a fresh skillet, transferred a little bacon drippings from the old skillet and dumped the eggs back in to finish cooking. The bacon was a little overdone but salvageable. "You can fix some toast," she said.

He gave her a shamefaced grin and took the bread out of the breadbox. "I'm a lousy cook."

"I noticed." Smiling made her face hurt, but in a good way.

God had protected all of them, and she was alive. There was much to be thankful for.

"Did things go well with Jon's parents and Betsy?" she asked. She vaguely remembered their brief visit in her room.

"They only stayed an hour. Betsy seemed afraid of them. Has she not been around them much?"

"We used to visit every week, but they're so loud and bossy that they scare her. And me," she admitted. "Sunday dinners were just painful. Betsy could never sit quietly enough or eat nicely enough. I quit going about three months ago except for an occasional visit. They might be her grandparents, but they weren't helping her get well. She'd wet the bed for two nights after every visit."

Rick put his big hand on her shoulder. "They won't get her away from us," he said.

Smiling up at him, she thought about how she'd misjudged him the night they met. For all his size, his gentleness and caring were rare.

And very appealing.

Rick called the rest of the bunch for breakfast. Latoya seemed unusually quiet, and even the boys were morose. Fern didn't say anything, but that wasn't unusual.

"What's with everyone?" Allie asked. "You'd think someone died."

The kids just looked at one another, then their gazes went back to their plates. Allie met Rick's gaze across the table. He shrugged and raised his brows as if to say he didn't know what was up.

"One week, and we're checkin' out," Devon said finally. "Gotta go back to the city."

Latoya put out her lip. "I wanted to learn to barrel race first."

"How about if I teach you before you leave?" Allie stood and began to clear the table.

"You're not well enough to do much with that," Rick said, taking the plates from her hands. "Go rest."

"I'm not an invalid." She tried to snatch the plates back, but he held them up out of her reach.

"Then go do your book work."

Her hands fell to her sides. She was so far behind on that book work. Did he know? She examined his face. There was something in his eyes that made her wonder if he realized how out of her element she was with paperwork.

"I'll do that," she said evenly. She turned to the teenagers. "You guys go curry the horses and get them saddled. We'll practice some barrel racing."

"Can I take Betsy with me?" Fern asked in her soft voice.

Allie grappled with the thought of Betsy being out of her sight. "She'd better stay with me."

"I'll be out there," Rick said. "It's okay."

Allie opened her mouth to protest, then closed it again. Rick had been on her to quit coddling Bets, and he was right. Nothing would happen to her daughter with Rick there.

"I'll guard her with my life. You know that."

Allie nodded. "I'll be out in a little while." She headed to the office, and her head began to ache with every step toward the torture chamber. The bright sunlight cast spears of pain into her eyes, and she crossed the room to close the blinds. When she turned back to the desk, she saw a box on it.

It was addressed to her. Dread seized her throat. Could it be another message from the killer?

Taking a step back, she stared at it. She wasn't going to let him terrorize her. She grabbed a letter opener and held it like a knife. Flipping it around, she slit the tape and opened the box. She didn't want to look inside.

He might have put a dead snake or something in it.

She should probably call Rick, but she told herself not to be a ninny. It was only a package. Snapping open the top, she peered inside. Wads of bubble wrap obscured the contents. Unable to help herself, she popped a bubble before lifting it out. Under it was an eyeglass case. Under that was a folder.

A movement by the door caught her eye, and she looked up to see Rick leaning against the doorjamb with Betsy in his arms. They were both smiling.

"Open the case," he said, crossing the room to join her at the desk. He set Betsy on the floor.

"This is from you?"

He nodded. "It's to celebrate our new beginning." His smile widened.

Then she realized what this was. "Overlays for reading, and pink glasses?" She didn't wait for him to answer but picked up the case and opened it. The glasses were as precious as gold. She perched them on her nose, and the soft color washed the hard glare out of her vision.

"Rick, they're wonderful." She whirled and leaped at him. He caught her, and she wrapped her arms around his neck. "Thank you, thank you!" Before she could have second thoughts, she kissed him.

His lips were firm and gentle. She pulled away and looked into his eyes. "It's the nicest present anyone ever got me."

"I'm glad," he whispered.

"You can put me down now." Her feet dangled at least eight inches off the floor.

"What if I don't want to?" He grinned, but his eyes told her he was serious. He brushed her lips with a soft kiss, then set her on the floor.

Allie stepped away and looked around the room. Her eyes widened as she took in details of the room she'd missed before. The soft patina of oak bookshelves, the detail in the oriental rug on the floor. "Everything is so much clearer!"

"Glad they help you." He shoved his hands into the pockets of his jeans.

"How'd you get them?"

"Ordered them online at the library. I want to give you what you need," he said.

Her exuberance gave way to self-consciousness. Did he expect something from her for them? She wasn't ready to do anything more than share a quick kiss.

His gaze searched hers as if he were looking for something. A heavy sigh eased out. She wasn't quite sure what he'd hoped to see, but it hurt that she'd disappointed him.

The light in his eyes dimmed. He took Betsy's hand and disappeared from the room. Allie sighed and got to work. She found the book work a breeze with her new eyeglasses and the overlays. The numbers and letters didn't jump around, and she quickly input the data in the account book and wrote the checks for the bills.

It only took an hour, then she shut the book and locked it in the desk. The kids would be ready for their first barrel-racing lesson. She stepped to the door. The phone rang, and she backtracked.

"Bluebird Ranch," she said into the receiver. There was only silence on the line. "Hello, is anyone there?"

A song began to play. Eddy Arnold's rich voice came to her ear, singing, "Gonna Find Me a Bluebird." The phone dropped from her fingers.

How did he know she loved that song?

She backed away from the phone, then bolted from the room. In her haste, she banged her shoulder against the doorjamb, but the pain barely slowed her down. Her boots slid on the polished wood floor of the hallway, but she managed to stay on her feet and ran to the front door. Throwing it open, she stepped out into the sunlight and stood blinking on the porch.

The hills had a watching quality, as if he stood hidden among the rocks with binoculars trained on her. Maybe he did. How could he know so much about her unless he was nearby?

RICK LENGTHENED THE STIRRUPS ON THE SADDLE HE HAD PUT ON BETSY'S mare. "We're going to see how she likes being ridden, Betsy."

The little girl had an uneasy frown between her eyes, but she nodded. Her gaze cleared, and she looked up at him with such trust that he felt ten feet tall and bulletproof.

"Don't you think she needs a name?" he asked. "It would make her feel more at home."

Betsy hesitated, then nodded. The tip of her tongue came out, and she wetted her lips. Rick held his breath.

Say something, honey. He didn't dare say the words for fear of breaking the spell.

"Bluebird," Betsy said in a voice so soft and hoarse it barely carried above the sound of the wind.

Rick wanted to sweep her into his arms and lift her high, but he tempered his excitement. He glanced toward the house, wanting to run and tell Allie, but if Betsy thought it was a huge deal, she might clam up again. "Okay, Bluebird is what we'll call her. She's a blue roan, so it fits." He ran his hand over the horse's neck. "How do you like your new name, Bluebird?"

The horse turned and looked at him, and he could have almost sworn the mare recognized how important it was that Betsy had named her. He rubbed the mare's face and ears. "I'm going to get on your back, girl. I'll try not to hurt you."

He fitted his boot into the stirrup. Bluebird didn't move away but stood still and quiet. Testing his weight, he stepped onto the stirrup, then back off, but again she didn't move. Though she'd been abused, she was going to let him mount.

With a smooth, easy movement, he swung onto her back. Mistake. The mare began to buck and snort, arching her back into the air like a rodeo bronco. She tossed Rick so high he could have snatched at the clouds. Seconds later, he was flat on his back with his mouth full of dust and staring up at the mare's underbelly. She was still bucking, and he rolled away before she could trample him.

Betsy ran to him and patted his face with her small hands. "Okay?" she asked in her rusty voice.

"I'm fine, Bets. We should go find your mother though."

Betsy must have thought he meant he needed Allie's help, because she took off like a roadrunner, running so fast she kicked dust back into his face. He spit it out and sat up as Betsy returned with her mother in tow. Allie must have already been outside and on her way. At least she hadn't seen his humiliating fall.

He bolted to his feet before she could help him. "Betsy, tell your mom what you named your mare."

Allie's eyes went wide, and her lips parted. "You gave your horse a name, Betsy?"

The little girl nodded. "Bluebird," she said again in her rough voice.

Allie dropped to her knees and pulled Betsy into her arms. "That's a wonderful name, Bets," she said in a choked voice. "It suits her."

"Bluebirds can be vicious if you've ever seen them shaking a worm. Bluebird isn't as sweet as she looks." Rick said, dusting off his jeans.

"She threw you?" Allie stood but kept Betsy's hand in hers.

"Like a roadrunner shaking a snake." He grinned and took Betsy's other hand, but the little girl pulled away from both of them and ran to climb onto the fence to watch her horse.

"Are you okay?" Allie asked.

"The only thing hurt is my pride. The old girl fooled me. Stood so quiet I thought she was used to being ridden." He looked at Allie then and realized she was on the verge of tears. Her hands were clasped tightly together in front of her. Her agitation wasn't the joyous kind Betsy's talking would bring about.

He took her hand, unhooking it from the other one. "You're shaking. What's wrong?"

"I don't know whether to laugh or cry." She rubbed her eyes. "Betsy's talking," she said. "But for how long? He called me while I was working."

"Who?"

She clung to his hand. "The guy who's after me."

His fingers tightened, and he drew her close to his chest. She fit so well in his arms, like she was made to be there. His hands stroked her soft hair, so fine and silky. The trembling eased. "Now tell me what he said."

"Nothing," she mumbled. "He played a song."

"What song?"

"'Gonna Find Me a Bluebird.' It's my favorite."

"How'd he know that?"

She pulled away and glanced up at him. "That's what scares me. He knows things about me, whoever he is."

He pulled her tight again. "You're safe here."

But was she? He looked out over her head and saw the glint of binoculars on the hillside.

He grabbed Gunner from the corral and rode up the hill. Jem ran along beside the horse. No weapons, he realized. His nightstick was in the umbrella stand by the front door.

Pebbles scattered and slid down the slope as the horse's hooves dislodged them. The wind nearly blew his hat off when he reached the top of the incline. Turning in his saddle, he looked down toward the ranch. It was about here he'd seen the glint of something.

He dismounted and led Gunner along the narrow trail. His gaze scanned the thin, rocky soil for tracks.

Jem growled, then took off toward a big rock that looked like a jackrabbit. Rick leaped after the dog. He heard a man's voice shout, then a figure shot up from behind the rock and backed away from the snarling dog. Jem never barked or snarled, so Rick grabbed a rock in each hand and rushed forward to see who would rile the dog like that.

A Hispanic man who looked like he was in his fifties was kicking at the dog and screaming in Spanish. He seemed oblivious to Rick's approach.

"Diablo!" the man shouted. *"Perro diablo."*

Devil dog. Jem was anything but that. Rick grinned when he realized the guy wasn't armed. He called the dog, and Jem trotted over to sit at Rick's feet.

"Who are you?" he asked the man.

The guy spread his hands out. "No Engless," he said in a heavily accented voice.

Rick switched to Spanish and asked the question again. The man told him he was heading to Mexico to take money to his mother. He was quick to pull out his card to prove he was legal.

It was only after Rick let him go and returned to the ranch that he realized the guy didn't have anything shiny on his person. So where had the glint come from?

21

WHILE RICK WAS CHECKING OUT THE HILLS, ALLIE PULLED BETSY ONTO her lap and smoothed her curls. "I'm so glad to hear your voice, sweetheart. I've missed it so much." Her own voice was choked, and she swallowed to regain control. She didn't want Betsy to feel bad. "Now when you play with Courtney, you can talk to her too."

Her eyes bright, Betsy smiled. Pride shone out all over her.

Rick had performed a miracle here. Allie still couldn't believe it, but the big guy had gotten through Betsy's defenses. And the horse helped too, of course. The ranch had worked its magic.

Betsy looked over Allie's shoulder. "Grammy and Grandpa." She pointed.

Allie turned to see the familiar car rumbling along the bumps toward them. Careful to hide her displeasure, she let Betsy stand, then groaned as she got to her feet to greet the Siderses.

Erika got out, smoothed her skirt, then started toward the corral. Hugh followed. Her gaze traveled from Allie's head to her jeans, and she grimaced. Then a pleasant smile dropped into view as if she changed masks. "Allie, my dear, should you be out of bed?"

Allie wanted to brush any dust from her clothing and hair, but she wasn't going to give Erika the satisfaction of knowing she felt self-conscious. "I'm fine. I'm about to teach the kids how to barrel race."

"I hope you're not letting Betsy participate in something so dangerous."

"Not yet," Allie said. "But she'll learn when she's ready."

A disagreeable expression twisted Erika's mouth, and she started to answer, then snapped her lips shut. When her smile returned, it looked forced. "We thought we might take you to lunch."

"It's only ten o'clock," Allie said.

"We can visit until then," Hugh said. "You need us to help out with anything?"

Like they were dressed for ranch work. Hugh's black suit was already picking up dust.

"No, we're fine," Allie said. What was she going to do with them for two hours? Her gaze settled on Betsy's head. "I've got good news—Betsy is talking again!"

She expected them to be overjoyed, but instead suspicion narrowed their eyes. They glanced from her to Betsy.

"Is this a scam?" Hugh demanded.

Allie rolled her eyes. "Betsy, say hello to Grammy and Grandpa."

Betsy didn't look up, but she shook her head.

"You're just trying to bolster your position with the court," Erika said. "You think if you can say Betsy is talking again, you won't look so incompetent. What do you take us for, Allie? The judge won't be taken in either."

"No, she won't. She'll see right through the two of you," Allie shot back before she could bite her tongue.

Hugh's face reddened. "I should have known you wouldn't accept an olive branch. Erika, get in the car." He stomped back toward the car.

Erika opened her mouth, then closed it again and followed her husband.

Allie ran her hand over her daughter's curls. "Why wouldn't you talk to Grammy?"

"She doesn't like me," Betsy said.

"Of course she does, sweetheart. She loves you."

Betsy shook her head, her chin taking on a stubborn jut. "She yells."

"That's just her way. Everyone loves you, Bets."

Betsy smiled up at her, and Allie felt a fresh burst of joy. Her soul had been so hungry for communion with her child. It was one thing to talk to Betsy and know she heard, but another thing for her to listen to her daughter's sweet voice answering back. She wasn't sure how she'd survived the silence this past year.

Rick came back down from the hills. "Just someone walking," he said. "Nothing to worry about."

But Allie saw how Rick kept glancing back toward the hills. She sensed his worry. Setting her focus on the kids, she decided she wasn't going to think about it. The kids were depending on her to have a fun day, and she was not going to let anything mess it up, not Jon's parents, and not some wanderer.

She went to the corral and joined the kids. "The most important thing about barrel racing is the connection between you and your horse. You've all been here long enough to figure out which horse is your favorite," she told the kids. "A good horse can go for fifty thousand dollars or more, so the horse means everything. None of these horses have been trained yet, but that doesn't mean they can't learn what you want and expect. All of you go get the horse of your choice."

She and Rick watched as the teenagers glanced at one another, then trotted off to take charge of a horse. Latoya grabbed Moonbeam's reins, and Fern gave a longing glance at Cupcake.

"You can ride her, Fern. It's been nearly a month, and she's doing good," Rick said.

The girl's smile beamed out, and she went to the mare. The boys chose Winston and Rebel. They all looked half-scared as Rick rolled barrels from the garage into the corral.

"Okay, the object is to go around the barrels in a cloverleaf pattern and to do it without knocking over any of the barrels. The winner is the one who takes the least time. Let me show you." Her muscles complaining, Allie mounted Jackson.

This was going to be hard with the way her body ached, but the exercise would be good for that. The gelding's hard muscles moved under her legs. She patted his sleek neck. "It's hard for the horse if you come at the barrel straight on," she said, urging her horse to a trot. "I'm going to go slow at first and show you the angles."

Jackson responded to the pressure of her knees on his sides and the reins on his neck. The gelding went around the barrel completely, then turned to cross to the other barrel. With his body tipping to the right, Allie felt the saddle give a little. She tried to adjust her position when she felt it give a little more.

What was wrong with the thing? Shifting her weight, she felt it give again.

Then it was sliding down the horse's belly.

She kicked her left foot free of the stirrup and tried to do the same with the right as she vaulted away from the horse, but her boot caught. Tugging on it, she slid down the horse's belly with the saddle. Dangling by her right foot, her back slammed into the dirt.

Allie tasted dust.

She tried to reach up and grab the reins, but Jackson went wild, racing over the hard ground with his hooves hitting dangerously near her head. Those wicked hooves flung pebbles and rocks up into her face, and one narrowly missed her left eye.

She flinched and twisted her foot in the stirrup, but it still refused to budge. Everything moved so fast, she barely felt the rocks and twigs dig into her back. She flailed again, trying to reach up to disentangle her boot, but it was impossible.

She became aware of Rick shouting. His voice sounded close, but all she could see was the ground quickly racing past her gaze. Then the landscape's passage began to slow, and finally she was lying stunned beneath Jackson's hooves while the sweat dripped from his neck onto her face.

She felt gentle hands release her foot, then Rick touched her face. "Are you all right?"

She blinked and tried to rise up, then groaned as her already sore muscles protested at the new indignities. "I think I'm alive."

"Thank God." He ran his hands over her limbs. "I don't think anything is broken. Can you stand?"

"Let me try." She really just wanted to lie there until she caught her breath, but Betsy would be worried.

He slipped his arm under her shoulders and helped her sit up. Her head spun, and pain stabbed at her neck, but with his help, she managed to get up.

"What happened?" he murmured in her ear as he helped her toward the house.

"I don't know. The saddle just slid. Who saddled him?"

"I did. The cinch was tight." He got her to the fence. "Here, sit down while I take a look at the saddle."

Hanging on to his arm, she bit back a groan as she lowered herself to a rock. The teenagers flocked around her with big, worried eyes. "I'm fine," she assured them. "Come here, Bets," she told her daughter. Betsy huddled at her feet and laid her head against Allie's leg.

"Dude, barrel racing ain't for sissies," Devon said. "That was awesome to watch."

"I thought you were toast," Leon said.

"Me too," Latoya said. She knelt beside Allie. "You need some water or something?"

"That would be good," Allie said. "I've got dust in my mouth. How about you all go inside while I wait for Rick? You could fix me some tea. There are cookies in the tin on top of the fridge."

"You're sure you're okay?" Latoya asked.

"Fine." Allie managed a smile. It was all she could do to tear her gaze away from Rick. From his clenched fists and tight jaw, she figured he'd found something ominous. "Go with Fern, Bets."

Betsy got up with a show of reluctance but took Fern's hand, and the kids all went toward the house.

Rick came toward her with the saddle in his hands. He tossed it at her feet. "Someone cut the cinch ring with snips," he said. He showed her the sharp, cut edges.

Allie didn't often cry. Tears were a weakness she didn't like to show, but her eyes burned with the need for release. "I'm so tired of this," she choked out. "If he would just show himself, or tell me why he hates me. I don't understand."

Rick went to his knees beside her and caressed her cheek with the back of his hand. "We'll find him. Somehow we'll stop him. I'll go see the border patrol. I meant to go before now."

The border patrol. Big deal. They weren't going to help her. "But what does that have to do with me?"

"I don't know, but it's the only place I have to look. I still wonder about the illegal alien thing. There was a lot of money run through your account. Whoever this guy is, he's got money to burn, and he had to earn it somehow. You want to go with me?"

She shook her head. "Maybe Betsy and I will go see Dolly." She wanted to forget the problems, to laugh and pretend everything was normal for just a little while.

"Okay." He rose and held out his hand. "Can you walk to the house?"

"I think so." She accepted his hand and struggled to her feet. Her legs felt shaky, and she leaned against his chest.

The thump of his heart's steady rhythm under her ear was as comforting as a hot water bottle to a puppy. His arms came around her, and without thinking, she wrapped her arms around his waist. The way his pulse accelerated made her look up to find him staring down at her.

She told herself to move, but she didn't want to. Lost in the vast blueness of his gaze, she clung to him.

Then his head came down, and his lips brushed hers. She inhaled his breath, the scent of his skin, and the response it brought in her caught her off guard. When he would have pulled away, she kissed him back and tightened her hold on him. She could sense his start of surprise, but then he pulled her tighter and kissed her until she was breathless.

Allie wanted to lose herself in his kiss, to forget the danger that threatened, to find a new path to walk with this husband she barely knew. *To live* when it seemed as though her life might soon be over.

Her knees trembled, and she would have sagged to the ground except for his strong arms supporting her. When his lips left hers, she felt abandoned, bereft. With reluctance, she opened her eyes again and gazed up into his face. His eyes blazed with a passion she hadn't seen in a man's face in too long.

Did they dare have a real marriage? Staring into her husband's face, Allie thought she might risk it.

SOME PROTECTOR HE WAS. RICK TUCKED BETSY INTO BED, THEN CAME downstairs and watched his wife's face in the glow of lamplight as the group played Yahtzee after dinner. Someone had tried to hurt her twice now, and he'd had to stand back and watch it happen.

It was hard to fight a phantom. He'd called Brendan several times, but his friend hadn't turned up anything yet on Mark Haskell or Ted Rediger. Too busy, he said. Tomorrow, when Rick went to Alpine, he'd stop at the library and use the computer to see what he could find out on his own.

Remembering the way she'd kissed him today heated his blood. He was falling for her in a big way, and it was enough to make him want to run. What if he failed her? He hadn't done good by her so far. The responsibility made him lick his lips and look toward the wine cabinet.

Elijah had always refused to get rid of the liquor. He said Rick would never conquer the need if he wasn't faced with making the right choice every day, but Rick wasn't sure he agreed with that. It would be so much easier to have temptation out of the way.

Elijah was gone now. There was no reason to leave the stuff there.

He could clean out that cabinet once and for all. Pour the liquor down the sink and smash the bottles. Tonight, after everyone was in bed, he'd do just that.

His gaze went back to Allie's face. Battered and bruised though she looked, she was a temptation he didn't think he could resist much longer.

The thought of it was driving him crazy. He stood and stretched. "I think I'll go to town for an ice-cream sundae. Want to come, Allie?"

"Sure. I'm getting stiff sitting here," Allie said. "I need to walk some of the pain out of my muscles." She held her hand up for him to haul her up. She winced as she maneuvered out of the chair. "I can't sit here much longer or I won't be able to move tomorrow." She put her hand on his arm and stared up at him with an appeal in her eyes.

When had his willingness to love begun to turn into the real thing? He'd tried Grady's advice, and by golly, the guy had been right. Love was about the action of loving. What a weird truth to discover.

He hadn't even been attracted to her when she'd first come here, and now his pulse soared like a bald eagle when he caught a whiff of her shampoo.

"Keep an ear out for Betsy," Allie told Fern, who nodded.

They went toward the door, Allie limping a little. He tucked her hand in the crook of his elbow, then grabbed a sweater from a hook by the door as they went past and slipped it around her. The soft glance of gratitude in her eyes made his palms grow sweaty.

They stepped out into the dark night, illuminated only by the stars. Only a sliver of moon showed. The night air was rich with the scents of the ranch: sage, creosote, hay, and a hint of horse on the wind blowing past the barn.

He helped Allie down the steps. "I'll bring the truck around. Wait here by the porch." He jogged to the vehicle and drove to the base of the steps. She slipped into the cab before he had a chance to get out and help her.

"I finished my paperwork for our next counseling session," she said once they'd started to town. "How are you coming?"

"Haven't had a chance." He knew his voice was a little sharp when he saw her flinch.

There was no answer from her at first. "Is—is there something you're not wanting to tell me?" she asked finally. "I hope you know whatever it is, it can't be any worse than the mess I've made of my life."

Tell her. The prompting dried his mouth. No way could he spill it. Not when they were just starting to get into a comfortable relationship.

"Nothing important," he said. "We'll get to know one another better every day."

Allie nodded. "I still can't believe Bets is talking. I guess you were right after all." She turned and looked out into the dark night. "Maybe I was babying her too much."

The tension drained from his neck and shoulders at the passing of the dangerous topic. "No maybe about it."

She stiffened. "I want you to quit tucking her into bed at night. It's . . . dangerous. She is beginning to get too attached to you."

His fingers tightened on the steering wheel. "Kids can never have too much love, Allie. You're trying to deprive Betsy of the most important thing in life. Jon's gone. He'll never be able to pull her up on his lap or read her a story." He knew his words were harsh, but she had to understand. "Look, I loved Jon too. And I admit it took me a while to get past the thought that I was taking his place. But he's not here to fill it. I am. And I'm going to."

"She can't forget Jon," she fired back. "I don't want anyone to take his place."

His inclination was to let go of his temper, but he took a tighter grip on it instead. "I know you don't want her to be hurt. Neither do I. You should know that. She needs me, and so do you."

"I think she's already forgetting," she whispered, her voice desolate.

"Allie, she's five years old. How much do you remember from when you were five? But at least both of us loved Jon. We'll talk about him, about what a great man he was. That's better than if I were jealous of him and didn't hold him up in her eyes."

She finally nodded, and her shoulder slumped against the door. "I guess it's inevitable."

They reached the drugstore and stepped inside to a nearly deserted space filled with the sweet smells of chocolate, whipped cream, and butterscotch. Nothing much was said over their ice cream. Rick knew she was mulling over what he'd said. Maybe she'd finally quit challenging him on every action.

After licking the last of his hot-fudge sundae from the spoon, he paid the bill and held the door open for her. A warm breeze blew across his face, and he inhaled the scent of the roses blooming along the tree lawn.

A sharp report echoed against the buildings, followed by a zip past his ear. "Look out!" Something stung the side of his face. He bore her to the ground and covered her with his own body. "Someone's shooting at us."

The night sounds of tree frogs and crickets went silent, then resumed. Rick strained to hear anything else: the footfall of someone walking their way, the harsh breath of someone running. There was nothing but the sound of the wind and the rumble of a truck passing them on the street.

Glancing behind him, he saw the lights go out in the drugstore. The door was probably locked. The rest of the businesses had closed down when the streets were rolled up at five. "We've got to make a run for the truck," he whispered in her ear.

She nodded. He rolled off her, bounded to his feet, then yanked her up and ran toward the vehicle. No rifle crack sounded, no more bullets zinged past his ears. He flung open the door and shoved her inside before running around to the driver's side.

"Lock your door!" He slammed the door and locked it, then started the truck. He tossed her the cell phone. "Call the sheriff." He rattled off the number to her.

She nodded and punched in the number. Listening to her tell the sheriff's office what happened, he began to shake at the close call.

The sheriff was waiting at the curb when Rick pulled the truck up and stopped.

By the time he and Allie recounted what had happened, it was nearly eleven. A deputy followed them home. He waved his thanks to the deputy and ran with Allie to the house.

Locking the door behind them, he left Allie in the living room to explain what happened while he made a beeline for the office. He went to the gun cabinet and stared at the weapons. He'd sworn never to take one in his hand again. The dark, frightened eyes of the boy he'd shot accidentally in Baghdad swam in his memory. Guilt made him slam the door again.

The boys congregated in the doorway. "Cool, dude, can I have some heat?" Leon asked.

"Not on your life." Rick peered out the window into the darkness. Who was in his neighborhood? And what was his game?

22

AFTER CHANGING INTO HER PAJAMAS, ALLIE SAT IN HER BEDROOM ROCKER
and watched her daughter sleep.

The thought of going to sleep after someone shot at them made
Allie shudder. He'd been in the house once, at least long enough to
slip a note under her door. What if he got in again?

She should have brought a gun up here with her. The madman
wasn't going to hurt her daughter. Allie pondered this. Maybe the
stalker wouldn't stoop so low as to hurt a child. He'd had several oppor-
tunities to harm Betsy but didn't. The realization only vaguely comforted her.

The man's attacks seemed relentless. If she only knew why he hated
her. All Rick's efforts to identify him led only to dead ends. Maybe

that's the way it was supposed to be though. Maybe God had put her in this position so she had to face this danger herself and deal with it. Nothing could happen to her that didn't first pass through God's hands. She had to remember that.

He'd protected them so far.

Her gaze lingered on Betsy. Rick wanted to be her daddy. Did she dare allow it? Her eyes burned, and she rubbed the moisture from her lashes. Rick was right—Jon was gone. It wasn't fair to Betsy to deprive her of love. But it was so hard to give up on Jon's memory.

A peck came at the door, and she got up from the chair. It had to be Rick, and the way her blood pressure rose made her shake her head at her silly self. She was thirty-two, not seventeen.

When she flung open the door and looked into his eyes, she *felt* seventeen and giddy though. How did he manage to do that to her? She felt anything but a sedate widow when she was around him.

"Everything's buttoned down," he whispered, stepping into the room. "But I don't want the two of you to stay here alone. I've moved a cot into my room, and we'll all stay there." Without waiting for her to agree, he stepped past her and lifted Betsy from the bed. She stirred but didn't awaken.

Allie's pulse hammered in her throat. There was only one bed in his room, and he'd brought in one cot. Did he mean to sleep on it?

She trailed down the hall behind him to his bedroom. Her gaze fastened on the big bed that dwarfed the room. She'd made up the bed that morning when she changed all the sheets in the house and washed them, but she'd never expected to sleep there tonight.

Rick laid Betsy on the cot and pulled the covers around her. After pressing a kiss to her forehead, he backed away and turned to face Allie. "I'll sleep on the floor. There was only room for one cot."

It was *his* bed. It didn't seem fair he should sleep on the hard floor. "I'll sleep there," she said. "Where are the blankets?"

His chin came out. "No way I'm letting my wife sleep on the floor."

His wife. The words started a warm feeling in the pit of her being. She glanced at the bed. "The bed is big. If you stay on your side, I'll promise to stay on mine."

His lips twitched. "What if I don't want you to stay on your side?"

Her laugh felt a little hollow. "We could put a board between us."

The glint of laughter in his eyes dimmed. "Not necessary. I'll be good."

"Okay," she said, not yet ready to explore what he meant by his comments.

Avoiding his gaze, she went around to the left side and pulled back the quilt and top sheet. A picture of a young boy sat on the stand beside the bed. "Who's this? He looks a little like you."

"My brother, Chad." His clipped tone told her he didn't want to talk about it.

Allie let it drop. "I hope I'm not taking your favorite side."

"Nope. I always sleep on the other edge." He went to the dresser and took out pajama bottoms, then disappeared through the door. A moment later, the bathroom door down the hall closed.

Allie slipped between the sheets. She rolled onto her side with her back to the center of the mattress. It was going to be impossible to make herself breathe like she was asleep when all she wanted to do was gulp in air through her tight throat.

Her eyes slammed shut when she heard him come back into the room. The bed springs groaned when his bulk settled onto the mattress. The covers tugged, and he settled into the bed. The musky scent of his presence filled her senses, and soon the warmth of his body drifted toward her as well.

Her tension began to ease when he made no attempt to roll toward her and embrace her. The day's events had worn on her. Every muscle in her body ached.

"Allie?" Rick's whisper came near her ear.

Her eyes flew open, and she rolled to the center to find herself nose to nose with Rick, though in the darkness, she could barely make out his features. "What's wrong?"

"I wondered if you'd like me to rub your back. Are you sore?"

"Yes, but you're tired too. Rest is the best thing." She didn't dare let him touch her. Her responses to him were too unpredictable.

Or maybe totally predictable.

"I like having you here," he whispered. His lips brushed hers.

Before she could respond, he rolled over, presenting his back to her. She touched her fingers to her lips and closed her eyes.

Though she'd been determined not to trust her heart again, he was battering down her defenses.

It was after three the last time she looked at the clock, then the sun was streaming in her eyes. Allie blinked against the brightness. She tried to move and found something heavy lying across her waist.

It was Rick's arm.

She stared in fascination at the thick black hair growing on his skin. Her gaze traveled up his arm to his strong shoulders, bare above his pajama bottoms. The dark stubble on his face made him all the more appealing.

His eyes were closed, and she let herself look to her heart's content. Always before she'd been afraid he'd notice her studying him. His hair curled a little where it touched his neck. He needed a trim, but the extra length combined with the morning beard made him look a bit like an outlaw. And only inches away. He'd rolled onto his side with his arm flung over her. If she leaned forward a few inches, she could kiss him.

She'd always been attracted to the bad boys.

Even Jon had had a wild streak, one that caused him to leave her and Betsy and go off to save the world. Allie wondered how many of those impulses Rick had. He seemed so upright, so steady. Someone to depend on. Jon certainly had trusted him.

His eyes opened, and she found herself staring into the depths of those blue pools of light. He stared at her with a steady gaze she couldn't look away from.

"Good morning," he said. He made no move to pull his arm away.

She wet her lips. "Good morning." She barely breathed, let alone moved. One part of her wanted to bolt from the bed, and the other wanted to move closer.

His arm shifted, and she felt a stab of disappointment until she realized he was moving his hand up to cup her face.

"You're beautiful even in the morning," he said. His thumb rubbed her bottom lip.

Warning bells screamed in her head, but she ignored them and shifted closer ever so slightly. His eyes darkened at her response, and he pulled her closer, his lips seeking hers. She fit so perfectly in his arms.

"Mommy?" Betsy's voice was still rusty and hoarse.

Allie jerked from Rick's arms and rolled over to stare at her daughter, whose face was by the pillow. "Hi, baby. Did you sleep well?" Her cheeks burned, and she was sure her face had to be red.

Betsy nodded. She tugged on Allie's hand. "Can I have pancakes?"

"Okay, I'm coming." With a rueful glance at Rick, she threw back the covers and climbed out of bed.

She wasn't sure if the reprieve was good or not.

THE TEENAGERS TALKED EXCITEDLY OVER BREAKFAST, AND RICK DIDN'T get a word in edgewise—a good thing since he wasn't sure what to say to Allie.

He'd totally fallen for her. Five foot two and maybe a hundred pounds soaking wet, she had a heart as big as Texas. She'd take down a tiger in defense of her daughter too. He liked that kind of courage in a woman. Okay, loved that kind of courage.

He grabbed the keys to Elijah's Jeep. "Charlie, I'm going to town today. I'll be gone most of the day, so you're in charge," he told the young man. Eyeing the boy's plate, he grinned. "That has to be your tenth pancake. You can sure put them away."

Charlie grinned and shrugged. "The kids want to practice barrel racing. That okay with you?"

"Fine. Just be careful."

"Always." The kid gave him a cheeky grin.

"You ready?" Rick asked Allie. She nodded but still hadn't looked him fully in the face since she'd scrambled from the bed.

He couldn't blame her. Everything was so weird and off kilter right now. She'd slept in his bed, and they hadn't really acknowledged the depth of their relationship yet. Between the guy terrorizing her and Rick himself trying to win her heart, she must be confused.

But he wasn't going to let this continue. He would find that man and get him out of Allie's life. Then they could plan for the future.

Future. The very word set his teeth on edge. All his plans had been set spinning by her arrival. He hadn't had a single peaceful moment since she arrived. Maybe that was a good thing. He'd been getting complacent, settled on a course that might have taken him right into a life of more isolation.

He hadn't felt this alive since he'd been a kid.

Neither of them talked on the way to town. Instead of just dropping her off to spend the day with Dolly, he went inside with her to say hello to Grady. Betsy and Courtney ran off together, and Dolly and Allie went to the kitchen for tea.

He found Grady in his office. "Got a minute?"

Grady looked up from his Bible with a smile. "Sure, I was ready for a break." His grin faded. "Did God die or something, bucko?"

Rick managed a weak grin. "Do I look that bad?" He should have known Grady would call him to task.

"Worse." Grady pointed at the chair. "Sit."

Rick shut the door and dropped onto the armchair. "Someone shot at Allie last night."

Grady studied Rick's face. "What else?"

"Isn't that enough?" Rick was in no mood to be analyzed.

"You're all still alive, so no, me bucko. You look like someone died."

Rick gave a short laugh. "I can't seem to keep my wife safe."

"She's dead?"

"No, she's in the kitchen with Dolly." In spite of himself, a grin started to lift the corners of his mouth. Grady always did that to him.

"Then you've managed to keep her safe." Grady grinned. "You've fallen for her, haven't you? That's the real problem. The mighty Rick Bailey has finally fallen hard."

"Don't joke about it."

"Why not? You've gone through your life keeping everyone at arm's length because you think you might fail them. That's being only half-alive, bucko, and you're finally finding it out."

Rick pressed his lips together. "I'm scared," he admitted. "Why would she want to stay with someone like me? I've got no family, no real assets other than a strong back. I told her I wanted to work on making the marriage a real one, and she hasn't really given me a clear answer."

"Maybe she's scared too. Have you thought about that?"

He hadn't. "Why would she be scared? She's been married before. She knows more about it than I do."

"Exactly. She knows how bad it can hurt when things go wrong. Maybe she's afraid of being hurt again, of loving again."

"She's probably smart to be afraid I couldn't do it," Rick muttered.

"Have you told her about your problem?"

"Nope, and I'm not going to." Rick set his jaw. "It's behind me."

Grady pointed a pencil at him. "But it's shaped you. She needs to know the demons you deal with, just like you need to know hers. You need to tell her before the next counseling session. It will come out sooner or later."

"Then make it later. I'm just not ready to show her what a loser she married," Rick muttered, standing. "I'm going down to talk to the border patrol today. Maybe they've heard of something going on through here."

"I thought her troubles started before she came here."

"They did." Rick shrugged. "I've got nowhere else to look." And keeping busy was the only way to avoid running scared. On the outside, he was this strong, take-charge guy, and on the inside, he knew his shortcomings. The trick was to make sure no one else did.

23

THE TEA WAS AS STRONG AS HER HUSBAND. ALLIE CHUCKLED TO HERSELF
and sipped from her mug before setting it on the coffee table. The
girls were in Courtney's room, and she and Dolly sat in the living
room. Allie was hungry for some girl talk, and maybe she'd even find
out more about her fascinating husband.

"How long have you known Rick?" she asked, curling her legs
under herself on the comfortable sofa.

"Seems like forever." Dolly stopped knitting and wrinkled her
nose. "I guess it was about two years ago that he came to help Elijah."
She shook her head. "Man, he was such a case when he walked into the
church the first time."

"What do you mean?"

"He had this tortured expression, like he'd just come through the desert and survived. I think it was a month before he even spoke to me or anyone else. He'd slip into the back pew at the last minute, then rush out at the final amen."

"Was it the war?"

"I think it was more than that." Dolly's glance held curiosity. "You don't really know him very well, do you?"

"I'd never met him before we came here."

Dolly put her hand to her mouth. "I didn't know. Grady never tells me anything told to him in confidence." Her tone was injured. "I don't get it, Allie. How did you marry so fast?"

"Rick was my husband's best friend. Jon, my husband, told me if I was ever in trouble to go to Rick. My in-laws were trying to take Bets from me, so I ran to Rick."

"And that guy was after you."

Allie nodded. "Still is. I was most afraid for Betsy. When I told Rick about the custody issue, he told me he'd promised Jon he'd take care of us. The marriage was all Rick's idea."

Dolly sighed. "So romantic."

Allie's lips twitched with the need to laugh. If Dolly only knew how the marriage really was.

"He's quite a hunk." Dolly waggled her eyebrows.

Allie burst out laughing. "You're terrible."

"I tease Rick like that all the time. He knows I love my Grady." Dolly's smile was impish. "I just like to embarrass Rick. He is so clueless around women and doesn't know what to say. It's quite endearing."

Endearing was an understatement. Appealing, infuriating, compelling.

Allie couldn't stop thinking about Rick and what life was like for him while growing up. The little snippets Dolly had told her indicated his childhood wasn't pleasant. What about the scars on his back? How did he get them?

There was so much about her husband she didn't know. "I—I noticed scars on his back. Has he ever said anything about them?"

Dolly winced. "I've seen them. He always passes them off as nothing. If he's told Grady, I wouldn't know. I know he was removed from the care of his parents. He'd been in trouble—some breaking and entering, taking a car on a joyride. Elijah turned him around."

"I saw a picture of his brother on his nightstand. Where is he?"

"They were separated in the foster-care system. Rick used to look for him, but all the records were lost in a fire a few years back, and he ran up against a dead end. Chad was five when he was removed from the home, I think. Rick never forgave himself for it. He always felt if he'd taken better care of Chad, welfare wouldn't have moved him to foster care. Rick never saw him again."

"And he's searched for him all these years?" Allie's heart swelled at the thought of such devotion and dedication. There was so much more to him than brawn.

"He gave up about a year ago. Grady told him the kid could have changed his name. Maybe he was even adopted."

"I wish I could find him for Rick," Allie said. "What a gift that would be. A way to say thank you for all he's done to protect Betsy and me."

"You never know," Dolly said slowly. "Even though Rick has given up, Grady and I try now and again to find out something. Grady tracked down Chad's sixth-grade teacher."

A surge of excitement rolled through Allie. "Where is she?"

"She's retired now and is in an assisted-living facility in Alpine."

An hour and a half away. Still Allie had to try. "Maybe I could call."

Dolly shook her head. "Grady tried that. The woman has Alzheimer's, and she didn't make much sense on the phone."

So much for that idea. "It probably would be a worthless trip to try to go talk to her then."

"Maybe not. She probably has lucid times like most Alzheimer's patients. It's worth a try. We could leave the girls with Grady and run up there."

"You think he'd mind?"

"Nope. They won't be any trouble, and he's off today anyway."

"Then let's do it!" Allie found the more she dug under Rick's brawny surface, the more tenderness she found.

ONE OF RICK'S FRIENDS FROM CHURCH WAS A BORDER PATROL AGENT. RICK knew Walker Rivera would be his only hope of getting some insider information. After stopping at the checkpoint, he was directed out to one of the landings along the Rio Grande.

Cactus tore at his tires and bumper, and he nearly bottomed out in the potholes along the narrow dirt road down to the river. The area was a desolate desert until he got close to the water where trees grew and vegetation sprouted, grabbing onto the moisture the river gave up. The fresh scent of water made the day brighter.

Walker's SUV sat on hardpan clay. A large patch of prickly pear cactus sprouted from under it. Rick parked behind his friend's vehicle, then followed the voices he heard echoing off the red canyon walls that lined the river. The walk down to the river was a little steep and treacherous, with small pebbles sliding away from his boots.

Walker and his partner were interrogating two handcuffed men.

About five ten with stocky features and a handlebar mustache, Walker had been with the border patrol nearly twenty years. The other agent was younger, blond, and scared.

Walker fired questions at the prisoners in Spanish, then turned to march them to the SUV. The Baggies of brown weed in his hands told the story.

When he saw Rick, he motioned for his partner to take the prisoners on to the vehicle. "Hey buddy, what are you doing out here?"

"Looking for information. Drugs?" he asked, nodding toward the men who were nearly to the top of the slope.

"Marijuana."

"Seen any evidence of coyotes running illegals through the area?" When Walker raised his eyebrows, amused, Rick added, "More so than usual."

Walker's gaze sharpened. "How'd you know? There have been nearly three times what we usually see."

Rick told him about the group he'd seen on the ranch and about Allie's situation. "I even checked out the brother of the guy she sent to prison, and he seems clean. He was up in Albuquerque."

The men had started walking up the hillside. Walker stopped and grabbed his arm. "Albuquerque. What's his name?"

"Luis Hernandez."

Walker began to smile. "He's been on our radar, and I've got a search warrant to deliver. That's my next stop."

Rick could have sworn the young man was clean. He was losing his touch. "I'd like to tag along."

Walker studied Rick's face. "You know, maybe you can get us in the door without him running. I've got a pilot ready to go. You free right now?"

"You bet. Let's hit it."

The men climbed back in their vehicles and headed to the post. Walker and his partner turned over the prisoners, filled out their forms, and came out to join Rick at his truck.

Two hours later they parked outside the same dilapidated apartment house that smelled of black beans and tacos.

"Let me go to the door first," Rick said. "Once they open the door, I'll motion to you." He still worried it might be a waste of time, but Walker obviously had something on the kid.

He got out, veered around four Hispanic children playing dodgeball in the street, then went to the door and pounded on it. "Luis? It's Rick Bailey again. I've got a couple of questions."

The baby wailed, and a woman's voice spoke soothingly. The door swung open, and Luis didn't look nearly as patient and understanding today. His glare stabbed at Rick, and his mouth was pinched.

"What now?"

Rick flicked his fingers at his side. Moments later, the two border patrol agents were showing the warrant. Walker had his foot stuck between the doorjamb and the door to keep Luis from slamming it in their faces.

Luis turned to run, and Walker grabbed his arm. "Not so fast, *amigo*. We've got some questions." The men shoved inside.

Rick shot an apologetic glance to the young woman, who stood off to one side, her dark eyes full of fear. The wails of the baby added to the chaos as Walker pushed Luis into a chair and stood over him.

"Keep an eye on him," Walker said. "I need to help Mike search."

Rick stood between Luis and the door. The young man sat on the edge of the chair like he might bolt. Waves of animosity rolled off the kid, and he kept glaring daggers of betrayal at Rick.

Rick stared down at the young man. "Did you try to implicate Allie Siders in running illegals through the rodeo?" he asked quietly.

Luis turned his head, but not before Rick saw a knowing smirk twist his lips. Rage simmered along Rick's nerves. If this guy had been terrorizing his wife all this time . . . He heard the border agents tapping along the walls, dragging drawers open, looking in cabinets.

Nervous energy jittered along Luis's body. His hands shook, and Rick could see he had something to hide. A boulder began to form in Rick's stomach at the thought he might have ended this nightmare days ago if he'd been able to see through the guy. Allie was suffering, and he'd had the power to stop it.

He was losing his touch. A few years ago he could read these degenerates like reading spoor in the forest. He'd let this guy bamboozle him. Some protector he was.

Walker came back holding a ledger book. "It's all in here." He flipped it open and showed Rick the money trail. Hundreds of thousands of dollars. When he handed the book back to Walker, something fell from between the pages. He picked it up and found a picture of Allie standing by a horse trailer at a rodeo.

"It was you," he said. "You were trying to frame her."

"She killed his brother, destroyed his business," the woman said, taking a step forward.

"*Cállete!*" Luis snarled.

The woman clamped her mouth closed at Luis's command to be quiet. She scuttled back to the couch with the baby.

Rick let his contempt show in his eyes as he stared at Luis. The young man looked down, but his mouth still held a line of defiance.

It was over. Rick's relief couldn't be described. He could go home, tell Allie to let the fear drift away like puffs of cottonwood seeds. They could begin to work on making a new life together. Once the adoption was final, he would have a real family.

The thought made him smile.

24

THE CARE FACILITY WAS ONE OF THE NEWER ONES THAT LOOKED LIKE A Victorian mansion rather than an institution. Allie could hardly wait to get inside. What if she was able to find Rick's brother? What a kick it would be to reunite them and see Rick's face.

She and Dolly stopped at the nurses' station and got directions to Rosanna Hilgers's room. They found her seated in a chair, her beefy arms propped on a side table and five cards in her hand. The green sweater she wore over her housedress had more pills than straight fibers.

"Mrs. Hilgers?" Allie said.

"I'll call you," she said in a shrill voice.

Allie glanced at Dolly and touched the woman's shoulder. "My name is Allie Bailey, and I'd like to ask you about a former student."

The woman's bleary eyes blinked, then she pulled her gaze from the cards in her hand and focused on Allie. "I taught you?"

"No, ma'am, not me. But you taught a boy named Chad Bailey. I was wondering if you knew how I might get in touch with him."

"Who wants to know?"

"I do. My name is Allie Bailey."

"You're his sister?"

"His sister-in-law. Do you know where he is?"

The woman shuffled her slippered feet. "Who wants to know?"

"Me, Allie Bailey."

"Want to play poker? I promise not to take too much of your money."

"I don't know how to play."

"Sit down and I'll show you."

Allie gave Dolly a helpless look and pulled over a chair from under the window. "About Chad," she said.

"Such a good boy," the woman said. "Terrible he had to go to Africa."

Dolly rolled her eyes, but Allie leaned forward. "He went to Africa?"

"With his parents. I was so upset. He came to see me on his giraffe when he got back though. So grown up and handsome."

"When was he here last?" Allie knew this was likely all false, but she might find a glimmer of reality in the stories somewhere.

"Just last week. He came on his elephant this time. He could name every part of that beast. I taught him well." Her eyes glazed over, then closed, and her mouth sagged. A snore ripped from her throat.

"She's not making any sense," Dolly whispered. "Let's go."

"I'm going to talk to the nurse." Allie rose and followed her friend from the room.

"Poor lady. She's delusional. All that talk about elephants and giraffes. I doubt you'll learn anything from the nurses."

"Just a quick question." Allie stopped at the hubbub of activity by the entrance and waited until one of the women was free. "Excuse me. I was wondering if you knew if Rosanna Hilgers gets many visitors?"

The young woman's tired smile brightened. "Oh, Mrs. Hilgers! Isn't she a sweetheart? We just love her. Some of her former students drop by from time to time, though since her mind has failed more, not so many."

Allie allowed herself a glimmer of hope. "I'm looking for a young man who would be in his early twenties now. Chad Bailey?"

The woman frowned. "Bailey. The name isn't familiar. There's another Chad that comes by though. He's about that age."

Allie exchanged a glance with Dolly. "Do you know how I might get hold of him?"

"No, I'm sorry. Visitors don't leave their information or anything."

Allie dug in her purse for a pen and paper. "Listen, could I leave a note for you to give him if he comes in again?"

"Sure. I'll put it in her file."

Allie scribbled out a note explaining who she was and what she wanted, then folded it and handed it over. "Thanks so much."

"No problem. I hope you find him." The woman tucked the note into a file folder.

It was the best Allie could do, but it felt like a pitiful attempt. Still, God was in control of this, and he could move mountains.

The women drove back to Dolly's house, but the conversation was much more subdued on the trip home. They stopped at the corner grocery and bought some milk, then went to the O'Sullivan home.

As they pulled into the driveway, she saw Rick's truck parked along the curb. "Don't tell him where we were," she told Dolly.

"I won't. I warned Grady to keep it mum too." Dolly held up the gallon of milk. "We'll tell him we went after this."

"I hope he hasn't been here long," Allie muttered. She got out and followed Dolly to the house. "Rick?" she called.

His voice came from her left. "In the living room."

Allie went to find him. "Did you find out anything?" She eyed him, noticing the triumphant grin he wore.

He stood from his seat on the couch and stepped to where she stood.

"It's over." Rick folded Allie in his arms.

She could hear his pulse thumping against her ear, sense the elation that filled him. "What do you mean?" she asked against his shirt.

His hands gripped her shoulders and pulled her out so he was staring into her face. "It was Luis Hernandez. They found the money trail and a picture of you at the rodeo. He put money in your account and tipped off the authorities, then pulled out the money and moved it around to some other accounts of his own offshore."

She felt giddy, and her knees threatened to buckle under her. She clung to Rick's strength. The nightmare was over. "How did he know I'd come here?"

Rick shrugged. "I suppose he tapped Yo's phone or something. The border patrol will figure it out. Let's celebrate. I'll take you to supper."

She wanted to smile, but it didn't seem real. "Are you sure? I never met him."

"He had a picture of you, and the money trail was clear."

For someone to hate her so passionately when she'd never even met him saddened her. "He must have loved his brother very much."

"You're feeling sorry for the guy? Get over it," Rick said. "He deserves what he's got coming to him. He murdered your family."

Allie shuddered. "It's hard to understand."

"I think the two of you need some time alone," Dolly said. "The girls would love to be together tonight. Why not let Betsy stay with us? There's no need to worry about her now."

It felt strange to let go of her anxiety, to let loose of her daughter. She felt light, airy, as the reality sank in that the danger was behind her. The future stretched ahead like a beautiful blue sky.

"Allie?" Rick said. "It's safe. You can leave Betsy with no worries."

"She's not used to being without me." Going off without Betsy would be like losing her arm.

Dolly laughed. "Listen to the girls chattering. She won't miss you."

Sure enough, Allie could hear the high, sweet sounds of the girls talking. *Talking.* Betsy was talking again, and life might actually return to normal, whatever that meant. "If you're sure." She couldn't look at Rick.

"I'm positive." Dolly made a shooing motion with her hands. "Get out of here, you two. Go celebrate."

Rick took her arm, and his warm fingers jump-started her pulse. "We'll get her first thing in the morning."

"No rush," Dolly said, smiling.

Rick led her from the living room and out the door. "What sounds good for supper? Let's walk. It's not far."

"Do we have a choice?" She turned to smile at him. The air suddenly smelled fresher, clean with the scent of citrus from the groves along the path. The sunset cast a subdued light over the tiny village, bathing it with a heavenly glow.

Free. She was free to love Rick and build a new life with him. And that's what this emotion she'd been unwilling to name was. Love. How did he feel? She glanced at him from the corners of her eyes.

He'd said if he acted love, maybe he'd feel it. Sure enough, the transformation had occurred in his heart as well. How was she to know about her own heart though?

The emotion swelled within her, lodging in her throat, choking off anything she might say. Not yet. She couldn't tell him yet. Maybe after supper.

He kept possession of her hand as they strolled along the sidewalk to the little café two blocks down. Allie glanced in the windows of the homes they passed, noticing the families living and loving. She wouldn't have to envy the other families any longer. She had a place of her own.

Carrying this much joy felt overwhelming.

Rick held open the door of the café for her, and she stepped onto the battered wooden floor. Red-and-white checked tablecloths covered the square tables, and the air was thick with the smell of chicken enchiladas, tonight's special according to the chalkboard. A few locals looked up and spoke to Rick, tipping their hats to her as well.

Rick led her to a corner table that looked out on the patio where pots of flowers bloomed. He sat across from her and smiled with so much contentment that she had to smile back.

His smile changed as he looked over her shoulder at someone. "Judge," he said.

Judge Thompson was smiling, and Allie let herself hope. The older woman stopped at the table. "You two look awfully happy."

"The border patrol just arrested the man who's been giving Allie so much trouble," Rick said. "And if that's not enough, Betsy is talking again, so we're celebrating."

The judge's smile widened. "Glad to hear it. Come see me

tomorrow, and I'll give you the ruling. I think you'll be pleased." She winked and walked away.

"Ah, the joys of small-town living," Rick murmured. "No tightly held secrets." He laughed, then stretched his hand across the table to take Allie's. "Enchiladas just doesn't sound like a celebratory meal. I think we should have steak."

"Me too." Though right now she felt she couldn't eat a thing. They placed their order, and the waitress left them alone.

"What are we going to do about Jon's parents?" Allie asked. "They are going to still want to see Betsy, even if the adoption goes through."

"How do you feel about it?"

"They're her grandparents. I'd like her to know and love them, but I hate for her to be forced to visit when she doesn't want to."

"Sometimes blood can't make family," he said. The sun dipped below the horizon as he spoke, and the shadows deepened on his face. His voice darkened as well. "Adoption can. Love is what counts."

"You never talk about your family," she said. Maybe he would open up now. She wanted to know more about this man who'd slipped into her heart when she wasn't looking.

The triumphant smile he'd worn since she first saw him tonight took a dip. He pulled his hand away and took a gulp of his water. "Not much to say. I haven't seen my parents in years. Last I heard, my dad was in prison for assault and battery over a dispute at work, and my mom was waiting tables in San Antonio and living with man number six."

"Dolly told me about your brother, Chad."

His brows drew together. "You could have asked me instead of gossiping behind my back."

Her cheeks heated. "You're right. I'm sorry. So tell me now." She held his gaze.

He took her hand again, rubbing his thumb over it. "I haven't seen him since he was five. I looked for him for a long time, ever since I threw over my career with the military and came back to Bluebird. Every door was shut though, and I finally had to accept it. Maybe he'll come looking for me someday."

Her trip today was on the tip of her tongue, but she so badly wanted to surprise him. She choked back the information, imagining his expression when Chad finally stood before him. No matter what it took, she would find his brother.

"Why so serious?" he asked.

She put as much of her love into her gaze as she dared. "What happened to your back? The scars, they're dreadful."

A slight smile tipped his lips. "My mother didn't take kindly to me burning the chili when I was ten. She took a whip to my back."

Tears burned Allie's eyes. "Oh, Rick." She squeezed his fingers. "I can't imagine a mother doing that."

"Most people can't," he said dryly. "It was one reason I swore I'd never marry. I didn't trust women. But watching you with Betsy has shown me how a real mother loves her child."

With his thumb rubbing her palm, she found it hard to think. "My parents were good to me," she said.

"Then why are you frowning?"

"My mom lied to me about Elijah," she said. "She said he kicked her out when he found out she was pregnant, and that she lost the baby. Instead, she gave my sister up for adoption, and Elijah brought Maria to the ranch. All these years I could have known her. I don't know why my mom broke ties with Elijah. It was only after she died that I realized he was even still alive."

"Maybe she didn't want your father to know about the baby."

"Maybe. But why did she refuse to have anything to do with Elijah? It doesn't make sense."

"Now that things have settled down, maybe we can try to find out."

The waitress brought their food, and the conversation lulled as they ate their tender steaks. It was the best meal Allie could remember. Maybe because she wasn't looking over her shoulder for danger every minute. Or maybe because of the loving glances Rick sent her way.

Replete with hot food, Allie leaned back in her chair. "The kids will be gone in a few days. When does our next batch come?"

"In a couple of weeks. The rest of the bunkhouse will be finished, and we'll have a group for the month of April. Summer is busy, even though it's hot. The kids like swimming in the river and riding the horses early morning before the sun heats everything up."

Allie's sigh was a happy one. Life was going to be good. "I'll be right back." She took her purse and walked to the bathroom.

The room smelled fresh from a pine detergent. Thankful it was empty, Allie found a chair and opened her purse. She pulled out a small photo of her and Jon together on their wedding day. They both looked so young and happy.

Rick wasn't Jon. Maybe it was best they were so different. Rick had his own place in her heart. "Good-bye, Jon," she whispered. "I hope you're looking down from heaven and are happy Rick and I are together. I think you are." Tears pricked her eyes as she put the picture away.

RICK HELD ALLIE'S HAND IN THE TRUCK. THE STARS AND THE MOON LIT THE vegetation on both sides of the road with a golden glow. With his window rolled down, the fragrance of creosote and sage filled his lungs.

He parked in front of the house. "Looks like the kids are watching TV." The blue glow of the television flickered through the window.

Rick's spirit deflated a bit. He'd hoped for the evening alone with Allie. Peeking at his watch, he saw it was only seven. It would be an hour before he could send the kids off to bed.

The security light illuminated the corral around the barn. They could be alone in the barn. He got out and went around to open her door.

Allie looked up at him with such trust it scared him. What if he failed her? She was bound to find out he had feet of clay soon.

"Let's make sure the kids took care of the horses," he said. Allie slid out, and he took her hand again. Jem ran to greet them, doing his little air dance of joy.

Allie stopped to pet the dog. "Hey, Jem, you keeping everyone safe for us?"

Rick led her toward the barn. "He'd only lick someone to death."

"Poor Jem, did you hear that? Rick has no faith in you."

"Oh, I have plenty of faith." Rick squeezed her fingers. "Faith that he's the friendliest dog on the planet."

The cougar screamed from a rocky hillside, and he saw Allie shiver. "It's probably two miles away," he told her.

"I know. I worry one of these days it will come after one of the horses. Or even worse, Betsy."

"Jem protects us pretty well from animal intruders. It's the human ones that were the problem." He rubbed the dog's head as he trotted beside them.

"That he does," she said, smiling.

They reached the barn, and he slid open the door. The scent of horse and hay greeted them like old friends. A mouse scurried away from their feet, then a dark shape swooped down.

Allie screamed and ducked behind him as the bat barely missed her hair, then cruised on out the door. "I hate bats," she said.

"They're interesting," he said. "There's a big colony in an old mine shaft about five miles from here. They're western pipistrelle bats, and they only eat insects, not pretty girls."

She shuddered. "Interesting to you maybe. Nasty things."

"They eat tons of mosquitoes," he said. "And scorpions and centipedes."

"They're still not my friends." She went past him to the stall that held Moonbeam. "Hey boy, you doing okay?" She rubbed the white blaze on his face.

Rick did a quick walk through, and all was quiet. He eyed the stack of hay in the corner. With a blanket over it, they could settle there and . . . talk. Suppressing a grin, he grabbed an old quilt they kept in the barn for sick horses. When he sniffed it, it smelled slightly horsy but not bad. He spread it over the hay and fell back onto it. He propped his head up with his arms folded under it.

Allie turned toward him and smiled when she saw his comfortable pose. "I take it you are in no hurry to go check on the kids?"

"Emilio is with them." He patted the spot beside him. Her smile widened, and she approached his little nest. "The kitchen is probably a mess."

"I'll help you with it later." Reaching up, he grabbed her hand and tugged her down onto the quilt with him. He put his arm around her, and she snuggled against him. Her hair, smelling like a yucca blossom, tickled his nose, but he didn't mind.

He settled his chin against the top of her head. The words he wanted to say hovered behind his teeth.

I love you.

He'd never told anyone that except his little brother. His parents weren't ones for soft words, and he'd learned that early. But Chad was different. And so was Allie. He'd never imagined he could be so happy, so content. But how did she feel? If she left him, he couldn't handle it.

She still didn't know the role he'd played in Jon's death. And he couldn't tell her. Not right now, with the hay so soft and sweet-smelling, and her trust in him so heady.

"Are you happy, Allie?"

"Very happy." Her voice had a little hitch in it. She pulled away and looked into his face. Her hand came up to cup his cheek. "I love you, Rick," she whispered.

Joy exploded in Rick's chest, radiating heat through his body. "You do? Really?" He sounded like a sixteen-year-old kid, and he nearly groaned. His lips found hers. So soft and yielding. He drank in the love she poured over him like the desert drank up rain.

Tell her. The words lodged behind his teeth. Three little words. I love you. Why couldn't he say them? He was afraid to let them loose in case they grew into something he couldn't manage.

Love made you vulnerable, tore your heart out when you weren't looking. If he said the words, they might bite him later. So instead he poured how he felt into the kiss. Surely she would understand.

They necked like two kids at the drive-in until he heard the kids laughing as they went past the barn to the bunkhouse.

"Let's go to the house," he whispered. "The bed is softer."

Her questioning gaze softened, and she nodded. Hand in hand, they slipped out of the barn and moved through the pools of moonlight to the house.

25

CONTENTMENT SOFTENED RICK'S BONES. HE PROPPED HIMSELF ON ONE elbow and watched his wife's face in the morning light. Had he ever been this happy, even once? He didn't think so.

His conscience had torn at him all night in spite of it. Until she knew the truth, how could he trust her vows of love? Before he got in any deeper, he needed to know how she'd react to the truth.

And he still hadn't told her he loved her. Rick believed in showing how he felt with action. She rolled closer, tucking her head onto his shoulder. He pulled her closer.

"You okay?" Her voice was husky.

"Fine."

His hand rubbed against the flesh of her upper arm in a loving caress. He had to tell her. Tension tightened the muscles in his back and arms. It wasn't fair to keep it from her. If only he had some whiskey to bolster his courage.

"What's wrong?" she asked.

"There's something I have to tell you," he said. Her smile bloomed out, and he knew she thought he was going to say something sweet, like the three little words that hovered on his tongue.

He rushed on before he lost his courage. "It's about Jon's death. My part in it."

Rolling onto her back, she propped herself up on the pillow and stared at him. "What are you talking about?"

He sat up and ran his hand through his rumpled hair. His courage began to fail. How could she forgive him when he couldn't forgive himself? "Forget it."

"No. No, I'm not going to forget it. Something is between us, Rick, even after last night. If we are going to build a future, we have to knock down the wall."

He knew she was right. "It's my fault he's dead."

She folded her arms across her chest as though to ward off whatever he was trying to tell her. "How can it be your fault?"

"Allie, I'm an alcoholic. A recovering one, but it's something I struggle with every day." He couldn't look away from her stunned face, though he wanted to.

"An alcoholic." Her blue eyes cleared, and she touched his arm. "It's okay, Rick. We all have something we're ashamed of in our past. I'll be here for you."

She wouldn't be so glib once she knew the truth. Rick held her gaze. "You don't understand, Allie. I was drunk the day Jon died." He looked away, unable to watch the words he was about to say pierce her. In an instant he was back in Iraq with the raw sewage making his eyes water and the stink of gunpowder lingering on his clothes.

THE SOUND OF THE TROOPS' BOOTS CLOCKED ALONG THE PAVEMENT. RICK staggered when they stopped at the end of the street. The rest of the unit hunkered down behind some trash barrels. Rick fell clumsily beside his buddy. Some hair of the dog would clear his mind. He fumbled for the little flask he'd slipped into his pocket.

"You've had enough," Jon hissed. He grabbed the flask from Rick's hand and started to put it in his own pocket.

"No sermon," Rick slurred. "Give it back." He made an awkward swipe at Jon's arm.

A shadow loomed over them. Colonel Preston glared down at Jon. "I knew you weren't as pure as you tried to seem, Lieutenant Siders. Hand it over. You'll be brought up for courtmartial on this."

Rick tried to slide out of the way. He had enough presence of mind to know that if the colonel saw him like this, he'd be placed under arrest. Jon was too good of a buddy to squeal on him.

"Yes sir," Jon said, straightening. He passed the flask to his superior. "I'm sorry, sir."

"Sorry doesn't cut it," the colonel snapped. "Stand up. Walk a line for me."

"I didn't drink any of it, sir. I'm competent to fight." Jon leaped to his feet, walked a line, turned, and came back.

Shame clutched Rick's gut. He'd make it up to Jon though. His buddy had been eyeing a dress for his wife but didn't have the money to buy it. Jon sent every cent back to his little family in El Paso. Rick would buy it and send it, then tell Jon what he'd done.

"Enough. But this isn't over." The colonel grabbed the flask and moved away with a final contemptuous glare.

"Thanks, buddy," Rick muttered. "You saved my bacon there."

Jon's gaze held pity and love. "You've got to quit the drinking, Rick. It's going to kill you."

"I know, I know." Rick stood, still wavering. "Let's get this job done." He couldn't stand to look his buddy in the eye. Jon was the best friend he'd ever had.

"Stop!" Jon grabbed Rick's arm when he started toward the house that had pieces of plaster missing and no windows. "Wait for the order."

Rick shrugged off his friend's hand. "No glory in waiting," he said, his words slurred. Before Jon could grab him again, he leaped to the door and kicked it open.

His gaze collided with the five insurgents pointing guns at him. He brought his own weapon up, but slowly, too slowly. Expecting to feel bullets tearing through his skin, he closed his eyes. The next thing he knew, Jon's rebel call echoed into the small room. His buddy leaped into the house in front of the men.

The bullets meant for him entered Jon's chest, and his blood-spattered body fell across Rick as the other soldiers came through the door.

HE COULDN'T LOOK AT HER AS HE RECOUNTED THE STORY. WHEN IT WAS over, he lifted his gaze to her face. "Don't hate me, Allie. I hate myself enough for both of us."

A stunned expression dulled the brightness of her eyes. "No," she said. "You're lying. You're afraid to love me, so you're trying to drive me away."

"It's the truth, honey," he said, his voice barely above a whisper. "It's eaten me up all this time. It's the reason I had to help you. I owed it to Jon."

She clapped her hands over her ears. "No, I won't listen."

He grabbed her wrists and pulled her hands down. "If we're going to go on from here, it has to be with truth between us. I killed him, Allie. I need you to forgive me. Can you do that?"

"That's the only reason you married me?"

Her whimper cut him to bloody shreds inside. "The only reason. But it's not the reason I want to stay married now."

"Then why?" She held up her hand. "Wait, don't say anything. I have to think about this. It's too much to take in." She got out of bed and gathered her clothes from the floor. "I've got to get out of here for a while."

He watched her walk away. Saying the words "I love you" might have stopped her, but he still couldn't get them out past his tongue. Maybe it was a good thing. If she couldn't forgive him, he wasn't going to run the risk of rejection.

MOONBEAM MOVED SMOOTHLY UNDER HER. ALLIE BARELY NOTICED THE clouds overhead, the blackness deepening as the storm approached. Her second husband had killed her first.

Murderer.

She couldn't stop the tears. Why couldn't he have kept the truth to himself? Dealing with it was going to be impossible. She had loved Jon, and now she loved Rick.

Oh, how she loved him.

But he had kept this one vital piece of information to himself until she threw everything to the winds and gave herself to him. Had he thought if he told her last night, he wouldn't get her into his bed?

Her hard laugh turned to a sob as the wind picked up pieces of sand and flung them against her face. The stinging attack broke her from her thoughts, and she looked up to see the towering thunderheads still building.

She had some time before it hit. The cabin where Rosa Garcia lived was just over the hill. She could head there to escape the coming rain. It would be an excuse to ask Rosa the questions she needed answered.

The tiny cabin looked barely bigger than an outhouse, a mere fifteen-by-fifteen square. Flowers bloomed beside the porch, and the rocker looked worn and well used.

Glancing at her watch, Allie saw it was barely six thirty. The old woman might still be in bed. But before she could decide what to do, the front door opened, and a tiny, wizened figure stepped into view. An apron covered the dark dress that touched her boot tops, and the woman wore her white hair coiled in a knot at the back of her neck.

"Finally, you have come for a visit." Rosa's dark eyes examined her. "You have the look of Maria, *sí*, and of your mother. Coffee is brewing. Come." She hooked a finger toward Allie.

Allie dismounted, tied the reins to the porch railing, and followed the woman inside. The tiny cabin was as spotless inside as out. A bright rug covered the worn floorboards, and three candles burned on the fireplace mantel. Coffee boiled on a woodstove in the corner.

Rosa wrapped her hand in her apron, lifted the coffeepot from the heat, and poured two cups. "Cream and sugar, *sí?*"

"Yes, please." Allie accepted the coffee the woman handed her, then went to sit on the ladder-back chair. "You sounded like you were expecting me."

"*Sí*. I knew you would come in your own time. You want to know of your mother." Rosa settled at the table with Allie. "I am the only one left who knows all the story. The rest—all dead."

Rain began to patter against the metal roof over their heads. "You were at the ranch when my mother was a child?"

Rosa nodded. "*Sí*. From the time your *madre* was crawling on the floor."

She might as well start at the beginning. "What happened to my grandmother?"

Rosa's dark eyes softened. "Ah, Francesca was a darling girl. Elijah, he loved her very much. I thought he would die himself when the pneumonia took her from him. But he had your *madre* to care for."

"I saw some pictures of my mother growing up. She looked so happy until she got to her teens. What happened? Who was Maria's father?"

Rosa winced. "It is an unhappy story. Elijah carried the hurt to his grave. He blamed himself."

Wrapping her fingers around her warm cup, Allie tried to prepare herself for whatever information was coming. Thunder rumbled overhead. She would be trapped here all morning unless Rosa hurried up.

"Elijah had a partner. Nolan Webster. Handsome as *el diablo* himself. His wife was Francesca's best friend. He took a special interest in Anna, showed her rodeo tricks, took her to her first rodeo. Elijah thought nothing of it until his daughter told him she was pregnant. And Nolan was the father."

Allie shuddered, suddenly cold. "How old was this Nolan?"

"Forty, he was. And Anna was fifteen."

A lech. "He should have been shot," Allie said fiercely. "He could have been prosecuted for statutory rape."

"*Sí*. Elijah did just that, dear girl."

Allie opened her mouth and shut it again. "Did what? You don't mean Elijah shot him?" That couldn't be what Rosa meant. Elijah was no murderer.

Rosa's lively dark eyes narrowed. "*Sí*. Elijah, he shot Nolan and buried him in an old well. Anna was the only one who knew. She left the ranch that night and never returned. It was the only way she could cope with knowing her father was a murderer."

Allie swallowed hard. "Elijah seemed to be such a good man."

Rosa grabbed her hand with tough, sinewy fingers. "*Sí*, he was a very good man. But even good men have their breaking points. He spent the rest of his life atoning for his sin. That is when he converted the ranch to a place for hurting young people."

"And Maria?"

"Elijah had many eyes and ears. When Anna left, he found her again a year later. By then she was beginning to make a name for herself in the rodeo. She refused to come home. When she had no *bebé* with her, Elijah found out what had happened to the little one. She was to be adopted, but he fought and won custody and brought her home."

"My mother never objected?"

"No." Rosa shrugged her wizened shoulders. "Perhaps she never knew. She abandoned the *bebé* at a church."

"How could she do that?" The action didn't compute. Her mother had always been so caring and supportive of Allie and her sister. It just went to show how so many people wore a mask. Like Rick. She pushed the memory of his face away.

She took a sip of her coffee. It wasn't as bitter as her heart.

Rosa stood and went to rinse out her cup at the old hand pump. "I do not know, *mujercita*. Perhaps by then, she had come to hate everything about Nolan and the ranch, all the past memories. I am glad she was a good *madre* to you. She learned from her past, as we all should."

Had Rick learned from his past? She hadn't seen him take a single drop of liquor. But he had hidden his alcoholism from her. It would be hard to get past that failure if she was even willing to try, and right now, she wasn't too sure about that.

ALLIE HAD BEEN GONE AN HOUR. RICK KNEW SHE NEEDED TIME, BUT HE couldn't hang around and watch for her or he'd go crazy. Maybe he could see what Walker had found out about Luis Hernandez since yesterday.

Hoping to catch him before he went to work, he drove to Walker's house. Splashes of rain peppered the windshield, and he flipped on his wipers. Looked like they could have a real gulley-washer. Rick parked behind his friend's truck and honked when he saw Walker exiting the house.

Walker waved and walked back to stand beside Rick's open window. "I was going to call you when I got to the office, Mr. Impatience." His easy smile came. "We did good work yesterday. The money trail checks out. The ring raked in over five hundred thousand dollars."

"And it definitely went through Allie's account?"

"Yep."

"And he killed Allie's family. Man, that took a lot of hate."

Walker's brow clouded. "Uh, actually Rick, we're not finding evidence of any murder. He was in Mexico when the plane crash happened, and then when the sister was killed, he was in Canada."

"Maybe he hired someone."

"Maybe. But if he did, there's no money trail pointing to a hit man."

"I'm sure you'll find the connection. He's good at covering his tracks."

"Maybe." Walker glanced at his watch. "Listen, I've got to run. I'll call you if I find out anything new."

"Thanks." Rick backed out of the driveway and turned his truck toward home. He should get Betsy, but considering the weather, she'd be safer with the O'Sullivans. They had a basement, and this storm just might have a twister in it.

He mulled over what he'd found out. Luis had to be the murderer. Rick might have to help pin this down himself. The last thing he wanted was for the man to get off on a lighter charge and come looking for Allie again.

The clouds drew his gaze again, thunderheads building in the southwest. As purple-black as a bruise, they towered over the landscape. They were in for a bad one. He needed to make sure Allie wasn't out in this weather. He tried to reach her on his cell phone, but she didn't answer. The best he could do was get home as soon as possible. If she was still out, he'd take Jem and go find her.

His cell phone rang and he flipped it open. "Bailey."

"Rick, Betsy is gone." Dolly was babbling, nearly hysterical. "The bedroom window is open, and she's just gone."

Time froze.

Rick jammed on the brakes and pulled to the side of the road. What should he do? Go look for Betsy or find Allie? He started to turn the truck around. Allie would want him to find Betsy.

But for some reason he couldn't name, he veered the wheel the other way and headed to the ranch. "Call the sheriff," he barked into the phone. "I'm going after Allie, and we'll be there as soon as we can."

Allie was roaming on her own, but Rick had a feeling the guy would take Betsy to flaunt his power over her. He could only take the impulse as direction from God and trust he was reading it right.

THE SPLATTERS OF RAIN CHILLED HER ARMS. ALLIE LOOKED UP INTO THE rolling underbelly of a monster. A doozy of a storm was going to hit any minute, more than just the rain that had eased off before she left Rosa's. She was exposed to the vicious lightning flickering in the clouds. A rumble followed that made Moonbeam startle. She could sense the horse's agitation as the storm grew nearer.

She probably should have stayed at Rosa's. Her gaze swept the landscape as she looked for a place to get her and the horse in from the storm. There was nothing in the rock face, and the ranch was an hour's ride behind her.

She saw something in the distance and realized it was Bluebird. She whistled to the horse, and the mare turned toward her. Allie trotted Moonbeam over to the other mare and grabbed her halter. "What are you doing here, girl?"

The horse snorted but didn't try to run away. Allie leaned her face against the mare's neck and inhaled the aroma of horse. Rosa's words came back to her.

Maybe she learned from her past.

Didn't everyone have regrets for things they'd done in the past? She sure did. Who was she to judge Rick? She hadn't lived his life and been faced with his hurts. Love was a choice, he'd said. He'd chosen love early on and proven it by his actions.

She could do the same. The anger seeped out of her heart. Rick deserved the best she could give.

"Allie!"

She turned in the saddle to see Charlie coming toward her on horseback. She waved and waited for him. He would help her.

"Are you crazy? Coming out here in the middle of a storm," he said, stopping his horse about five feet from her. "The lightning will get you if the wind doesn't."

"You're out here too," she said, smiling.

"I was looking for you. Rick was worried, and so was I. He went to town to get Betsy and asked me to try to find you. You two have a fight?" His smile suggested he'd be glad to hear the juicy details.

"Something like that," she said shortly, irritation wiping away her initial happiness at seeing him. "How'd Bluebird get out?"

He shrugged. "No clue."

"Any idea where we can hole up?"

"I've got the perfect spot. Follow me." Digging his heels into his horse's belly, he led the way up the hillside and disappeared around the curve in the trail.

Muttering under her breath that she wanted to go down, not up, Allie followed with Bluebird. As soon as she got past the creosote bush that stuck halfway into the path, she saw Charlie waving from the opening to an old mine shaft.

She rode up to join him. "I don't want to go in there. Bats." She shuddered.

"They're sleeping," he said.

A brilliant flash of light superimposed itself on her eyes. Her hair stood on end, and the lightning crackled a hundred feet away, where it split a piñon tree right down the center. The smell of ozone burned her throat.

Bluebird snorted and tried to jerk away, but she hung on. Moonbeam pranced along the wet ground too, his eyes rolling to the whites.

"Come on!" Charlie and his horse disappeared into the shaft.

The hot scent from the burning tree and the way the wind picked up made Allie dismount and follow, leading Moonbeam and Bluebird in with her. The cool muskiness of the mine made her instantly want to go back outside. She hated closed-in spaces. The rough walls and low ceiling made her chest feel tight.

"Over here, Allie," Charlie called.

He was brandishing a flashlight. The friendly beam pushed back the edges of the darkness. Allie dropped Moonbeam's reins and sat beside Charlie on a big rock near the ashes of an old campfire.

"Looks like someone uses this place." Kicking at the ashes with the toe of her boot, she glanced around the space.

Black things in the corners made her shudder. Bats, but they weren't moving. The storm would blow itself out soon, and she could get home to Betsy.

Once she figured out what to say to Rick. Tears welled in her eyes again, and she turned her head, but not fast enough to hide her emotion from Charlie.

"Hey, you okay?"

"Fine." She sniffed and gulped back her pain.

"Rick have a drinking binge or something?"

She looked up then. "You knew?"

"Well, sure. The whole ranch knows. Elijah was waiting for Rick to fall, but he hasn't so far. Maybe you weakened him. You have that effect on men."

She wasn't going there. Uh-uh. Charlie seemed to have words of confession hanging on his tongue, and she wasn't going to give him a chance to tell her he was crazy about her or something equally embarrassing.

Standing, she walked around the cavern, though she was careful not to look up at the bats. If she saw one move, she might scream. "What kind of mine is this?"

Charlie stood and joined her. "Mercury." He kicked an orange rock with his toe. "Cinnabar rock carries it."

"Why isn't it mined anymore?"

"I don't know, do I look like a park ranger?" He laughed, but there was an edge to it. "I've been wanting to talk to you. Sit down." He took her arm in a surprisingly hard grasp and marched her back to the rock.

There was no getting around it. She was going to have to hurt his feelings. Just what she needed on top of an upsetting day. "Look, Charlie, let's not go there. I'm happily married."

His laughter barked, echoing off the sides of the mine. "Get real. You're not as pretty as you think you are."

She drew back at the derisive edge to his voice. "My mistake," she said in a cool voice. "So what's on your mind?"

"Women like you can twist a guy until he doesn't know which way is up." Charlie swore and stomped at the ashes and charred wood, scattering them in all directions. Vile words spewed from his mouth as he waved his hands and roared around the space.

Allie wanted to grab Moonbeam and run, but the storm had descended in full fury. The wind howled outside the mine opening, and the thunder boomed in a continuous roll. Rain sluiced over the entrance like a waterfall.

"Calm down, Charlie. Tell me what this is all about." She tried to speak in a soft, calm voice, and it seemed to work. He quit kicking at the ground and turned to look at her.

Then she saw his hand come up with a gun.

"Put that away." She spoke in her strongest, most assertive voice.

"You killed my brother." His voice was calm and reasonable.

"Jimmy Hernandez is your brother? Bu—but you're not Hispanic."

His short laugh made Moonbeam prick his ears and step back. "This has nothing to do with *Hernandez*. You're so stupid. I gave you plenty of time to figure it out."

"Who's your brother? I thought you said he was a politician."

"He wanted to run for office, but you killed him. The name Mark Haskell ring a bell?" He watched until she flinched, then he smiled.

"Mark's dead? I didn't know."

He leaned over her, yelling at the top of his lungs, "Of course he's dead, you heartless witch! He hung himself when you broke his heart. You led him on, then tossed him aside like a piece of trash when you were done."

Allie winced as spittle sprayed from his mouth over her face. "Charlie, it wasn't like that. We weren't romantically involved. He never even kissed me."

"You're a liar! He'd come home at night and tell me what you said about loving him forever. Then some new cowboy walked in and whisked you away from him."

"He lied to you," she said, trying to edge away. Her back was up against the wall of the mine. "You have to believe me."

The storm was beginning to abate. She could hear the thunder moving off. They had to get down off this mountain and through the wash before a flash flood hit.

Charlie quit looming over her. He stepped back, and she took hope that maybe he was listening to the truth.

"Please, you have to believe me, Charlie. I only went out with him a couple of times." Did Charlie kill her family and Yo? Staring into his face, suffused with red, she could believe it.

And she was stuck here in a mine with him training a gun on her. Praying, she tried to think of what to do. She couldn't leave Betsy alone.

26

THE WIND RATTLED THE TRUCK LIKE A COUGAR SHAKING A RABBIT. RICK gripped the wheel and fought to keep it on the road. He kept shooting cautious glances at the sky. While tornadoes weren't common in the Big Bend area, they weren't unheard-of either.

Lightning snaked across the sky, and thunder chased it, a rumble that he felt clear through the vehicle. Allie and Betsy were out in this. He had to find them.

Squinting through the driving rain, he struggled to see the road. With the storm obscuring the landscape, he had no idea where he was. Then he saw a lane off to the right and recognized his neighbor's drive. The ranch was still ten miles away. He should pull off and wait this out a few minutes.

He wanted to press on, but if he ended up in a ditch, Allie and Betsy would be lost. He angled the truck into the lane, keeping it on the high part so runoff wouldn't flood him out. With the truck shut off and stationary, the storm battered the vehicle so much, he thought it might tip over. There could be a twister in this sucker.

His cell phone rang, and he fished it out of his shirt pocket. "Bailey," he said. He heard a voice on the other end, but the storm was so loud, he couldn't hear well. Then he realized it was Brendan.

"Got word about—"

"Say again, Brendan?" he shouted. "I'm in the middle of a spring thunderstorm."

"Mark Haskell," Brendan said, the connection suddenly clearing. "He hung himself, which is why Allie didn't hear from him again."

"Holy cow. Listen, Brendan, this is important." Rick had to shout over the sound of the wind. "Betsy's missing. I thought we found the guy who was after Allie, but I was wrong. Did this Haskell have any family?"

"Just a brother he was raising. Half-brother actually. The kid ended up in a mental hospital for a while. Charles—" The rest of the name disappeared in a crackle of static.

"What was that, Brendan? You cut out. What's Charles's last name?"

"Reyes," Brendan said. "Charles Reyes."

Charlie!

His friend Charlie, who was out looking for Allie. Could they have been wrong? Maybe Luis had nothing to do with the deaths. He claimed he didn't.

The static in his phone grew louder. The connection was about to die. "Brendan, I don't think my phone is going to hold. If you can hear me, call the sheriff in town. Tell him Charlie Reyes has Betsy and is going to kill her and Allie. I'm going to the ranch now."

Brendan's response was garbled, then the phone went dead. Rick could only hope and pray his friend got the last of the words. He started the engine, backed out onto the road he still couldn't see, then sped back toward the ranch as fast as the buffeting rain would allow.

He couldn't believe it. Not Charlie. He was just a kid. But then murder didn't seem to have an age requirement.

He reached the turnoff to the ranch. A new river had sprung into existence while he was gone. The wash across the road ran heavy and deep. He was going to have to try to make it through anyway. The truck shuddered as Rick gunned it. The tires found purchase in the mud under the water, then a wave slapped against the door. The truck bucked again. The tires lost their grip, and the water lifted the vehicle.

In seconds, the truck was riding the waves in the middle of the current. Hurtling toward the Eye of the Needle, as they called the hole between two huge boulders. No way would the truck fit through there.

Rick unfastened his seat belt and prepared to abandon the truck. With the force of the current, the vehicle would slam into those rocks, and he didn't want to be trapped in the cab when it happened. He might be unable to get out with the doors and windows jammed up.

The truck slewed sideways, and the passenger door became the leading edge. Rick tried to open his door, but the water pressure was too great. He jerked around to see the approaching rocks, then ran the window down to try to get out that way. Sitting on the top of the window opening, he grabbed the top of the truck and hauled himself up until his feet were on the armrest.

Then he was atop the truck, looking down at the red-brown, swirling water. The bank was fifteen feet away, and it would be a hard swim to make it, but he had no choice. The rocks loomed ahead, and the impact would knock him in the water anyway.

The rain continued to drench him. He shot up a prayer for help, then leaped. The water closed over his head, and then his feet touched the bottom. He kicked with his heels and shot up to the surface, where he gulped in air. He couldn't see which way was to safety, but he saw the truck barreling toward the rocks and struck out perpendicular to its trajectory.

Flotsam and debris battered him as he struggled to swim in the turbulent water. Pieces of sheet metal barreled by, and he ducked out of their way, but one raked a sharp edge across his arm. He grabbed a piece of wood and hung on to it for buoyancy. Fatigue was already beginning to slow him, and he wasn't sure he'd make it. Then his boot touched bottom, and he used the stability to propel himself forward. His arm struck a tree limb, this time not one floating in the water but anchored in the soil.

He grabbed the limb, hauled himself to shore, and lay in the mud with the rain pounding on his back. Half-unconscious, he coughed up the dirty water from his lungs.

Allie. Betsy.

They needed him. He managed to get onto his hands and knees, then finally to his feet. Patting his pocket, he realized his cell phone was still there, though it was probably useless.

The rain began to slow, and he blinked water out of his eyes. He needed a horse and Jem to try to find Allie. The barn was three hundred feet up the lane, but on the other side of the water. He'd have to climb the rocks and sidle across the Eye of the Needle.

Gathering his strength, he started for the rocks. With his boots wet and the rocks slick with water and mud, it would be a hard trail.

He reached the base of the hillside and started up. Cold mud and muck clung to his hands and caked his boots. Several times he fell on the slippery surface. Finally he was at the summit.

Below him, the truck rocked and scraped against the rocks as the roaring flood battered it. The door had crumpled in, and the rolling of the water had smashed it from all sides. He straddled the narrow rock and began to scoot along toward the other side. The water rose higher and higher on the face of the cliff until it touched the soles of his boots.

But by then, he was nearly across. With a last shove, he gained the boulder on the other side and began his descent. It was just as treacherous going down as it had been going up. One false step, and he'd hurtle to his death.

There weren't as many finger holds on this side. When he was about ten feet from the ground, his hand slipped from the rock, and he began to slide down. Scrabbling for a finger hold, he tore the nail from his thumb but continued to fall. His other hand flailed out but found nothing to grab hold of.

The next thing he knew, he was lying on his back in the mud, staring into roiling black clouds. On either side of him were more rocks, but he'd fallen into the only safe spot. *Thank you, God.* He struggled to his feet in spite of his screaming muscles. Hobbling toward the ranch, he finally managed to break into a run. The barn and house were just ahead.

First he should see if Allie was back. Maybe his fear was for nothing. He rushed up the steps, threw open the door, and stepped inside. The welcome respite from the storm made him pause, then he hurried to the living room.

Empty.

He turned and ran back outside. His boots smacked through the mud puddles as he ran to the barn. The doors to the barn hung open, and so did the gate. He heard voices around the back of the barn and veered to the back paddock.

The horses were gone. He could see several of them at the far edge of the field. Several of the hands and the teenagers were chasing them.

He caught sight of Fern coming from the barn with a halter in her hand. "Have you seen Allie?" he asked.

"What's wrong?"

He hesitated, unsure if he should alarm her. "She went out for a ride this morning, and I don't want her caught in this storm."

"I haven't seen her all day," Fern said.

"Me neither," Latoya echoed, exiting the barn behind Fern.

"Hang on. I only want to say this once." Rick waved over the rest of the group.

Devon and Emilio jogged toward him with Leon coming up a few paces behind. The ranch hands gathered around too.

"Look, Betsy and Allie are missing, probably out in this storm," he said.

"Dude, you need help?" Devon asked. "We can go out too."

"I can organize them into a search party," Emilio said.

Rick hesitated. While he could use the help, he didn't want the kids in danger from Charlie. "Just pray, guys. Emilio, call the sheriff. Tell him I found out Charlie might be a danger to Allie, and I'm looking for them now."

"Charlie? No way," Devon said.

"It looks like he's behind the attempts on Allie's life. And someone stole Betsy out of the bedroom early this morning. I've got to find them."

"Let me come," Emilio said.

"The kids need protection in case he comes back. You'd better stay here." Rick turned toward the house. "Get in the house. Lock the door, and don't let Charlie in if he comes back."

He jogged across the muddy yard to the house and rushed into the office. The glass in the gun cabinet gleamed. The key was in the desk. He fished it out and opened the cabinet. The black barrels looked deadly. Rick touched the gunstock, so smooth and slick.

He'd sworn never to point a gun at another human being after the accident that killed a child in Iraq. But this was his wife, his child. Didn't he have the right to protect his family?

His hand hovered over the gunstock, then dropped. He couldn't do it. God would have to provide another way. Grabbing up the nightstick, he wheeled and ran to save his family.

THE GUN'S BORE SEEMED TO GROW BIGGER WITH EVERY SECOND. NOW THAT the rain had stopped and moisture shimmered in the air, Allie felt the danger growing. He would do something now that they weren't trapped here.

"What do you want me to say, Charlie? I'm sorry Mark is dead. I never meant to hurt him. Or you. I thought we were friends."

"Friends?" He laughed. "I'm a better actor than I thought. I don't want you to say anything, Allie. I want you to die. But first you'll watch Betsy drown."

All the air left Allie's lungs. "What are you saying?"

He laughed. "Got your attention now, don't I?" He grabbed her arm and dragged her toward a small opening. The hallway was so tiny, she had to bend over to walk through it.

He forced her in front of him, the gun digging into her back. Then she stepped through into a smaller circular room about twelve feet in diameter.

Betsy leaped to her feet. "Mommy!" She ran to Allie, but Betsy's hands were tied behind her, and all she could do was lean against her mother's leg and cry.

Allie's fingers tore at the rope's knot, and even before Charlie emerged from the corridor, she had her daughter freed.

"Here, brat." Charlie grabbed at Betsy.

Allie pushed her daughter behind her and faced him down. "Leave her alone! What kind of monster does this to a child?"

"I didn't want to," he said, a sulky pout to his lips. "You forced me. Always around Rick, never coming out for a ride with me. I told you I was going to strip you of everything you loved. I would have settled for the adults if you hadn't been so smug." He sneered. "All joy and light. You had another fish on your hook, and I couldn't take it anymore."

"Let her go, Charlie. Please. I'll go with you, do anything you want, anything to make amends. Just don't hurt her. She's just a little girl, and you've hurt her enough."

"I haven't done a thing to her yet."

"Didn't you wonder why she didn't talk? It was seeing the—the accident." She lowered her voice, hoping Betsy wouldn't be able to make out her words. "For a year she didn't utter a word. Don't you think that's enough?"

For a minute she thought maybe her plea had gotten through to him. His gaze fell on Betsy, and his mouth softened.

"She's a cute kid," he said. His lips pressed together. "I'm sorry, but the sins of the mother fall on the child too." He reached around her.

Allie screamed and beat at him with her fists. She leaped onto his back and pummeled him. "Run, Bets! Run!"

Her daughter leaped past her, squeezed between Charlie's legs, and darted into the tunnel. Charlie whirled around and around in the chamber. He fell against the wall, slamming Allie's back against rock. The pain made her loosen her grip, and he managed to throw her down to the floor.

"You'll pay for that." He dragged her to her feet and forced her into the tunnel.

Praying for God to save her daughter, Allie moved slowly. Betsy needed as long as possible to run for help, to escape. Charlie shoved at her with the gun, and she stumbled to her knees, then took her time getting moving again.

All too soon, her head emerged into the high-ceilinged room. But there was no sign of Betsy, and Allie closed her eyes with thankfulness. All three horses were gone too.

"I'll find her," Charlie said, his teeth gritted together. "You can count on that." He shoved her out of the mine opening onto the ledge outside.

The storm had passed, and she could see a glimmer of blue in the clouds, smell the freshness in the air. Allie breathed in the life, knowing it would be only a few minutes until she lay broken and drowned at the bottom of this cliff where the flood raged. Her gaze swept the valley until she saw a small figure on horseback at the bottom of the path, still above the water's reach. A gulf separated Betsy and Bluebird from the safety of the other side.

Charlie had seen them too. He started toward them, but Allie grabbed his arm. "I admit it. I wanted to hurt your brother. He was such a nerd, and he deserved everything he got."

Charlie stopped and turned his gaze on her. It was odd, looking death in the face. Allie had never expected to see it so clearly. Cold and implacable, his eyes reflected no humanity that she could see.

Then he smiled. "You can't distract me that easily."

He turned toward her daughter again, but the mare and little girl melded into one blur as the combined figure leaped the gulf and gained the safety of the other side.

"Thank you, God," Allie whispered. With her daughter safe, she could handle what came next. She wasn't afraid to die, though she desperately wished she'd told Rick she forgave him.

He'd feel guilt over her death, and she regretted that.

She sagged to the ground, her legs like rubber. Charlie's fingers tightened on the trigger, and Allie squeezed her eyes shut, expecting a bullet to slam into her skull at any moment. When nothing happened, she opened her eyes and stared up at his smiling face. The smile made her shudder.

She could find no pity or remorse in Charlie's set face, but she wasn't dead yet. Maybe she was giving up too soon. He wasn't going to shoot her, so she had hope. Slim hope, but a tiny sliver at least. The only weapons at her disposal were rocks and her own hands.

"I want you to suffer like Mark did," Charlie said. "He climbed that chair, put the rope around his neck, knowing he was about to die. He kicked over the chair, but his neck didn't break and he slowly strangled to death. It wasn't clean and easy."

He grabbed her arm and yanked her to her feet. Grabbing her hands, he pulled them roughly behind her back. She felt rope chafe her wrists, and he tightened it down until she groaned.

"What are you going to do?" she asked when he shoved her closer to the edge of the cliff.

"Make the most of a storm like this." He propelled her to the very edge of the cliff.

Rivulets of water ran down the hillside to join an ocean of rushing, tumbling water. Churning brown waves tossed up pieces of wood and debris before sucking them under the deadly current again. The flash flood stretched from the base of the cliff across to the next rocky outcropping, a distance of three hundred feet.

Allie caught just a glimpse of her daughter's curls on top of the hill. Rick was standing beside her!

She turned to face Charlie. "You won't get away with my murder. You'll be caught and tried. You'll go to prison or the electric chair, Charlie. Stop this now before it's too late."

"It's already too late. I've killed five people. One more won't make a difference." He smiled, a brief gleam of teeth. "But they won't know I killed you. They'll think the flash flood caught you. It's perfectly understandable. I'll find Betsy and dispose of her before she can tell. All neat and tidy."

He meant to toss her into the raging water.

Lord, help me.

She struggled then, fighting his grip on her arm. "They'll know I was murdered," she gasped. "My hands will be tied."

She spared a glance toward her daughter and found Rick atop the horse with Betsy. They were turning this way. What was he thinking to bring her back into danger?

Charlie turned her around and untied her wrists. "You won't be able to fight the waves anyway." He flipped her around to face the water again.

His hand shoved her in the small of the back, and she was standing on the very edge of the rock. Looking down into the swirling water, she knew Rick wouldn't get here in time.

She wasn't a strong swimmer. The waves would overpower her in seconds. Her only chance was to not go there at all, but Charlie was prodding her. Only a few inches kept her from plummeting down the slope to the hungry waves.

Her gaze fastened on the roots of a tree jutting out from the rock above her head. The closest one looked strong enough to support her weight. She might be able to reach it.

Without waiting to consider the outcome, she leaped up. Her palms slapped onto the thick root, and her fingers closed around the support. Drawing her knees to her chest, she snatched her legs from Charlie's grasp as he lunged for them.

"Allie!"

She heard Rick's voice, and her head turned toward the sound. He was dismounting from Bluebird, who had leaped the gap again. Once he was on the ground, he smacked Bluebird's rump, and the horse carried Betsy back to safety.

Rick's voice made Charlie falter in his lunge. His leap brought him closer to the edge, and she kicked out, her left foot connecting with his head. His arms pinwheeled as he tried to catch himself, but his right boot slid out from under him.

Rick's nightstick sailed through the air. It struck Charlie on the head, and in that instant, he lost his battle for balance. His face turned up to her, and she saw terror in his eyes. Out of instinct, she let go of the roots with one hand and started to reach down for him. She couldn't let him die without at least trying.

"Allie, no!" Rick dove toward Charlie too, but it was too late. Without a sound, he pitched over the side and disappeared in the brown foam.

Allie dropped down and flung herself onto her stomach beside Rick to peer over the side. "Charlie!"

Charlie's head bobbed up, and one arm flung toward the skies before he disappeared again. He never came up.

THE FRESH SCENT OF RAIN WASHED AWAY THE DANK SMELL OF FEAR. IT was truly over now. Rick held Allie as she curled onto his lap and clutched at his shirt as if to assure herself—and him—that they were both really alive. He still wasn't sure if they were alive or just in heaven.

"You're safe," he murmured in her hair.

"You're wet," she said, pulling her head away.

"I had a little swim in the river to get here." He smiled down at her.

"You swam *that?*" Her gaze went to the raging floodwaters below their perch.

"I'd swim the ocean to get to you." His arms tightened around her. "I—I love you, Allie." He wanted to say the words before he lost his nerve. Even if she couldn't forgive him for keeping the truth from her, he had to tell her.

She didn't answer for so long, he thought she would pull away and tell him she was leaving. His muscles tightened for the blow.

Her fingers toyed with the buttons on his shirt, but her eyes stayed downcast. "I hated you for all of fifteen minutes," she said. Her gaze finally lifted to lock with his. "I wanted to dig the love up by the roots and fling it back in your face, but the tentacles went clear to bedrock. You're stuck with me."

"You forgive me?"

"Yes." She curled her fists into his shirt and gave him a slight shake. "Just don't ever hide anything from me again."

"You've got a lot of room to talk," he said, his grin breaking out. "I seem to remember all kinds of things you didn't tell me in the beginning."

Her smile was shamefaced. "That's different." She swatted his arm. "Okay, I was wrong too. Let's go home. I need to see Betsy. You're *sure* she was okay when you saw her?"

"Riding like the wind. She'll be proud she played a part in your rescue. I would never have been able to get across that water without a horse to jump it."

"Why did you bring Betsy with you?"

"Bluebird wouldn't let me on without her. You know how Bets calms animals. It was with Betsy or not at all. They're back to the ranch by now, and this place will be crawling with cops any minute."

"We need to go. I have to hold her."

"In a minute." He gathered her closer and bent his head. There was nothing between them now. Everything was out in the open. He loved and was loved in return. It was too much to hold in.

His lips brushed hers. She wound her arms around his neck and kissed him back. His. She was all his. Now and forever.

EPILOGUE

THE BIRDS FILLED THE MEADOW WITH SONG. THERE HAD BEEN NO NEED TO buy flowers for the ceremony because God provided them himself. The rains had brought the wildflowers into full bloom, and their fragrance and color flooded Allie's senses.

She glanced at her watch. Where was he? The ceremony was about to begin, and she wanted to give Rick his surprise first. It was supposed to be bad luck to see the groom before the wedding, but it hardly counted since they were already married.

"You're more jittery than me," the young man at her side said.

Allie smiled at her newly met brother-in-law. "Chad, don't be mad if he doesn't recognize you, okay? It's been fifteen years. You look a little different than you did at five."

Rick had shown her the last picture he had of his younger brother. Chad's hair was blond then, and he had mud on his face. This quiet young man with starched hair and clothes didn't even come close.

"I know." Chad's nervous smile chased away the picture he'd presented of a polished young yuppie. "I just barely remember him, but he was like Superman to me."

"There he is," Allie whispered when her husband's broad shoulders moved through the crowd. "Stand behind me and turn around so he only sees the back of your head."

She blocked the view to Chad as Rick spotted her. His face brightened, and he wagged a finger at her to indicate he wasn't supposed to see her yet. She waved him to her, and his smile beamed out.

He glanced around. "If Dolly sees us together, we're in trouble."

"I have a present for you," she said. She couldn't stand it much longer. Rick's face would be a picture.

"I have something for you too, but you can't have it until after the wedding." He waggled his brows at her.

She laughed and felt heat on her cheeks. "Shh, people will hear."

He laughed. "Girl, your mind is in the gutter. That's not what I meant, but it's not a bad idea. This is something more—um—substantial." He glanced at her hands. "So where's this big present?"

"Right here." She stepped aside. "I'd like you to meet someone."

Chad's face was pale, but he mustered a smile. "Hi, Rick."

Rick looked perplexed for a minute, then his gaze locked with Chad's before sweeping up and down the young man. "Wh-who are you?" A dawning hope filled his eyes.

Allie grabbed his arm. "If you could have one person here to witness our wedding, who would it be, Rick?"

"Chad?" he whispered.

Chad nodded jerkily. "It's me, Rick."

Rick stepped forward first, his arms coming up awkwardly. Chad embraced the bigger man, nearly swallowed up by Rick's muscular arms. Though the older man was bulkier, the resemblance was impossible to deny. Chad had Rick's nose and thick hair. The shape of the eyes was the same too.

Allie swiped at her wet cheeks. She wanted to sit down and just howl with indescribable joy. She couldn't help but think how she'd feel if the sister she knew was dead walked up to her. That was a little how she imagined Rick felt right now.

Then Rick was pounding his brother on the back, and saying over and over, "Chad, I can't believe it." His voice was choked with emotion.

Chad had wet eyes. His knuckles were white with the clutch he had on his older brother.

Rick finally stepped back and gripped him by the shoulders. "How did you find me?"

Chad wiped his face with the back of his hand. He nodded at Allie. "Your wife found me through an old teacher. She got a message to me through a nurse." He looked down at his perfectly shined shoes. "I thought you'd forgotten all about me."

"Never, Chad." Rick gave him a little shake. "Never for a minute."

"I know that now. My foster parents adopted me when I was twelve. They were missionaries, and we went to South Africa six months after the adoption. I was there for five years, then came back here for college. I'm in San Antonio."

"No wonder I couldn't find you," Rick said, his grin rueful. He swiped at his eyes. "Man, you're a sight for sore eyes."

Allie couldn't stop crying as she watched the reunion. Rick had known his brother with one look.

Betsy tugged on her hand. "Why is Daddy crying?" she whispered. "I'm scared."

Allie knelt beside her daughter. "Those are happy tears, Bets. Like when Mommy heard you talk again. Sometimes the happiness just bubbles out, and you can't help it." Her vision was blurry, but her daughter was still the most beautiful thing she'd ever seen.

Allie had come so close to losing everything, and she didn't think she'd ever take anything for granted again.

Betsy nodded, but she still looked wary as she watched the two men. Allie stood again, unable to get enough of the joy that filled the meadow.

Rick's gaze locked with hers over his brother's shoulder. "Allie, you did this? How did you know where to look?"

"Dolly had a lead on the teacher. I went to see her, and she rambled about missionaries and Africa. It made no sense, but I left a note at the nursing home in case he came by to see her again. He called me two days ago."

Rick left his brother then and grabbed her up so her toes dangled above the ground. He dropped a kiss onto her lips. "Thank you," he said. "That's all I can say. I have everything I've ever wanted right here, right now."

He set her back on the ground, and she let her love shine through her eyes as she stared up at him. She had another present for him later, a very special one, but that would have to come when they were alone. Her hand dropped to her tummy in a protective gesture. He was going to be buried with new family.

She saw Rosa standing apart from the crowd. Allie waved to her and went to join her. "Thanks for coming, Rosa. It means the world to me."

The woman smiled. "You must wear something old, so I bring you this, *sí*?" She held out a soft christening gown and bonnet. "It belonged to your *madre*. You can fold the bonnet and tuck it into your garter. Your *bebé* will wear it."

"How did you know?" Allie whispered.

"It is in your eyes," Rosa said, her smile soft.

Allie's throat closed. She took the bonnet. Turning her back to the guests, she lifted the edge of her dress and tucked the hat into her garter. The soft fabric felt like a touch from her mother. "Thank you, Rosa," she said. "If you'll keep the gown, I'll get it before we leave."

"Of course." Rosa pressed her lips to Allie's cheek. "I pray for you, just like I pray for your *madre*."

Dolly called for them to get started. Rick walked to Grady's side under the gazebo they'd moved into the clearing. From somewhere, the wedding processional began to play, the sound a perfect blend with the birds chirping and the song of the wind in the trees.

Jon's parents stood along the sidelines, their faces reflecting their unease. But at least they'd chosen to support her, and Betsy was gradually warming up to them. The teenagers they'd helped crowded around. They'd come so far in the few weeks they'd been here. Allie hated to let them go, but she knew they'd be all right. They'd learned important lessons here, ones they'd never forget.

Just like she had.

Fern's tremulous smile filled Allie with joy. She smiled back, and Fern's blush held joy.

"Go on, Bets," Allie whispered, giving her daughter a little shove.

Betsy moved out from her mother's side. She dropped flower petals along the path to join her new daddy. They were bright splashes of blue against the yellow sea of wildflowers.

Then it was Allie's turn. Her white slippers trod the petals underfoot. She was Cinderella, though her fairy godmother had been Dolly, who had made her dress with her magic sewing machine. Though the bluebirds hadn't come to help her make her dress, she caught flashes of their blue feathers from the corner of her eye and smiled.

For once in her life, Allie actually felt beautiful.

As she and Rick repeated their vows, this time with meaning and intention, she couldn't look away from the promise in his blue eyes. They might have troubles in the future, but together they could weather the storms.

"I now pronounce you husband and wife. Rick, have at it," Grady said.

Laughter rippled through the guests standing around the clearing. Rick's hands came down on her shoulders, and he drew her to him. His kiss was a gentle caress full of forever. Allie drank it in without fear of the future.

When she lifted her head, she saw her husband nod to Dolly. Cages snicked open around them, and Allie saw blue feathers every-where. A sea of bluebirds filled the air, their wings fluttering past her ears, their bright flashes of color mimicking the blue in her hus-band's eyes.

She'd found her bluebird of happiness. Now and forever.

ACKNOWLEDGMENTS

I ALWAYS KNEW I WAS A TEXAN AT HEART. IF YOU'VE NEVER VISITED THE Big Bend region in southwest Texas, you should make it a priority. My brothers, Rick, Dave, and Randy Rhoads, have always been Wild West nuts, and their love of all things western transferred itself to me long ago. I started out writing western romances, and my first book in that genre came out in 1998. Writing this book was almost like going back to the good old days for me. Though this book is set in contemporary times, a ranch is a ranch.

My thanks to Andrea Doering at Crossings for suggesting I set this book in the Lonestar state. I'm almost ready to move—well, if it weren't for the tarantulas!

They may get tired of me thanking them, but I've got the best possible publishing team at Thomas Nelson. Allen Arnold, Ami McConnell, Natalie Hanemann, Amanda Bostic, Jennifer Deshler,

Carrie Wagner, and Lisa Young are always cooking up new schemes to gain me new readers. My love and thanks to you all, especially Allen for this particular book. And my fabulous cover designers, Mark Ross and Belinda Bass, deserve a hand of applause as well. I'm always excited to get a new cover from Nelson because of all the work they put into it. And thanks to Erin Healy, my terrific freelance editor who is always pushing me to stretch and be better than I think I can. You all rock, and I thank God for you!

No author rises or falls on her own talent (I'd be in trouble if I were expected to!), and in my case I've got a great team that extends beyond my Nelson family. It all starts with my great agent, Karen Solem, who makes me dig deep in a story for the things that matter. My critique team is a constant source of encouragement and handholding, and you deserve a medal! Thanks to the girls (www.girlswriteout.blogspot.com): Kristin Billerbeck, Diann Hunt, and Denise Hunter. And thanks to Robin Miller, who holds me up to high standards on the suspense thread. If she figures out the killer early, I'm in trouble!

I wouldn't be writing today if it weren't for the support of my family. My great husband doesn't mind when the laundry isn't done or dinner isn't on the table because I'm off somewhere roping bulls. My love and appreciation go out to my great family and to my wonderful Jesus, who has kicked open so many doors.

And you, dear reader, are a constant source of light in my day with your e-mails and letters. You're the focus of much of what I do every day. Thank you for the joy you bring to my life. Stop by my Web site for a visit at www.colleencoble.com or e-mail me at colleen@colleencoble.com. If your book club of twenty members or more is reading one of my books, I'd be happy to call in if you contact me.

READING GROUP GUIDE

1. The perennial question is why bad things happen to good people. What gets you through times like Allie suffered?
2. We all have things that we struggle with. For a while Rick turned to the bottle to deal with his guilt over Jon's death. What other crutches do you see people use?
3. Have you ever given up a dream for someone you love? If so, what was it and how did it turn out?
4. Rick was passionate about the plight of abused horses and abused children. What are you passionate about? Does anything move you to action? If not, what is stopping you?
5. As parents we can tend to overprotect our children. Discuss Allie's relationship with her daughter, the good and the bad.
6. Rick believed love is an action word. Was he right?
7. Can secrets ever be good?
8. The villain allowed revenge to rule his life, and it's hard to forgive someone who has hurt a loved one. How do you manage it?
9. How do you feel about the fact that Elijah never went looking for his other granddaughters, Allie and Tammy?
10. Is there a dream for a better life that God has never let die in your heart? What are you going to do about it?

ESCAPE TO BLUEBIRD RANCH

ALSO AVAILABLE FOR YOUR eREADER

"The Lightkeeper's Bride is a wonderful story
filled with mystery, intrigue, and romance.
I loved every minute of it."

— CINDY WOODSMALL —

New York Times best-selling author of *The Hope of Refuge*

THE BEST-SELLING MERCY FALLS SERIES.
ALSO AVAILABLE FOR YOUR eReader

VISIT COLLEENCOBLE.COM

LOVE IS ON THE WAY.

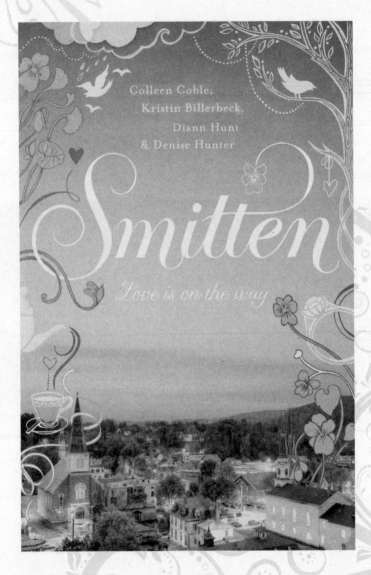

Colleen Coble,
Kristin Billerbeck,
Diann Hunt
& Denise Hunter

Smitten

Love is on the way

When a failed logging company threatens its town's survival, four friends devise a plan to turn Smitten, Vermont, into the country's premier romantic getaway.